Marheh of the Silberay, Book 4.

I0533669

Water Road Challenge

By

Rosalind Kentwell

L'Optimisme

Melbourne

Marheh of the Silberay Series

Book 1. Water Road Apprentice

Book 2. Apprentice Still

Book 3. Apprentice in Clanning

ISBN: 978-0-9874868-5-1

DEDICATION

To the kind friends who have read and enjoyed Marheh's previous
adventures.

ACKNOWLEDGMENTS

Thanks especially to Elwin, Elenor and Noni who listened and Sally and Dorothy who read the uncorrected version and made corrections and suggestions.

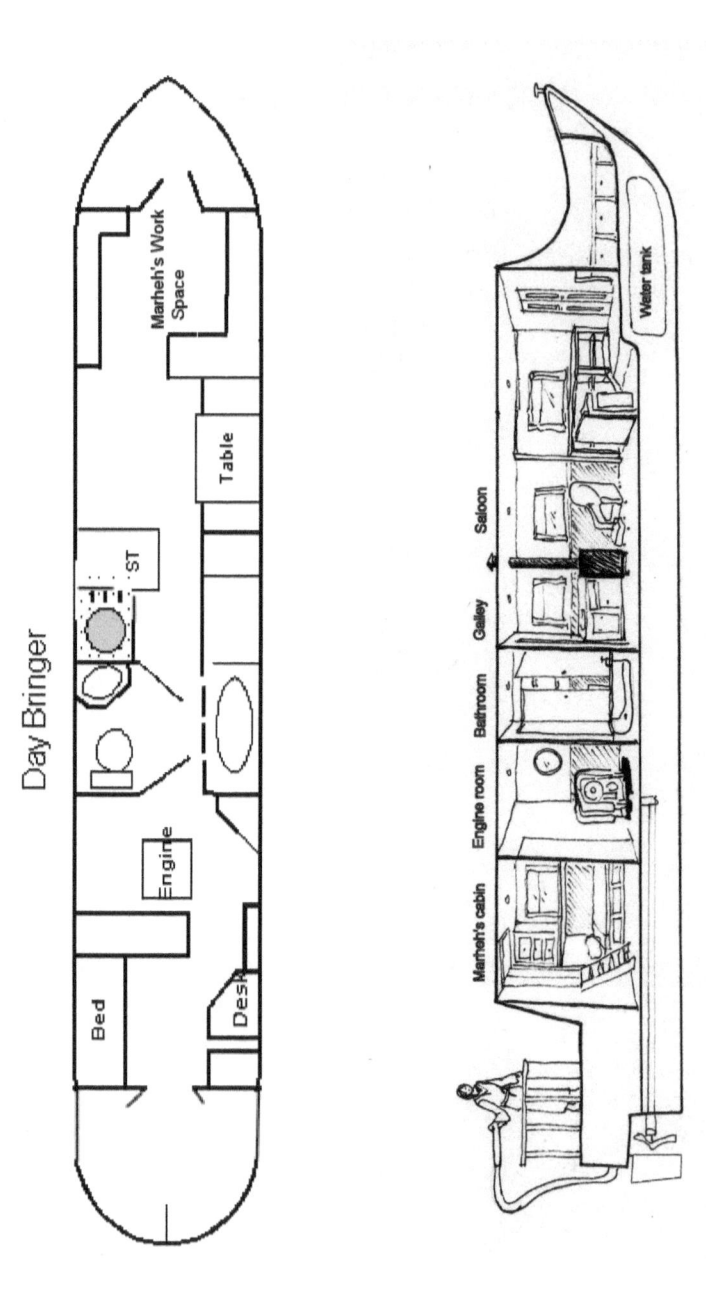

Day Bringer

A favourite mooring

Chapter One

Marheh recognised the mooring place she and Nemle had always used when they came this way. She eased the throttle back and steered towards it. A short burst of reverse slowed *Day Bringer* even further and she glided into the bank, touching lightly so she could step off with the centre line and steady the boat before taking the mooring pins and making her fast.

This daily task was second nature now and she rarely remembered how difficult it had been at first. Nemle had been a patient and loving teacher on the whole. Marheh gave a little grimace. She had always wanted to run before she could walk and she knew she had tried Nemle severely at times.

Now Nemle was at the Harbour with the old ones and she might never see her again. She had not realised how much she would miss her.

She tucked the mallet into its holder in the locker and stood for a minute looking out over the fields around her. This had always been a favourite mooring of hers. There was something about the shape of the low hills that was particularly satisfying. Dimples in the land held shadows and secrets. Tree tops glimpsed beyond the hill beckoned her and did still although she had walked to visit them many times.

It was four weeks since she had left the Harbour and the Gathering of

1

Silberay. Four weeks ago she had graduated, receiving *Day Bringer*'s tiller from Nemle in the Consigning Ceremony.

She rested her elbows on *Day Bringer*'s roof, let the fields and the wide sky soak into her, and remembered.

Tippa and Pon had been before her. It had always been that way since they were first apprenticed twenty years earlier; Tippa, then Pon then Marheh. Until now it had never occurred to her to wonder why she was always last but perhaps it was because of her reputation for arrogance. She could see it now and recognise it as something she would always need to guard against.

The Silberay sang through the Consigning Ceremony. She knew the songs well, they were the same each Gathering, a song of farewell for the retiring mentors, a song of welcome for new graduates.

"You are the old, our wisdom, our strength,
As you pass let our love wrap you well."

The words sang themselves in her head.

Nemle had been her wisdom for twenty years, now she would need to use what she had learned. It would not be Nemle's fault if she failed.

Tippa had made her lap of the Harbour, then Pon, and the Silberay had sung to welcome them. Then Nemle had handed her *Day Bringer*'s tiller arm. She had aged in the last few years, suffered badly from arthritis and Marheh had been glad to care for her. For this moment though she had stood straight, without the stick she had taken to using.

"My dear good daughter," she had said, her mind reaching in to Marheh's to communicate her love. "This is yours."

Marheh had taken the tiller arm and fitted it carefully before setting out on her lap. She had wept.

She had been thinking only of Nemle and *Day Bringer* and the change this ceremony would make to her life so she was completely unprepared when the welcome song flowed over her accompanied by tumultuous applause. She glanced towards Nemle who was not clapping but looking at her with loving attention.

"Yes," she seemed to be saying. "You are one of us and we love you."

She pushed herself away from the roof and stretched. Her apprenticeship had been tumultuous at times. She had more than once challenged the surface smoothness of the Silberay and she supposed she would go on doing it, yet they had welcomed her as if they cared for her. She let her attention return to the landscape, clean and fresh in its spring colours. It was the life she had chosen and she had known the shape of it from the beginning but knowing the shape of it was nothing. It was living it that mattered.

For a few moments more she rested in the landscape then made her way below. *Day Bringer* had been thoroughly over-hauled for her but the small back cabin that had been hers since she became an apprentice was unchanged. The narrow hard bunk where she slept was neat and tidy, its bright cover shadowed by the cupboards above it. She had soon learned to be meticulous about putting things away. It was the only way to manage the tiny space where she lived.

From her cabin she moved through to the engine room, stopping briefly to turn the stern tube greaser and hang her windlass in its accustomed place. The bathroom was next. It had a very small hip bath replacing the tin basin she had washed in for the last twenty years. She could have hot water too after a day's boating, heated by the engine. Nemle would have appreciated that. At least the old bucket toilet had been replaced with a closed chemical one ten years ago. Marheh had known about bucket toilets when she became apprenticed because her Uncle Jik was Silberay and she had been on his boat. However, she had been appalled when she was told it would be her job to empty it, sometimes even having to dig a hole in a nearby field for the purpose. She gave a rueful smile at the thought of her younger self, what a spoilt, self-important brat she had been. Poor Nemle!

She washed her hands and went through to the galley with the saloon beyond it. Even after four weeks she could be surprised by the changes here. Nemle's cabin, which had occupied space at the bow, was gone, and the saloon led into Marheh's new work space. There were storage bins for her clay and drying shelves for the little sculptures she made as well as a functional work bench with a place for her tools and her working smock.

It was light and bright and best of all, to Marheh's way of thinking, the doors into the well deck could be opened for the outside to come in.

It was only after she had seen this for the first time that she realised what Nemle had given up when she took her as apprentice. No wonder she had found the relationship difficult at first.

She went to the stove and moved the kettle over the fire. Today she was to open the envelope Jik had given her the last night of the Gathering. She would make herself a mug of sperit and take it and the letter to the well deck.

"Open it in four weeks," he had said when he gave it to her.

Jik was in the middle of a four year term as Harbour Master and she had wondered briefly whether the envelope contained an official communication or an uncle's greeting. Then she had resolutely decided against speculation and put the missive aside until the appropriate time.

Now the time had come. While the kettle was heating she took the cushions from the front locker and arranged them on the bench in the well deck. She spooned a mixture of spices and dried berries into her mug and poured on the boiling water. Sperit was still the Silberay drink of choice, but it was going out of fashion with other people. The drink prepared, she took it and the letter and made her way outside. She placed the steaming mug on the gunnel and settled herself on her cushions. Another refreshing acknowledgement of the landscape and she was ready.

It was a very ordinary envelope made from crisp white paper. Her name, Marheh Carron, was written on it in Jik's bold script. To have included her family name made it seem more official, she thought, turning the envelope over to ease one finger carefully under the flap. It came away easily and she drew out a folded sheet of paper and another envelope.

"*My dearest niece,*" she read, unfolding the paper. "Only niece," she commented to herself. "*First let me be a proud uncle and congratulate you on you graduation and give you my love. I hope you know you will always have that.*"

She nodded thoughtfully and sipped from her mug.

"*Second, let me, as Harbour Master, ask for your help. The water road is not in very good health. I think perhaps you noticed that water levels in the harbour are a good two inches below where they should be at this time of year. Your assigned route takes you to Deerford to visit your family (and mine) to show off your new status. Some way beyond Deerford, kept carefully secret even from most of the Silberay, is the source of the water road. I don't believe it is urgent and I may be over reacting, but I'm concerned that there is some kind of blockage at the source and I'm asking you to go and look. I've drawn you a rather cryptic map, but I wouldn't be surprised if you already know where it is. The very adventurous small girl you once were explored widely around her home.*"

Marheh studied the map for a few moments and a slow smile spread over her face. Of course she knew where it was. It had been her own special hiding place. The letter lay on her lap unheeded as she lost herself in remembering. It had been the summer between primary school and secondary school so she must have been twelve when she found it.

Jik had been passing through Deerford and had moored overnight at the bottom of the garden. The rest of the family knew he was there, but she was the only one who could see the water road clearly, so no one noticed that she had hidden in the well deck of *Autumn Wind* while he was saying good bye to her parents. She had stayed hidden while they went through the tunnel out of the village and then made her way along the gunnel to the back deck. He had been cross with her at first and threatened to put her off immediately but she had pleaded with him to let her stay for a bit longer and he had given in.

"You'll be the one who gets the spanking," he had said.

For two hours she had travelled with him. He had even allowed her to hold the tiller. Then he had moored, given her something to eat and set off again without her. He had expected her to go straight home, but she couldn't bear the day to end. Back home she would have a scolding and three younger brothers to mind, here she was free, the day was bright and fresh and the fields and woods beckoned. So she had not hurried home but gone exploring, found a narrow stream and followed it to its source.

The water had welled up around a large rock, bubbling deep and mysterious to make a pool that was partly in sunshine and partly shaded by an overhang of rock that was almost a cave. She had drunk from the pool and washed her face and listened to the silence, and because all water was the same to her, she had not known until now that this was part of the water road and not some natural stream that all the world could see. No wonder the place had drawn her again and again despite the long walk to get there.

She had been very late home that first time and her parents had been worried. They had explained at length just how worried and sent her supperless to bed, but nothing could really tarnish the happiness of that day.

For the next two years the place had been her refuge and delight. It was too far to visit often but there were other Silberay passing through Deerford and mooring at the bottom of the garden and sometimes she was allowed to ask for a ride. Sometimes, during a bad patch at school, she truanted, walking both ways, her school bag on her back, just for the chance to spend an hour there, to eat her lunch and taste the stillness.

She had formed the habit of making the little jump to reach the rock in the pool. It was the perfect place to be alone, to think, to watch and listen, just to be. One day however the rock had been damp and slippery and she had fallen. The water had been deep and turbulent as well as bitterly cold. It had not been easy to save herself and she had lost her school bag and a shoe in the process.

That was the end of course. When she did not reach home at the proper time inquiries had been made. Her parents learned she had not been to school all day and had put a stop to her explorations. For a whole month she had been escorted to school, handed over and escorted home again later like an infant.

Marheh shifted uneasily and sipped at her sperit. Her mother's white face and her father's explosion of anger when she reached home, limping and bedraggled, had made her feel both guilty and defiant and she had shouted back. Then her father had put his arms around her, hugged her while she fought him and when she collapsed into sobbing. She hadn't thought about the incident for years and years. She thought she might tell them she knew how lucky she was to be loved when she saw them again.

She sighed a little and turned back to the letter in her lap. It was hardly likely that her shoe or her school bag were a problem after all this time. What could it be? And why had Jik written to her about it instead of talking to her at the Gathering?

She turned her attention to the other envelope. It was neither addressed nor sealed but as she held it with attention she knew it was from Nemle.

"*Dearest Marheh,*" the letter began.

Marheh let her eyes dwell on the words. She knew she was indeed Nemle's dearest and it had sometimes irked her, as if it demanded more from her than she wanted to give.

"*Here I am, still interfering in your life.*"

Marheh smiled at that. Nemle's love had mostly been very clear sighted.

"*Jik spoke to me about what he wanted you to do but I wouldn't let him ask you at the Gathering. It didn't seem fair that you should be burdened with a difficult task before you had a chance to taste your freedom. Don't protest at my use of that word. I know that you care for me. You demonstrated that most lovingly over these past five years when the afflictions of age began to take their toll, but you were not free. Now you are, in as much as Silberay are ever free. Perhaps freedom is only ever freedom to choose the path you follow, the challenge you accept.*

But I didn't mean to embark on a dissertation on freedom. Jik and I both agree that you are best fitted for this task and that it is a necessary one. It is not something you need to hurry over. Take your time to enjoy your first solo voyage, spend a little time with your family at Deerford. All this good advice and I didn't mean to give you any! Forgive me. I am uneasy about this task we have given you. Take care my dear, good daughter and know that my mind will support you and my soul sing with yours as long as I live."

Was she freer now than she had been when caring for Nemle? Marheh let the letter lie in her lap and looked out to the horizon, the sky clear and pale, the line of hill and tree defined in an infinite range of greens and browns. It was not so much freedom as opportunity and independence. Now it was up to her to use all she had learnt, to grow with it, building on the skills she had, perhaps developing new skills, choosing what to keep and what to discard.

She looked down at the letter again and smiled. Nemle knew her so well. There was a postscript which read.

"No doubt you have already removed all my lovely plants from Day Bringer's roof. I forgive you!"

Cottage by the bridge

Chapter Two

Marheh sat for a few more minutes sipping her sperit and pondering the task they had given her. It did not occur to her to wonder whether Tippa or Pon had been given a particular task. She knew it was not customary and understood from her letters that Nemle at least was concerned about it, Jik too probably. If Jik thought she was particularly fitted for the task, then it was her talent with the discipline of the mind that he expected her to need, or perhaps hoped she would not need.

She stared into her mug then suddenly drained the last few mouthfuls and stood up. They had both said it was not urgent and she was not to hurry. She would make her way with the usual slow, steady pattern of progress Nemle had established with her, and not even think about it until she reached Deerford.

She went inside and collected the heel of the loaf and the slice of cheese she had planned for her lunch. She might be good at the disciplines, but the domestic arts did not interest her and it was even harder to be interested now she did not have Nemle to cook for. She would need to bake though if she wanted bread for tomorrow.

She took her lunch into her workspace and ate it standing as she studied the piece she was working on. It was a bit more challenging than the bread and butter pieces she took to the village markets. She had wanted to do something that would ask more of her than the little studies of animals she sometimes thought she could do in her sleep.

It was a group of three figures, carefully balanced, one squatted with a trowel, one bent forward with a pruning knife and the third stretched up to pick fruit. Gardeners they were and she thought now that they were all the same gardener, planting the seed, nurturing the young plant and receiving the fruit. It was for Nemle really, although she would probably never receive it. She had not intended it, but now she saw she was acknowledging Nemle's loving mentoring with a metaphor that was particularly appropriate for her.

She swallowed the last, dry mouthful of bread, pulled on her smock and began to work on the faces making them serious, intent on their work and giving them a look of Nemle as she had been twenty years ago, when Marheh first joined her as an apprentice.

The work took hold of her and she knew nothing else for a couple of hours. Only then was she aware of weariness and knew she should do no more. Another hour will finish it, she thought, wrapping it carefully in damp cloths. She would wait until she reached Deerford and home before having it fired. Although she had built up a network of small potteries throughout the water road, where she could exchange her labour for a firing, she felt most comfortable going home to her family pottery, where she had learned her craft and where her father and her youngest brother Tep welcomed her. They helped her market her best pieces too, through the shops that sold the quality crockery they made.

A month should see her at Deerford if she stuck to the steady, unhurried pace she was accustomed to. She could get there in a week if she spent all day every day boating and for a moment she was tempted, but underneath she understood that it would be foolish. If the task they had set her was in any way dangerous she must make practicing the disciplines a priority. Silberay did not rush through the landscape without listening either, or without offering themselves in the discipline of the soul.

She stretched and took off her smock. Laundry was always a problem on a boat so it made sense to save her uniform from the clayey fingerprints she made without being aware of doing so. She hung it on its hook and went to move the kettle onto the fire. Another mug of sperit would be good, then she must think about her evening meal and do some practice.

This was the time she missed Nemle most.

When Nemle was with her there was reason to prepare dinner. Even when she became too frail to do much, she would sit in the arm chair by the fire and keep her company. Sometimes she teased or joked, sometimes she talked seriously about what they were learning about the places they had passed through that day, sometimes they were silent together. The armchair belonged to Marheh now and she couldn't turn back the clock.

She took her drink to the armchair and reached for her journal where she kept it in the rack on the wall. She couldn't talk with Nemle, but she could clarify her thoughts this way.

"*An uneventful journey today*," she wrote and placed a neat and deliberate full stop.

Well it was, she protested to Nemle's imagined disapproval. Journal writing did not come naturally to her, but Nemle had pushed her into keeping one during the last couple of years, saying she would need something to talk to when she was alone. She looked at the page and its single line of writing.

"Go deeper," Nemle would have said. "Your mind is not a blank page."

"Yes it is," Marheh wanted to say, but instead she sighed, drank from her mug and began again.

"*The days are getting longer now and as usual I woke with the sun. It is still chilly in the mornings though so I took my clothes through to the saloon and got dressed by the fire.*"

Suddenly she was away, writing to Nemle, telling her about the heron that had seen her through its territory, flying ahead of her then stopping, poised on the bank until she caught up. She loved its elegant grace and had tried many times in the past to capture it, but clay was too heavy a medium and her sketches were just for fun.

This had led her on to speculate about the animals that saw the water dimension. All the wild ones, except rabbits, she decided, and most of the others, only sometimes she had seen a rider push his horse through the water road, oblivious. Perhaps it depended on the rider with horses or the master with dogs.

Then she remembered her letters and wondered how she could have said the day had been uneventful, and before she knew it she had written a page and revisited all the events that made up her day.

She put the journal away and wrote up *Day Bringer*'s log, how long she had travelled and where to. Then she peeled a potato and a carrot, chopped them into a pot with an onion and a bacon bone and set them on the edge of the fire to cook slowly while she entered discipline of the soul.

This was her true work. This was the place where she could sing light as well as enrich her own soul with music and she gave herself to it totally. Even after twenty years of practice, entry to the song did not always happen easily, but today it did. She had barely visualised the candle flame that was her portal before she was through and singing.

At first it was only her own song she was aware of, singing light within light, melody like a thread of gold. Then other songs swelled around her, some distant, softly going about their own business, others closer making a pad of harmony that would become distinguishable as melody only from within it. Then came one song that danced around hers, weaving its own thread of gold so that together they made a brilliant pattern of light that extended outward to enrich those places where the light was dim.

Sometimes she sang into darkness and then the song was difficult, painful and exhausting but necessary for the health of the world around her, or so she believed. Today, however, there was no real darkness, just places that were less light and the song remained joyful and uplifting.

When finally she emerged from the place she had been, she was tired, but pleasantly so, and she understood Nemle's song had been there, complementing her own.

Twilight was deepening into evening and *Day Bringer* was full of shadows and the smell of her supper. She rested for a few moments in the half light then got up to light the oil lamp and decant the contents of the saucepan into a bowl. She was tempted to eat straight from the pot, but the sense of Nemle's closeness forbade this slipping of standards.

Washing up followed the meal, then she made up the fire and treated herself to a chapter of the book she had chosen from the library at the Harbour. She was enjoying it and it was tempting to read on, but rationing the chapters made it last longer, so she restrained herself. The lack of space for books was the only drawback to living a on boat.

She closed it reluctantly and rested for a moment in the world where it had transported her before making her way slowly through to her cabin and to bed.

Next morning she woke to the sound of gentle rain. For a few minutes she was tempted to indulge in some more sleep, but she remembered she had to bake. By the time she had breakfasted and put the loaf to rise by the fire the rain had stopped and the sun come out, so she was glad she had not succumbed.

She did the engine checks, placed everything she needed to hand, then set off. The whole world seemed newly washed, every leaf, every blade of grass sparkled. The sky was clear and pale and the water road shone before her like a silver ribbon. The light breeze caused by her forward passage caressed her cheeks and lifted the tendrils of hair that always seemed to escape from the confines of the long dark plait that hung almost to her waist. She was aware of the occasional thread of grey now, but the knowledge did not disturb her greatly. Mirrors did not feature largely in her life.

She had been travelling for perhaps an hour, watching, listening, enjoying the sight of a water vole perched on a floating island of weed scratching its whiskers, or the occasional flash of blue fire that was the flight of a kingfisher. There had been little sign of human life, a couple of distant farm houses and once a man and a boy who appeared to be mending a fence.

Ahead of her now however was a bridge, a narrow arch only a few inches wider than *Day Bringer*. Not far beyond it, she remembered, was a cottage situated quite close to the water road with a sweep of mown grass edged with azalea bushes. They should be in flower now, she thought, looking ahead to see if she could catch a glimpse through the bridge hole.

The old couple who had lived there could see something of the water road. Marheh could remember a time, perhaps ten yours ago, when they still kept a cow. She and Nemle had been able to buy fresh milk from them. The cow was long gone and it was a couple of years since *Day Bringer* had been given this route. She wondered now whether they were still living there, so far from anywhere.

She turned her attention to her steering as *Day Bringer*'s prow entered the bridge hole and slowed a little. This one was quite a tight fit, though she noticed there was a water mark about two inches above the current level. Then she was through and looking eagerly to the right where she would see the cottage.

She realised at once that the old couple had gone. The cottage had been newly painted, most of the old, sheltering trees around it had gone and it sported a smart new conservatory. The welcoming mooring the couple had provided for the Silberay had gone too, and now the long sweep of grass ran down the water's edge and, Marheh guessed, continued beneath it. The azaleas were still there though, a bank of bright colours flaunting themselves against the green.

She eased back the throttle a little so she could enjoy the flowers for longer. She could not help wondering about the new residents and feeling sad for the passing of the old and the loss of the trees.

Day Bringer was just drawing level with the cottage when the back door burst open and a young child came running across the grass. She looked to be about four years old and Marheh realised that she was running with a purpose. The child could see her and was excitedly waving and calling. Marheh waved back and pushed the throttle into reverse so she could stop and greet her.

For a few minutes, as Marheh eased *Day Bringer* into the bank, the little girl watched round-eyed then she approached the boat and smiled at Marheh.

"Hello."

The greeting was shy and Marheh recognised the child's curiosity.

"Hello," she replied, smiling in her turn.

The child reached out and lightly touched *Day Bringer*'s painted hull.

"Pretty," she said.

"She is isn't she," Marheh agreed. "Be careful though, we don't want you falling in."

The child laughed.

"Falling in the water," she said and then again. "Water."

It occurred to Marheh then, that perhaps the child's parents did not see the water road and tried to persuade her she was imagining it. It happened she knew and could leave the child confused and vulnerable.

She looked up at the cottage but there was no sign of any adult.

"Is your Mummy home?" she asked. "Or Daddy?"

"Mummy."

"Do you think she would come and say hello to me if you went and asked her?"

The child looked uncertain then shook her head.

"Mummy is busy."

Marheh hesitated for a moment then took the centre line and stepped off *Day Bringer* onto the grassy bank. She felt it was important that she speak to the child's parents and at least try to convince them that the water road ran past their garden and that their child could see it.

The little girl moved back a few steps looking earnestly at Marheh who crouched down to be on a level with her.

"My name is Marheh," she said. "And my boat is called *Day Bringer*."

It was the first time she had said *my boat* aloud to anyone, and it gave her an unexpected thrill.

"Do you have a name?"

The child giggled.

"Of course I do. You're silly."

Marheh nodded with mock sadness.

"I am silly aren't I?"

"Are you pretend?"

"I don't think so. What do you think?"

"Mummy said the water is just pretend."

"Perhaps she can't see it," Marheh was beginning to say, when there was an angry shout and the sound of agitated feet.

"Debbie, come here!"

The child looked anxiously at Marheh then drifted towards the angry, rather breathless young woman who had run from the house.

"Who the hell are you? What do you think you're doing in my back garden with my child?"

Marheh stood up slowly.

"I'm sorry if I've given you a fright," she said, trying to find words to explain herself.

"Clear out not! Who do you think you are?"

"The people who used to live here let us moor," Marheh said. "But perhaps you can't see the water."

The little girl had been looking at Marheh from her mother's side.

"Water Mummy, and a boat," she said in a small, sad voice.

"Debbie, you know the water is just pretend."

The woman looked angrily at Marheh.

"Have you been telling her it's real?"

"It is real," Marheh said quietly. "It's just that you can't see it."

The woman stared at her.

"You must be some kind of lunatic," she said contemptuously. "Just clear off before I call the police."

She grabbed the child's hand.

"Come along Debbie."

Marheh watched for a moment, fighting down an angry response. The woman marched towards the house pulling Debbie behind her. Marheh wanted to jump onto *Day Bringer* and leave, but Debbie kept turning back, her face puzzled and pleading, and she knew she could not give up yet.

"Couldn't you just listen," she called. "For Debbie's sake."

The woman stopped and turned to stare at Marheh, who stood looking quietly at her.

"Please," she said. "I promise I'll go then, if you want me to."

The woman looked down at Debbie and back to Marheh. Then she took a step back towards her, then another.

"There is water Mummy," Debbie said, tugging at her mother. "Come and see."

The woman returned to within a few feet of Marheh and stood looking at her, one hand still grasping Debbie's, the other on her hip. Marheh studied her, trying to find the right words.

"Go on then," the woman challenged Marheh. "I'm listening."

"I'm Silberay," Marheh said, but this obviously meant nothing to the woman. "I live on the water road."

Again she paused, hoping for understanding.

"I suppose you could call it a slightly different dimension, aligned more with the spiritual world than the physical."

"So?"

"Most people have to be helped to see it, but some see it naturally, like your Debbie."

The woman's anger seemed to have eased, but she continued to look puzzled and uncertain. Marheh looked at Debbie.

"Will you tell Mummy what I am doing?" she asked.

Debbie nodded importantly. Marheh smiled at them both and turned to step back onto *Day Bringer*. She heard a gasp from the woman and Debbie's little voice talking earnestly.

"She's on the boat now Mummy. There's a little house on the boat."

Deliberately Marheh opened the door to her cabin and reached in for her heavy cloak, placed where she could get it easily in case of rain. She swung it round her shoulders and smiled at Debbie.

"She's got her coat on now," Debbie said.

"Tell Mummy what colour it is," Marheh said.

"It's a sort of green," Debbie said. "It's pretty."

Marheh returned to the bank still wearing her cloak. The woman stepped back from her, her face white.

"I'm sorry to frighten you," she said gently. "But I couldn't just disappear because of Debbie."

"Who are you?" The woman's voice was fearful, almost awed.

"My name is Marheh, I'm Silberay."

"I told you there was water Mummy." Debbie's pleased tones seemed to bring her mother back to some semblance of normality.

"So you did." She turned to Marheh. "You said most people have to be helped to see it. Can you help me?"

"I think so, if you want me to." Marheh still held the centre line. "It would be easier for me if I could moor. Then I won't have to think about the boat."

"Yes, if you want to."

She had let go of Debbie and was staring at the place where she thought Marheh had come from.

Marheh gave the centre line to Debbie to hold and busied herself with mallet and mooring pins. When *Day Bringer* was secure she thanked Debbie gravely, coiled the centre line and placed it back on the roof. She knew Debbie's mother would have seen her actions because this bank was not part of the water road, but she did not see *Day Bringer*'s ropes or the mooring pins.

When she turned back at last Debbie had pulled her mother down so she could whisper something to her.

"Debbie wants me to ask you to come up to the house for a cup of tea," the woman said stiffly.

"Do you want me to?" Marheh's voice was gentle.

The woman thought for a minute, studying Marheh all the time.

"Yes, I think I do," she said at last.

"Then, thank you. That would be lovely."

Debbie reached out to take her hand and the three went together across the grass to the house.

It took a little time for the kettle to boil and the tea to draw. Marheh, seated at the kitchen table, looked around curiously. It all looked very new and shiny and she guessed it had been refurbished recently. There was even a large white cupboard that gave off a soft humming sound. When her hostess opened it to bring out a bottle of milk a light went on inside it. Marheh guessed it might be a refrigerator, something she had heard about but not seen and never expected to own given the limitations of living on a boat.

Debbie had been given the job of putting some biscuits on a plate which she did very carefully from a big tin of home baked treats. Between each deliberate action she looked at Marheh as if she thought she might disappear. Then everything was ready and they were all sitting around the table. The teapot, in a bright floral cosy, and two delicate cups and saucers, were set down and a glass of milk poured for Debbie. Marheh smiled into the moment of awkward silence.

"I'm Marheh, and this is Debbie, but I don't know your name."

"I'm Marion," she said, then added abruptly. "You said something else, sil…something."

"Silberay," Marheh said. "It's what I do, sort of like my job, and it's who I am."

"Silberay," Debbie repeated carefully and took a big drink of milk.

"Would you like me to tell you a story about the Silberay?" Marheh asked her.

Debbie nodded, looking at Marheh over the rim of her glass.

"Once upon a time," Marheh began, wondering whether she could do this. Nemle had been the story teller.

"Once upon a time," she repeated. "There was a woman called Sila. She and some friends of hers used to meet together to talk about things they thought were important, like how to live their lives so that they would help to make the world a good place."

She continued on, telling how Sila had dreamed of the water road being created to carry things of the spirit and support those who travelled it as messengers, advocates and enablers. She tried to tell it in a way Debbie would understand, but it was not always easy to find simple words. She wanted Marion to understand too, and that required a deeper telling.

"But that was nearly two hundred years ago," she finished. "And Silberay have travelled the water road ever since."

"Are you two hundred?" Debbie asked.

Marheh laughed.

"Am I looking very old today?"

She leaned towards the little girl.

"I'm just an ordinary person, like you. If I'm lucky I might live to be ninety, Silberay usually do. Right now I'm forty."

Marion was looking suspiciously at her.

"It sounds like some kind of fable. If it's all true, how come I haven't heard of you?"

Marheh shook her head.

"For about the first hundred years we grew in numbers and people recognised us and understood a bit about us, but since then we've declined. There are only 75 boats in the water now and no new apprentices this Gathering."

Marion stood up to remove the empty tea things.

"Well I still don't really understand what you do, but I suppose it's harmless. Only I'm not happy that I can't see what Debbie can. What if there is some kind of danger to her?"

"That's why I stopped really, even when you didn't want me to. She would be vulnerable to other influences, especially if you are not aware."

"What do you mean vulnerable?"

"We have enemies. I suppose it is inevitable really. If we are in any way successful in what we set out to do, we attract the attention of others who want power for themselves rather than to empower others, who believe that they are justified in exploiting others because they can, when we consciously reject exploitation and try to advocate for the exploited."

Marion frowned.

"I don't really care about anything except keeping Debbie safe."

"And I want that too," Marheh said, standing up.

"Come and I'll try to help you see something of what Debbie sees."

"Can we go on the boat?" Debbie bounced off her chair. "Can we go into the little house?"

"If Mummy says so."

"Can we Mummy, can we?"

"How would I know, I can't even see it'" Marion snapped.

Debbie recoiled a little from her tone and she bent to her apologetically.

"I'm sorry Debbie, I can't see what you can see and it makes me feel muddled."

"I'll help you Mummy."

Marheh smiled at her.

"That's right Debbie. We'll show Mummy what a pretty boat *Day Bringer* is and help her to see the water."

They walked together across the grass towards the water road. When they reached the edge Marheh stopped.

"Debbie you hold Mummy's hand very tightly so she knows without looking that you are right next to her."

She held out her hand to Marion.

"Close your eyes and try to picture what I describe. Forget what you think is there."

She paused to order her thoughts.

"The water road lies almost at your feet," she began. "There is very little flow so it looks calm and still, like a silver ribbon unrolled across the landscape. It is not very wide, but it stretches for a thousand miles. It mirrors the sky so today it looks blue, but it is not very clear so you can't see what lives beneath the surface. My boat is moored right in front of us. The gunnel is only inches from your feet. It is painted dark green, like the hull and the sides. There is a sunrise painted on the side and the name, *Day Bringer*, written beneath it. She's long and thin, like the water road. I'm on the deck now," she said, moving quietly. "I'm inviting you to join me." She tightened her hold on Marion's hand. "Keep your eyes closed and lift your right foot up. Picture the gunnel. Now put your foot on it."

Quietly, calmly, she talked Marion onto the back deck, Debbie following.

She wouldn't let her open her eyes until she had guided her down into the back cabin. Debbie's face was one big smile as she looked around Marheh's neat little bedroom. Marion stood stunned at first, but Debbie's excitement helped to put her at ease and soon she was taking pleasure in the clever fittings that made the most of the small, narrow space. Marheh led them through the engine room and the bathroom to the galley, with the saloon beyond. She guided Marion to the armchair and left her to sit and look while she filled the kettle, took up her forgotten loaf to punch it down and shape it, and be on hand if needed.

It was quite some time before Marion spoke. Marheh had finished with her loaf and seated Debbie at the table with paper and pencils.

"Will I be able to see the way Debbie does now?" she asked.

Marheh shook head.

"I'm afraid not, but now you know what is there you can practice looking."

Marion sighed.

"I don't understand."

Marheh smiled sympathetically but did not respond directly.

"Do you use your soul name?" she asked. "It would help your practice if you acknowledged it sometimes."

"My soul name?" Marion looked puzzled. "What's that?"

A Broken Stile

Chapter Three

"Your soul name is…" Marheh searched for the words. "It's the name that belongs to what is good in you, the essence of you. It names the part of you that will live on after your body dies."

"More weird stuff."

Marion sounded aggressive but Marheh understood it was part of her confusion. She smiled sympathetically.

"It's a lot to take in, I know."

"I don't even know why I'm listening to you. I still don't really believe you exist."

Marheh laughed at that.

"You probably wish I didn't."

"I've done you a picture Mummy."

21

Debbie slid off the seat and brought her paper across to Marion.

"See," she said. "That's M-mar-heh." She stumbled a little over the unfamiliar name. "And she's standing on the boat."

"That's lovely Debbie," Marion said, looking at Marheh as if to acknowledge her existence through Debbie's eyes.

"Is Marheh your soul name then?"

Marheh nodded. "Mary is my ordinary name, but Silberay use the soul name most of the time."

There was silence then for a little while. Marheh slid her loaf into the oven and moved into her work area. Debbie climbed onto Marion's lap and gazed contentedly at her drawing. Marion put her arms around Debbie and leaned back. She closed her eyes for a few moments, then opened them and let her gaze wander over the small, neat interior.

"Why don't I have a soul name then?" she asked at last, as Marheh came back to the saloon carrying one of her little sculptures that had been fired ready for sale.

"You do, every one does," Marheh said. "It's just that you don't know what it is."

She held out her sculpture to Debbie.

"Would you like to have this to keep?" she asked.

Debbie's face lit up and she put out one finger to touch it lightly. It was a mother duck with her ducklings under her wings.

"Look Mummy."

Marion nodded absently.

"How can I find out what it is?" she asked Marheh.

"It's a duck Mummy."

Debbie sounded disgusted.

"Yes darling, it's beautiful," Marion said, but she was looking at Marheh for the answer to her question.

"I can help you if you like," Marheh said.

"And Debbie?" Marion asked, her arms tightening around her daughter.

Marheh looked thoughtfully at Debbie.

"She might be young enough to remember it for herself," she said.

She went to perch on the footstool beside the armchair where she was on a level with Debbie.

"Can you tell Mummy your inside name?"

Debbie studied her duck thoughtfully for a moment. Marheh waited, not wanting to prompt her any further.

"This duck calls me Rebah," she said, holding it level with her eyes and looking across it at Marheh.

"Does she?" Marheh said. "And is that what I call you?"

Debbie held the duck close to her ear and listened.

"You call me Rebah," she said.

"Thank you Rebah."

Marheh looked at the child with all her attention, the way Nemle had sometimes looked at her. "I'll think about you when I'm away."

Debbie nodded as if this was her due.

"I'll think about you sometimes," she said graciously.

Marheh and Marion exchanged smiles at this.

"Shall I call you Rebah too?" Marion asked.

Again Debbie listened to her duck.

"You call me Rebah at bed time," she said. "And some other times if I want you to."

Marion gave her a hug. Debbie enjoyed it for a few moments then wriggled free and climbed off Marion's lap.

"Can I look?" she asked Marheh.

"Look, but don't touch, alright?"

"Look but don't touch."

She wandered away into Marheh's workspace. Marheh, still perched on the footstool, looked a question at Marion.

"It feels right for her," she said.

"She has probably told you before now, only you didn't know there was anything to listen for. Another year or so older and she would have forgotten."

"As I have."

"I can help you remember if you want me to."

Marion looked away. Marheh waited, her eyes down.

"What would be the point? No one would ever use it now."

Marheh took time to answer.

"For us it is a safeguard," she said at last. "Our enemies deny the soul and don't use any names at all if they can avoid it. We use the soul name all the time to be continually reminded of who we really are."

Again a silence, broken at length by a long sigh.

"It won't do any harm I suppose."

Marheh smiled a little at that.

"Only good," she said.

"What do I have to do?"

"Relax and listen and tell me when you hear it."

It was work Marheh had done often before, and she was good at it. She slid her mind into Marion's and called to her, a compassionate, loving yearning towards the half forgotten soul, drawing it forward to be acknowledged by Marion's mind.

To Marion it seemed as if something as delicate and beautiful as a flower, or a snowflake, was blossoming deep inside her, offering itself to her. She reached for it and heard it welcome her by name. For a moment it lay vulnerable, unresisting in her grasp, then slipped away, leaving only the memory of its greeting. There was a space then, empty and filled, a moment beyond time.

"Imni," she said into the silence. "I am Imni."

Marheh looked at her and smiled and she saw again for an instant the fragile flower. Then she saw how Marheh had paled and understood a little of what her gift had cost her.

"Are you alright?" she asked abruptly.

"I'm fine." Marheh brushed aside the concern and stood up.

"Would you like a hot drink?"

Marion shook her head.

"Just to sit for a few minutes so I will remember this in my bones.'

"Of course."

Marheh drifted into her work space and smiled at Debbie, who was still examining the contents of her drying shelves and talking, in a little murmuring voice, to the duck Marheh had given her.

She moved past her, opened the doors into the well deck and went out. In the past Nemle had been there to ease the way when she had done this work. Nemle had taken the burden of hospitality and given her time to recover herself. Nemle had made sperit and seen that she was fed. She had not understood until now when she had to do it alone. She sank onto the bench in the well deck and let the sight of the water road restore her. Then Debbie came out to her and few minutes later they went together to the saloon and Marion.

"Thank you Marheh," Marion said, taking care with her name. "I think Rebah and I should go now. Might you still be here in the morning?"

Marheh smiled.

"I could be Imni, if you are agreeable."

So it was arranged and they left. Marheh stood on the back deck and watched them go before she let herself sag again with weariness.

The smell from the galley reminded her of her loaf and she went to take it from the oven. It must be the worst she had ever made, over proofed and over cooked as well, but it would have to do. She would have to manage better than this. Leaving the loaf, she made her way back to her cabin, remembering as she passed the engine that she needed to turn the stern tube greaser, since she was not moving on. Then she fell onto her bunk, closed her eyes and slept.

It was probably hunger that woke her late in the afternoon. She lay for a while reflecting on the events of the morning. Nemle would say "I told you so," she thought with a rueful smile, and then, no she wouldn't she never had, but she would have every right to.

"There are some people who have to learn from experience," she said out loud.

She yawned and stretched and got up, wondering how much was left of the day and how she could organise herself to manage better.

"*I was a bit too pleased with myself,*" she wrote in her journal to Nemle, when she had eaten and washed up and done a bit of dusting. "*I thought I was managing so well, but I was really only getting by. When something out of the ordinary happened I was not prepared. Everything went to pieces, even the bread. It was certainly penitential! Actually I exaggerate, not quite everything went to pieces. I did manage the most important thing. I found Rebah and Imni and showed them the water road, not that Rebah needed to be shown, but she needed reassurance about what she could see and now she has it.*"

She put down her pen and leaned back. There was still a pale light in the sky, but *Day Bringer* was full of shadows. Through her window she could see lights going on in the house. They seemed to shut her out. She closed her eyes. It was stupid to think that way. She had chosen to be shut out. She would sing with Nemle and go to bed and in the morning the sun would be shining and she would be on her way again.

In the morning it was not quite like that. The sun was shining and she woke early, but she was still washing when she heard Debbie's happy voice calling her. She pulled on her dressing gown and went out to greet her. Debbie was dancing about on the grass, her little pink slippers and the legs of her pyjamas were damp with dew.

"Come and say hello to my Daddy," she said. "He has to go to work soon."

Marheh laughed and shook her head.

"I'm not dressed yet."

"Get dressed now," Debbie ordered.

Again Marheh laughed, but when Debbie jumped on board and marched down the steps into her cabin, she followed obediently and finished dressing as quickly as she could, though still not quickly enough to satisfy Debbie. Then she allowed Debbie to lead her up to the house.

They were met at the back door.

"You run upstairs and get dressed now Debbie or you'll catch a cold with those wet feet."

The man's voice was direct and Debbie's little resistance was dealt with firmly. She went inside and Marheh caught a glimpse of Marion hovering anxiously before the door was firmly shut and the man turned to confront her.

He was tall, blond and well-built. He looked to be about ten years younger than Marheh and was already smartly suited, ready for work. Marheh wished she had taken time to redo her plait. She stood a little straighter and lifted her head to meet his gaze. There would be no persuading this one, she thought, bracing herself as if to meet a blow.

"I'll give you one warning," he said. "If you approach my wife and daughter ever again I will call the police and have you arrested."

"I see," Marheh said quietly. "And have you discussed this with them?"

"I don't need to. You've already influenced them with your mumbo jumbo so that even my wife believes your lies. Now get out of here before I forget you are a woman and give you the hiding you deserve."

"I'd like to see you try," Marheh said, a hint of challenge in her voice.

He lunged at her but froze suddenly before he could touch her. She looked at him in silence for a moment.

"I don't think you deserve your wife and daughter," she said to the trapped, angry eyes.

She turned and walked away down the garden towards *Day Bringer*. When she was about half way there she sent a command to release him, but did not look around or change her even, unhurried steps. If he ran after her she would stop him again, but some how she didn't think he would. She stepped onto *Day Bringer* and turned then to see his angry, baffled face as he looked for her. A little shaken by his fury, she made her way below.

Deliberately emptying her mind of everything but the task, she made up the fire and put the kettle to boil. She felt in need of warmth and comfort.

She also felt guilty. She had been angry at his arrogance and deliberately provoked him so she could justifiably use her skill at the discipline of the mind to stop him. She was not permitted to use it against ordinary people except in self defence, so she had held to the letter of the law, but not its spirit. Now he would be even more her enemy and that would be hard for Rebah and Imni.

She made herself sperit and sank into the armchair thinking of nothing but the warmth of the mug clasped in her hands and the feeling of being held that the big chair gave her. Almost like sitting on Nemle's lap, she thought, a thing that had occurred once or twice in the early years of her apprenticeship.

She had lost her chance to persuade him of her good intentions. It would be best to be away as soon as possible for the sake of Rebah and Imni. She had perhaps done more harm than good. She wished she could discuss it all with Nemle who could scold, comfort and advise in a way that made her feel supported. How galling it was to realise that despite her forty years she could still act like a child challenged in the playground.

Breakfast next and then she would be away. It was not fair to Imni to stay any longer. She made porridge and sat at the table to eat it. The state of her store cupboard was woeful, nothing fresh, a few tins of this and that, some dried milk. She would have been ashamed to let things slip to this extent when she was caring for Nemle.

She was just doing the washing up when she looked out the window to see Rebah and Imni coming hand in hand across the grass. Debbie grinned at her while Marion stood looking anxiously through her, like a blind person, not sure where to step next. She put down her dish mop and hurried out to greet them.

"I'm so sorry," she said, stepping onto the grass. "I've made him angry."

Marion turned to her, a relieved smile on her face.

"I'm sorry too. He doesn't want to understand. I think the idea frightened him. I know I was frightened at first."

She looked at Debbie then back at Marheh.

"Debbie said you were still here. I'm glad. I wanted to give you this."

She held out a paper bag. In it were a couple of eggs, a carrot, a peach and a half a pound of butter.

"I don't know what to say." Marheh broke the silence that had fallen between them. "You don't know how much I need this, but I don't deserve it. I've just made trouble for you."

Marion shook her head.

"You've helped me understand Debbie and shown me something about myself."

"And there's this," Debbie said, holding out a little jar of jam. "It's apricot," she said proudly. "I helped Mummy to make it."

"How lovely," Marheh bobbed down to her level. "Thank you Rebah. It's my favourite."

All of a sudden Debbie ran at her and gave her a hug. Marheh wrapped her arms around the little girl and stood up, lifting her.

"You're going away," Debbie said. It was a sorrowful accusation.

"Yes," Marheh said gravely. "I'm going away, but I will think about you and one day I'll come back."

She put her down and picked up the jam and the paper bag from the ground at her feet.

"Thank you so much for these. You couldn't have given me anything nicer."

Marion smiled.

"I'm glad. You will come again won't you?"

"If you are sure you want me to," Marheh said, studying her face. "But it wouldn't be for sometime."

"I want you to," Marion said firmly. "And so does Rebah."

"Thank you Imni, thank you Rebah."

She stood on the bank and watched as they went together back to the house. Before they went inside they turned to wave. Marheh waved back then went below to finish her chores and be away as quickly as she could.

There was plenty to think about as she stood at the tiller. The day's bright promise had faded and a wind had come up, scattering clouds across the sun and making it necessary for her to concentrate on her steering a bit more than usual, but as well, she kept replaying in her mind the encounter with Imni's husband. How could she have managed things better? Why was it that people felt so threatened by Silberay now? Imni had been afraid of her in the beginning too. It seemed to be getting worse. Fewer people had even heard of them and only those already on the fringes of society seemed ready to accept them.

As she travelled on, both the weather and her questions, to which she had no answers, combined to make her feel more and more depressed. She moored after her customary two hours of boating, taking particular care with her mooring pins because the wind seemed to be strengthening by the minute.

She could still enjoy the wide, wild sky, but she could find no pleasure in standing against the buffeting wind and soon went inside to the fire's welcome warmth. She would use one of Imni's eggs and make herself scrambled egg on toast for her lunch, then she would get out her map and plan a long walk. The wind would make *Day Bringer* too unsteady to work on her sculpture and she needed to walk off her mood. She might even find somewhere to buy milk and a loaf that would be better than her own.

An hour later she was ready to set off. She had changed her tunic for a warmer one and slung a small back pack over her shoulders. If she felt a bit chilly it would just keep her moving, she thought, as she decided against her cloak. Six miles, roughly, if she had read the map correctly – she could scavenge for the fire, maybe if she was lucky she might find a mushroom or two and the exercise would lift her spirits.

She spent a few moments over *Day Bringer*'s mooring pins, speaking the words of the little rhyme the Silberay liked to think was a safeguard. Whether it actually helped she was not sure, but it made her feel better about leaving *Day Bringer*.

Her way took her through little used lanes and footpaths where spring was progressing well despite the day's chill. New green veiled the trees, bluebells and small starry celandines decorated the verges, and birds sang and darted and rode the wind. For a while she thought of nothing but the warming exercise and the beauty around her. She saw no one. Once or twice she needed to take out her map and refresh her memory of the way, once she came across a marked footpath that had been closed, forcing her into a short detour.

She found very little in the way of firewood, just a couple of pine cones that she put into her pack, but since that had not been the purpose of her walk she was not disappointed, especially when she found two big mushrooms as she crossed a field. Fried in some of Imni's butter they would make a lovely supper.

The thought of Imni's butter reminded her of Imni herself and then of the morning's confrontation. She had not handled it well. What she had done had only reinforced his anger and perhaps turned his dismissal of her into dislike or worse. He had been prejudiced against her, but she had made no effort to improve his understanding of whom she was. She shook her head as if to rid herself of the thought and tried to lose herself in the walking again, but with only limited success, until the sight of the small village that had been the target for her walk distracted her.

It was years since she had been there and it had changed almost beyond recognition. She was approaching across a field, but she could see the road from where she stood, or at least, the cottages that marked the road and they seemed to extend in clumps at either end. Going closer she realised that her footpath spilled into a lane with more new cottages and it was not until she reached the centre of the village that she actually recognised the old pub and the church on opposite sides of the green. There must be a school somewhere too, she realised, as a bell sounded. She preferred not to be about when school was dismissed, but she could not hide away today, so she continued on towards the sign that distinguished the village shop from the rest of the row of small terrace houses that had their front doors right on the footpath.

As she came closer she found that the village shop and post office had been supplemented by a butcher on a corner opposite the shop. Her thoughts turned to bacon and lamb chops and she was glad she had tucked an extra pound note into her purse. A bell rang as she stepped inside. The two customers ahead of her turned to stare and the butcher lifted his head from the package he was wrapping.

"Clear off," he said, giving her a hard stare but not raising his voice. "We don't want your sort in here."

Marheh straightened a little, but stood quietly where she was.

"What do you mean 'my sort'?" she asked, when she was enough in command of herself to speak without challenge.

"Dirty, thieving gypsy," the butcher said. "Now clear off before I throw you out."

One of the customers looked at Marheh and tittered. Marheh reddened under her despising gaze but kept her lips firmly pressed together. The other, an older woman, looked from Marheh to the butcher and said mildly.

"That's a bit hard Jack. She looks quite harmless to me." She turned back to Marheh. "What were you wanting my lovely? Jack gets a bit crotchety sometimes, and he doesn't like women in trousers."

"I just wanted to buy some meat," Marheh said, smiling at the woman. "But I don't want to cause a problem. I can do without."

She turned to go, grateful to the woman for allowing her to make a dignified departure. It was not the first time she had been called a dirty thief and she knew it would not be the last but it was never easy to accept it. Nemle had advised and scolded and counselled self-discipline until she had mostly learned not to show anger, but she doubted she would ever learn not to feel it.

She felt a light touch on her arm and turned back to the woman.

"If you've money to pay for what you want Jack's obliged to serve you," she said. "You wait with me until he's finished with Mrs Tarrant and then we'll get you sorted."

Marheh glanced between her and the butcher and saw that he was completing his wrapping. There was a rather surly expression on his face, but he no longer protested at her presence. He passed the parcel across the counter to her protector and money was passed back before he turned to deal with Mrs Tarrant. Marheh's new friend put the package in her basket and patted Marheh's arm.

"He's a very good butcher really," she said. "And his bark's worse than his bite."

Mrs Tarrant's needs were quickly supplied and she left with another despising look at Marheh and a brief warning against her to Mrs Armstrong.

"Don't mind her, my lovely." Mrs Armstrong gave her an almost mischievous smile. "I don't, and she's my next door neighbour."

Marheh grinned at that.

"It's kind of you to help me."

With Mrs Armstrong's benevolent assistance, she was soon in possession of half a dozen rashers of bacon, two lamb chops and a bone for soup. Mrs Armstrong had even prevailed upon Jack to cut it in two for her so it would fit comfortably in her saucepan.

When they were outside the butcher's Marheh turned to thank her. Mrs Armstrong patted her arm again.

"That's quite alright my lovely. You're Silberay aren't you?"

Marheh nodded. Her smile lit her face.

"I thought I recognised the uniform. There's a lot of ignorance about now and a lot of prejudice."

She paused to look at Marheh.

"Were you wanting anything from the shop?"

"I was planning to get milk, and perhaps a loaf," Marheh said.

"You'd best come with me then, just in case."

"If you're sure. I don't want to cause trouble for you."

"The village is used to me. I've never been one to keep silent if there's something I ought to speak about."

"It's years since I was last here. I don't remember feeling unwelcome then though."

"Lots of new people have come in the last few years and just lately we've had a spate of petty theft. People are a bit wary of strangers."

They began to cross the road. Behind them came the sound of running feet and a scatter of children ran past.

"School's out!"

Mrs Armstrong raised her eyebrows. More children came running, one or two calling a greeting as they passed. Marheh fielded some curious glances then one, bolder than the others, stopped in front of them.

"Who's she?"

"This is a friend of mine, so just you mind your manners Nicholas Johns."

"Why is she dressed like that?"

Mrs Armstrong glanced at Marheh to see if she wished to answer.

"This is my uniform," Marheh said.

At the sound of her voice more children stopped behind Nicholas to stare at her.

"Trousers are for men."

A girl child's disapproving tones came from beside Nicholas.

"Why?" Marheh asked.

"My mother says so," the child replied.

"My mother doesn't mind if I wear trousers." Marheh smiled at the child. "It's easier to do my work."

The child appeared unconvinced.

"You shouldn't be doing man's work," she said, clearly parroting an adult's opinion.

Marheh forbore to argue but followed Mrs Armstrong into the store.

"A very conservative family," Mrs Armstrong said apologetically.

Marheh gave her a rueful smile and stood with her at the counter to be served.

Soon a fresh loaf and a block of good strong cheese were added to her pack. She picked up her bottle of milk and thanked Mrs Armstrong for her help.

"I'll be grateful all over again when I'm cooking my chop," she added.

Mrs Armstrong smiled at her.

"It's a pleasure my lovely. I don't like to see my village turning in on itself.

You'll be alright for getting home?"

"I'm sure I will. The bulk of my walk is behind me and it's mostly downhill from here."

She parted from Mrs Armstrong in the high street and set off to complete her walk. There was perhaps a mile and a half to go and she stepped out briskly, pleased with her purchases and looking forward to her evening meal.

Once through the village she turned off the high street onto a narrow lane, rather over grown with high, ragged hedges of hawthorn on each side.

There should be a footpath soon. She pictured the map in her mind and slowed her pace a little looking for a stile.

"Hey, you!"

The shouts came from behind her, the shrill high voices of children. She turned towards them and received a half dried cow pat full in her face, then a stone caught her shoulder. There was the sound of laughter and more shouting.

"Get away witch, we don't want you."

Then the sound of running feet faded into the distance and she knew she was alone.

For a few moments she just stood, her eyes closed, aware of dirt and smell and discomfort. Carefully she reached for her handkerchief and tried to wipe her eyes, needing to open them, to see. It was better then. She took a couple of rather unsteady steps and stopped, straightened her spine. A couple of unruly schoolboys would not get her down. She had not even dropped her bottle of milk. She spat on a clean corner of her handkerchief, wiped her eyes again and set off.

Getting over the stile was a test that demonstrated how shaky she was, but at least crossing the fields she was in the open, no more surprises. It was easier not to think, just walk steadily onwards with *Day Bringer* her goal.

By the time she reached her the wind had dried much of the dirt to dust and blown it away. The smell had blown away with it, or else she had become accustomed to it but her shoulder throbbed painfully. Before stepping on board she eased out of her tunic and gave it a good shake. It would need washing but at least she would not be carrying cow dung onto *Day Bringer*. The action had awakened the throbbing to pain and she stood for a moment, concentrating on her breathing, before picking up her pack and her bottle of milk and stepping on board.

A couple of hours later she sat comfortably in the armchair, her journal on her knee.

The business of washing, herself and her clothes, of preparing her meal and clearing up had been an effort of will, but worth it now that it was behind her. Her long dark hair was still wet but drying in the warmth of the saloon. What was important now was to make sense of what had happened. It hurt, not the dull ache that remained in her shoulder, she could put that out of her mind. What hurt was the knowledge of hatred. Nemle had taught her the pain of that needed treating just as much as the painful shoulder she had smeared with comfrey ointment. It was not a new thing, but far more confronting than the encounter with Rebah's father because she had done nothing to provoke this attack, nothing except be who she was.

She picked up her pen, but at first she could not find words and made little doodles instead, a teardrop then another, a stile with a broken step, an empty basket. It was the caricature of her own surprised, dirty face that the released the words.

"I must have looked really funny," she wrote. *"And if it had been an accident I might have been able to laugh too, but they did it to me to make me less, to make me someone they didn't need to be afraid of. I need to understand what has made them afraid of me and I need to understand what being feared might do to me."*

She put down her pen and closed her eyes – a memory of childhood, as vivid as if it had been yesterday.

An elderly woman had lived alone in a rather dilapidated house with a large, wildly over grown garden. Marheh had led her brothers in exciting forays into that garden. They skulked in the undergrowth, climbed the trees and crept to the windows to pop up and shout. She'd made up stories that turned the woman into a witch and added a frisson of fear to their activities. They began to believe in the stories and became more daring. Then one day, five year old Tep had been caught as they ran from her.

Marheh had watched through the fence as the woman had taken the small, struggling figure into the house and closed the door. She had hovered, horrified, trying to find the courage to go and tackle the witch, but her two other brothers had run home to pour out to their mother how Tep had been captured and was about to be eaten.

There had been consequences then. Marheh had watched from afar as her parents met the woman as she was taking Tep home. His hand was happily in hers and his face smeared with chocolate biscuit. The three adults spoke together. Marheh remembered how this normal, everyday interaction had awakened her to reality. She had not wanted to go home and wandered about in the woods until nearly dark trying to persuade herself that the woman really was a wicked witch who deserved Marheh's treatment of her.

She had finally walked into the kitchen, holding herself stiff and proud and ready to flare out. The boys were finishing their tea and were careful not to look at her. Her mother had quietly sent her to her room. Serious talks and tears followed, but as well, her parents had invited the woman to a family meal. That, more than any scolding, had shown her the truth of the woman's humanity and enabled her to apologise with sincerity for the hurt she had done her.

Now she knew what it felt like.

She picked up her pen again.

"I was angry and vengeful. It would have felt good to have made them push their faces into a cowpat. Fortunately I didn't, because not only would I have broken the law, but I would have been sorry now."

She sighed deeply. There was more. She knew there was more to be learnt but she couldn't get her mind to address it.

"Why?" she wrote and added a big question mark, then again "**Why?**"

But she could find no answer now. Better to stop fussing and forget it, put her thoughts away with her journal and practice the disciplines.

Of course that did not come easily either. Her song struggled to spin any light in the darkness that seemed to surround her and at no time did she sense Nemle's supporting presence. She returned to herself exhausted, only just able to drag herself to her bed, too weary to even begin to consider the implications of the darkness she had found.

Although she slept, she woke unrefreshed, conscious of troubling dreams.

It seemed as if she had stirred up something malevolent and longed for Nemle's wisdom and common sense to guide her. She dressed, feeling a twinge from her shoulder as she pulled on her tunic. It was her job to deal with the darkness here but she had another job to do too. She couldn't seem to think. She ought to be able to cope surely. She had faced challenges before. Why couldn't she decide what to do?

In the end she knew the only thing she was capable of doing was leaving, at least for the moment, so she could find space to think through what had happened.

As soon as *Day Bringer*'s engine was throbbing beneath her and her hand on the tiller felt its vibrations, she began to recover her equilibrium. She didn't even succumb to the temptation to castigate herself for a fool and a coward. She had perhaps been to complacent, too confident in her ability to manage whatever came her way, but this retreat was to regroup, to gather herself. She would find a nice mooring and work and rest and sing again. Then she would be clearer about what she needed to do.

Yesterday' gales had blown themselves out and the morning was calm and warm. Summer was on its way. She would have fresh bread with butter and some of Rebah's apricot jam for her lunch, then a short walk, just to stretch her legs, then perhaps an hour to finish her sculpture and then she would be refreshed and could practice the discipline of the soul again. This time she would be strong enough to sing even if it was into darkness, even if Nemle could not find her to sing with her.

The water road made its quiet way through the countryside and she with it, breathing its gentle peace until there was no room for anything other. She had not really thought much about the other women who had lived on *Day Bringer* though Nemle had told her of them and she had dipped into Rinteh's journal in the archive at the Harbour. Now she was alone it seemed as if they were all present with her and she wished she had paid more attention to Nemle's stories. Rinteh, Tala, Hafa and Nemle, women of the Silberay and she was following, was trying to follow, their example of service.

She found her nice mooring and enjoyed her bread and jam, but when it came to a walk she was suddenly reluctant. After a small struggle she acknowledged to herself that she was afraid. That was enough to challenge her to action. Marheh the Great lifted her chin and stepped briskly off *Day Bringer*. She would enjoy her walk no matter what.

When she was young she had found it very difficult to admit to fear. Nemle had more than once demanded honesty of her in the past and now she had learned the wisdom of acknowledging it, so she could address it consciously. That did not mean giving in to it though, she told herself, deliberately choosing to take a path through a field rather than continuing beside the water road. She met no one and returned to *Day Bringer* refreshed and ready to lose herself, first in finishing her sculpture and then in entering the soul song.

Higham's Hill

Chapter Four

Next morning she took out Jik's and Nemle's letters and re-read them. Both enjoined her to take her time over the task they had set her. She would stay here a little longer and try to discover the cause of the darkness that had threatened her song, even in this place, though it was not as strong here at today's mooring as it had been the previous day.

Once her decision had been made her confidence began to return. This was her job. She was not an apprentice any longer. For twenty years she had leaned on Nemle, been foolish and headstrong, been adventurous, even courageous sometimes and the knowledge of Nemle's steady, supporting presence had been her rock and her anchor. Nemle's physical presence was gone, never to return. She had to be grounded now in her own long practice of the disciplines. These were the years when she must develop wisdom of her own or waste the years of Nemle's patient teaching and her own, sometimes painful struggles.

She spent half an hour quietly completing necessary chores, then she set herself again to practise the discipline of the soul, this time conscious of the presence of darkness, this time deliberately focusing her song against that darkness, hoping both to understand and diffuse.

It was a solitary struggle and when she emerged she understood that it would not be enough simply to sing light. In this place the darkness was active and her song alone would not be enough to render it benign. She prepared herself a small meal of bread and cheese, grappling with the realisation that she must return to the village and try to discover whether the source of darkness was lurking there. It was not simply a malaise born of negligence and self-centredness. It was stronger and more focused than that. Yareblis influence was at work.

Oddly, the understanding was almost reassuring. The villagers were being taught to reject her, which some how made their enmity less personal.

She ate sparingly, checked her map briefly and set out. She took nothing with her, not even her empty pack. She would have nothing to spare for any gathering for her own needs. She would walk through the countryside holding her candle flame lightly in the forefront of her mind, conscious of every influence acting on its small, steadfast glow.

Nemle had called it listening with her heart and there was a time when the arrogant young apprentice had scoffed at the idea. She knew better now.

At first, all was as it should be. The soft spring sunshine warmed her, a light breeze fanned her, the turf was firm under her feet. She stepped out steadily, not hurrying but keeping a pace she knew she could sustain for the long walk. Whereever possible she kept to footpaths, preferring to cope with an occasional field of cows than to take to the roads, quiet tree-lined lanes though they were.

Eventually though the roads became her most direct way. She was approaching the village from a different place and the road that led her there was rather more than a country lane, macadamised with a painted line of dashes along its centre and a deep, overgrown ditch on either side. It was uncomfortable walking, made more difficult by the need to be aware of the possible approach of cars. Listening with her heart became more and more difficult when her physical safety necessitated listening with her ears.

She leapt for the verge as a large black vehicle swept by with an arrogant blast of its horn. She had felt the wind of its passing and could still smell its exhaust as it raced ahead of her towards the village.

Carefully she extricated herself from the weeds in the ditch. Not much further. Surely she must be close now. For a moment she stood, looking and listening. Across the road the land fell away sharply. She could see, across what must be a deep gully, to a scar of rock topped by a tangle of scrubby growth. From somewhere not too far away a train whistle sounded. Beside her, beyond the ditch, was a rather neglected hawthorn hedge supplemented by a wire fence, and ahead, beyond the crest of the hill she glimpsed chimneys between groups of trees.

She closed her eyes briefly to concentrate on her candle flame then relinquished it reluctantly. It had no chance against the increasing darkness and she did not need its warning now. Who did she think she was anyway, expecting to make some kind of difference here? Still, she had come this far, she might as well keep going.

Just before the crest of the hill she came upon a painted sign, rather weathered, welcoming the traveller to Higham's Hill and informing her that the population was 341.

"I suppose it was once," she thought. "It must be double that now."

At the top of the hill the road swept around a corner and abruptly the scrubby hedgerows gave way to a terrace of small, bland houses, squashed together behind minute front gardens. She stopped to catch her breath and take stock.

They were quite new, the houses, made all at the same time to the same design, red brick with a central front door and a window on either side. Above there were three windows beneath a grey pitched roof. There was nothing really wrong with them only the proportions were a bit pinched and no one seemed to care very much about the gardens. Sighing a little, she continued to walk. At least there was a pavement now, though she still jumped as another car swept past.

Quite suddenly, like a wave, depression rolled over her. What was she doing here? What did she think she could achieve? The village didn't want her. They had made that perfectly plain two days ago. They probably thought their village was perfect.

Mrs Armstrong didn't though.

What had she said? "I don't like to see my village turning in on itself."

She was the stranger, the outsider. If the village had to look at her, what would they see?

She continued to walk, most of her mind busy with these thoughts, but aware enough of her surroundings to stop in delight before the one house where someone seemed to care. The front door had been painted a soft blue grey. A paler shade framed the door and the windows. On either side of the tiny path to the door was garden; cottage flowers, daisies, stocks, poppies, pansies all colours and shapes, splashed across the small space and, guarding the door, two tall standard roses bloomed in all their spring glory.

This gift of beauty was for her, the outsider, the passer-by. There was work in it, lovingly performed. She watched as a butterfly landed on a leaf, then on another. She saw a bee crawl to the heart of a flower. Then the front door opened.

"Hello my lovely," said Mrs Armstrong, smiling at her. "I saw you from my window. Admiring my garden?"

"It's beautiful," Marheh said, feeling her spirits lift at the friendly greeting.

"I'm surprised you're back. You didn't get much of a welcome last time."

"You welcomed me and helped me."

Mrs Armstrong studied her for a moment. Marheh wondered what she was seeing.

"Would you like to come in, have a cup of tea?" she asked at last.

Marheh hesitated.

"I would love to," she said. "But I think I had better continue just now."

She looked ahead to where the village awaited her then back to Mrs Armstrong.

"Perhaps, if it wouldn't be a nuisance, perhaps I could call on my way home."

"Come any time," Mrs Armstrong said, smiling again, before she popped back inside as abruptly as she had emerged.

Marheh continued on her way, cheered by the encounter. Perhaps it didn't really matter that she had no idea what she would do in the village. Perhaps what was important was her obedience.

She passed the new houses and came to a couple of bigger, older detached homes and then the row of small cottages near the shops. There were people about now, mostly women with shopping bags and she received a few curious, even hostile glances. She kept going without reacting however until she came to the village green. Here there was a bench seat placed under a big old oak with a view of the church. She went to sit down. The shade was pleasant after her walk and she felt less visible resting there.

After spending a few minutes watching the small comings and goings as villagers met and parted, entered or left the shop, crossed back and forth in the afternoon sun, she sought again for her candle flame. Almost immediately she wondered whether she had made a mistake. It was not so much that there was darkness, she had expected that, but now it was as if the darkness was aware of her. She drew back hastily and looked up.

At first it seemed as if nothing had changed. No one seemed to be taking any more notice of her than they had already. Then she saw a man come out of the shop followed by another man and three women. They grouped together in battle formation and headed towards her. She straightened, head erect, but remained seated watching them approach. What had she expected? She had brought herself here and asked to be noticed. She must not use her mind against them, she reminded herself, only if her own mind was threatened.

She bit her lip and noticed that one hand was gripping the seat. Carefully she relaxed it. The group were very close now and she would not show fear despite the anger and determination on their faces.

Another minute and she was surrounded. She looked from face to face all distorted by their dislike of her. One face held more than dislike. She looked again and recognised Imni's husband. What was he doing here?

"I told you I passed one of them on the road," he said now, speaking to the second man. "I didn't realise it was that one."

Marheh continued to sit quietly, her hands resting on her lap, but she allowed a mild question to appear on her face.

"Two days ago she was in my back garden attempting to corrupt my wife and daughter."

There was a muttering and a shuffling and "Disgusting!" burst forth from the lips of one of the women.

The group was close, almost close enough to touch her, but not quite and Marheh had the sense that they were a little afraid of her.

"What's she doing here then? Ask her, go on, ask her."

Marheh looked at the woman who had spoken and smiled.

"I came because I thought you needed me," she said.

There was a little gasp from the woman, as if she was surprised that Marheh could speak then Imni's husband thrust her aside.

"No one needs you – bitch and we're here to see that you get out of this village and stay out."

He wanted to touch her, but Marheh could see he remembered what had happened when he tried to before. He was almost dancing with rage and frustration. Marheh looked at each of the others before she spoke again.

"I don't believe this gentleman lives in your village. Are you sure you want him to speak for you?"

"Yes we are!" The woman's face twisted. "You and your kind are disgusting, corrupt."

The words poured out and over Marheh like the worst kind of filth. When they finally ended, the woman stepped closer to Marheh, gathered herself and spat full in her face.

This action broke whatever feeling had restrained them until now and the two men reached for Marheh, pulled her up off the seat and flung her face down on the grass. Someone kicked her as she tried to scramble to her feet and she went down again. Dimly she was aware of noise, shouting and running feet, but mostly she was trying not to react with her mind. She could stop them as she had stopped Imni's husband, protect herself and get away, but then they would fear her more, turn further against the Silberay. Not yet, she told herself, trying to get up again, not yet.

There was a different quality to the shouting now and feet and hands no longer invaded her. She lifted her head warily and saw Mrs Armstrong, flanked by a large young man. Their anger shone bright around them. She put her head down and closed her eyes. She would get up in a minute.

Mrs Armstrong's voice filtered through to her.

"What do you think you're doing? You would be ashamed to treat a dog this way. This is a human being."

Marheh thought she would not get up yet. She hurt all over.

"Peter Butterworth, your mother would be turning in her grave."

Gradually other noise died away.

"Amelia Tarrant, don't come asking me for a cup of sugar next time you run out. I don't know what this village is coming to. What harm did she do to any of you?"

The large young man crouched down beside Marheh and touched her shoulder hesitantly. She opened her eyes and tried a small smile.

"As for you," Mrs Armstrong continued. "Why should a commercial traveller, who only visits once a week, have any say in how this village conducts itself?"

Imni's husband reddened angrily.

"She's evil," he blurted out.

"Who's evil? Who's evil?" She stepped forward. "Now go away the lot of you and do some hard thinking about what you've just done and be thankful that Sandy and I got here in time to stop you doing something worse."

She flapped her hands at them as if they were unruly hens then crouched down beside Marheh and Sandy. She put a hand over one of Marheh's.

"Can you get up my lovely? Let Sandy help you."

Getting up was painful but possible with Sandy's strong arm to assist her. She stood a moment taking stock. Mrs Armstrong and Sandy watched her anxiously.

"Nothing that won't mend," she said to reassure them. "A few bruises. I'm very grateful."

Her sentences were short and producing them difficult. She couldn't think how she would get home, not all that long walk.

"You'll come home with me and rest," Mrs Armstrong told her. "Then Sandy will take you whereever you need to go."

Just getting to Mrs Armstrong's small house seemed impossibly far at first but she found walking easier as she went. Mrs Armstrong hurried on ahead and when Marheh arrived, leaning on Sandy's arm, she had already run a bath for her.

"Hand me out your tunic," she said. "I'll mend it while you bathe then we'll have tea and Sandy will go for his car."

Undressing caused a few twinges but sinking into the bath was perfection. The water was perfumed lightly with lavender. She breathed in the scented steam and felt it heal her spirit. She washed her face, and then again, until the woman's venom was cleaned away, then turned her attention to the rest of her. It was odd to see her body stretched out, naked like this. Washing was not usually something to linger over. She supposed she was in reasonable shape. She felt as fit as ever normally. Now she was aware there would be bruises. An especially tender place under her left breast might even be a damaged rib but there was not much to be done about it if it was. She did not want to think about what had happened, though she knew she would have to eventually.

The water began to cool and she levered herself painfully upright. Mrs Armstrong had left her a big fluffy towel and she dried herself carefully, discovering more sensitive places as she did so.

When she had dressed again she joined Mrs Armstrong and Sandy in the kitchen. Mrs Armstrong looked at her anxiously as she appeared and patted the seat beside her at the table. She had Marheh's tunic on her lap and was just completing her sewing.

"It was just the seam gave way," she said, holding it out to Marheh. "The fabric didn't tear. It will be as good as new."

"I'm very grateful," Marheh said again.

"Let me help you with that."

Mrs Armstrong got up to assist her.

"You will stay and have tea won't you? Das has just made a pot."

Marheh turned to smile at Sandy.

"Das?" she said, recognising she had been given his soul name. "And I'm Marheh."

"Marheh," Mrs Armstrong repeated.

She settled Marheh's tunic, pulling out the collar of her shirt and folding it over. Marheh was reminded for a moment of Nemle's loving care.

"Call me Blethan," she said.

Marheh smiled and sat as Mrs Armstrong pulled out the chair she had indicated before.

"Blethan and Das," she said looking from one to the other. "I can't thank you enough."

There was tea and bread and butter and homemade cake and Marheh ate and felt better.

"You're looking a bit brighter now my lovely," Mrs Armstrong said, pouring them all a second cup of tea. "Suppose you tell us what happened and why you came back. There's something wrong here in the village isn't there?"

Marheh lifted her cup and sipped, savouring the warmth and considering her answer.

"It feels as if something is out of alignment," she said slowly. "I listened and there was no song. I looked and there was only darkness. It seemed to be my job to come back."

Granny's friend's cottage

Chapter Five

Marheh sat around the table with Das and Blethan for quite some time. Whatever needed doing in the village could not be done by her alone. She could be a catalyst, but the village must change from within and Das and Blethan were obviously part of that change.

As they talked Marheh learned that Das was Blethan's youngest son. He managed the family farm on the outskirts of the village. He was not quite as young as Marheh first thought and had a wife and a small child. Blethan had moved to the new houses when they were built in order to give them the farm house. The family had farmed near Higham's Hill for four generations.

"I know small villages tend to become a bit insular," Blethan said. "But not like this. I don't know what's got into them lately."

"I think," Marheh chose her words carefully. "I think there is some, not control exactly, but influence that can catch the unwary. You and Das use your soul names. Just doing that helps you to keep hold of your values when they are threatened but perhaps there are others whose values are not as firmly in place."

"Is that why you came back?" Das asked. "Mother told me about meeting you in the butcher's."

Marheh nodded.

"I didn't know what I should do, but it felt like my job to return."

"So now what?" Blethan asked.

"Do you think any of them were a bit shocked at what happened, what they did?" Marheh asked.

"Peter Butterworth was," Das said. "I saw his face when Mother said that about doing it to a dog. He's got two rescue dogs and one of them had been really badly treated."

"He's not a bad man, a bit thoughtless and jumps in without considering first," Blethan said. "I've known him nearly all his life."

"Is he the man who owns the shop?" Marheh asked, trying to get it clear.

Blethan nodded.

"It's always been a family business."

"It's just that," Marheh spoke slowly. She was aching all over and longing for *Day Bringer* and solitude, but this was important. "I think it is my job to try to find the source of the influence, but it might be your job to use what happened today to help the village realise that there is an influence that is bent on twisting them."

There was a short silence when she finished speaking then Blethan stood up and began to gather the cups and plates.

"You're quite right, the village is our business, you've done enough. I think I can see how to go on."

She stopped and looked at Marheh.

"And I know I can see you've had enough. Das will go and …" She paused as if for effect, "…and borrow Peter Butterworth's delivery van to take you home."

It was a good idea, the delivery van, Marheh thought, when she was finally alone on *Day Bringer*. Peter Butterworth had been very willing to lend it and wanted to load her with gifts in reparation. She had accepted a big block of chocolate but that was all. Das had driven her down the hill and as close as she could guide him to *Day Bringer*. He had refused to leave her until he knew she was safe so she had allowed him to support her alongside the water road until they reached the boat. She'd not had energy enough to help him see her, but she had explained what would happen, how she would step into a different dimension when she boarded. Although he could not see her she had energy enough to make sure he could hear her quiet thanks for his aid. He acknowledged them with a lift of an eyebrow and a wry smile before turning to go back to the van.

Marheh made her way down into her cabin. She was bone weary and ached all over but there were things she had to do before she could rest. Some were little things; mend the fire, treat the worst of her bruises with comfrey ointment, but the important thing would take all her remaining energy. She must enter the discipline of the soul and find the courage to sing, even if all she encountered was darkness, because now the work of change had begun she must make sure that the enemy was not permitted to increase its influence.

The little things accomplished, she changed into her nightdress, wrapped herself in her dressing gown and settled into the armchair, trying to ignore the painful twinges that seemed to be lying in wait for any incautious movement.

He candle flame beckoned, burning brightly, so brightly that entering the discipline was almost painful. Her song faltered but she persisted and as she sang golden light seemed to surround her. It was the candle yet not the candle, she was the candle and the song and the light and there was no darkness anywhere. The song and the light seemed effortless although on some level she knew there was a cost.

At first she was alone in the light and the song was all her own, but gradually, almost imperceptibly, other voices joined hers. Some remained supporting her from afar but others came closer and one in particular wove glorious harmonies of celebration, under and over and between her song.

It ended of course, and she was left exhausted, but uplifted too, and next morning it seemed as if her sleep had been cradled in love and her dreams filled with music and light.

How had it happened? She wondered as she sat with her breakfast in the well deck, light and celebration where there had been darkness and struggle. She had not been wrong about the darkness, it had been there, only not now. What had happened? She had done nothing except go there because she had thought she should. She let her mind drift into the loveliness of the spring morning and away from the aches and pains that reminded her of Higham's Hill. She felt a little kernel of warmth at the knowledge that she had not allowed herself to hit out with her mind, not used her special power against those with no defence. Somehow she felt it made up a little for her failure with Imni's husband.

This business of the discipline of the mind, the practice of it and the use of the power she had was the hardest of all the Silberay teachings. It would be so much easier if she either had no power or if she could use it when and how she wanted. Instead she had been encouraged to develop the power, practising with Nemle until she knew she was more skilled than any other Silberay, and then shown how wrong it would be to use it except against the Yareblis.

She drank the last of her sperit and stood up. Perhaps her obedience had helped against the darkness. She could hope so anyway, and now she could move on towards Deerford and home and then to the task Jik had given her.

The next few days were gentle and healing. She resumed her usual pattern of boating, moving on each morning, spending the afternoon working at her sculpture and the evening practicing the discipline of the soul. Her body ceased to ache, though there were bruises of all colours in unexpected places.

Her sculpture of the gardeners was finished and she was working on a group of musicians now. At least there would be a group in the end, first she was trying out poses from sketches she had made at the Gathering. She thought the individual figures would be saleable too at the small markets she visited. She had completed a couple of concertina players and a guitarist and was enjoying the challenge of modelling a fiddler and trying to find a way to capture the light, mobile quality of the bow.

Beneath all this gentle activity she was conscious of thoughts and questions. Sometimes these thrust themselves into her notice. At other times they seemed to work away at the back of her mind. Now she began to understand the true purpose of her journal. When she took it up to write she could explore her thoughts and questions more deliberately, even constructively. She needed to make sense of her recent experiences, not just make sense, but try to learn from them. How could she have done things better? Had she needed to allow herself to be hurt? Could she have used her mind to diffuse the situation without them realising? Perhaps she had needed to suffer?

"You could hardly call it suffering," she wrote after a day of questioning. *"Other things have hurt more and achieved less. I can't believe that it is necessary for me to be hurt, though perhaps it is necessary for me to be willing to be hurt."*

She scribbled a little doodle, rubbed her hand over her face and sighed heavily. Then she continued to write.

"It sounds stupid to say that I want to add to the sum of goodness in the world. I don't know how to say it so it doesn't sound stupid. I thought life as Silberay was going to be a great, romantic adventure. I know in the past I've just responded to things as they happened and relied on Nemle to talk sense to me and support me when I needed it. This last week has shown me I have to do better than that now. If I hadn't treated Imni's husband the way I did, if I hadn't given him reason to hate me, then maybe things in the village wouldn't have escalated the way they did.

I am willing to put myself at risk if that is needed, at least I believe I should be and hope I am. A soldier would be and I suppose in a way I am part of a battle, but what I do, what I want to do isn't about fighting, not really. If anything it's about freedom."

She sat back and looked at what she had written. *"It's about freedom."* What had Nemle said in her letter, *"perhaps freedom is only freedom to choose the path you will follow, the challenges you will accept."* Once you've chosen though it's no good wanting something else and thinking you're free to chop and change. That's why Silberay talked so much about discipline. You have to follow the chosen path through thick and thin even if it hurts. What was more important, the path or the goal? She wrote that down in her journal in big letters then closed it and put it away. So many questions she had no answer for and yet she was no longer an apprentice. Somewhere she had to find answers for herself. Perhaps that was really the purpose of the next thirty years until she became a mentor.

Sometimes, as she went, she saw things, unwillingly, because she travelled unseen. Things people would not do if they thought they were overlooked. Over the years she had become adept at not seeing the small private moments of others, but occasionally there were moments it pained her to have to ignore; the sly aggression of a bully, the secret anger of the vandal, unkindness to a child or an animal.

Now she began to wonder whether she really needed to ignore them. The most important prohibitions in Silberay law were against the wrong use of the discipline of the mind. These had been drilled into her in various ways throughout her apprenticeship and she believed strongly in the validity of the idea behind these prohibitions. It was wrong to use the discipline of the mind to force people to act in certain ways, not only because it deprived them of choice, but because she herself would be damaged by thinking herself powerful.

But perhaps there were ways to help a victim without becoming a victim herself. Suppose she were to enter the mind of a bully and misdirect his punch so the spent force of it knocked him off balance. She could do that easily without him even being aware of her existence, but should she? Should she have the prospective vandal trip over his own feet? She could do that too, but should she?

She pondered these questions as she stood at the tiller each morning. They were not entirely new questions, but she was aware that she had been more ready to act than to think in the past, letting Nemle do her thinking for her. It was not arrogance to acknowledge she was the most skilled of all the Silberay in using the discipline of the mind. It was just the truth, but Nemle had encouraged her to recognise that she, more than anyone, needed to understand what that meant in terms of responsibility.

And she had to do it for herself. All the laws of the Silberay were external, learned and applied but perhaps not always appropriate. She had been in trouble as an apprentice for challenging some of the laws and things had changed a bit in consequence, but sometimes it still seemed to her that there were circumstances where the rules could not apply. Was it arrogance to think she knew better? Or was it the beginning of wisdom to be questioning?

It was important to ask the questions, but equally important to leave them and allow the discipline of the soul to guide her towards the answers. That was where the Yareblis had fallen. They denied the soul and so the guidance of the soul song was lost to them and their values became warped by the misuse of their ability.

There was Yareblis influence still at work here. Each day as she travelled to a new mooring and spent time listening with her heart and singing the soul song she was conscious of increasing dark held at bay. It made her anxious for her family at Deerford and she began to increase each day's journey until two hours became three and then four.

It was more than a year since she had visited her parents and her brother Tep and she found herself thinking more and more of them and looking forward to seeing them again. Was Deerford being influenced by the darkness too? She didn't think it would change her parents or Tep and his wife Fali, but what of the village itself? The water road ran through the village so they were used to seeing Silberay and they knew her. She had grown up there. Of course there would be those who remembered her fondly and those who did not, but surely she would not experience the same prejudice she had in Higham's Hill.

Days before she expected it she found she was approaching the mooring for Willow Rise, a small village about a week's journey from Deerford.

It was a pleasant place and one she knew well. The water road ran quite close which made it a useful source of provisions and she had visited it often as a girl. Her mother's parents had lived there then, though there was no family left now.

Although she had not been travelling long, barely an hour, she decided to moor and give herself a day off. *Day Bringer's* brass needed a bit of attention and it was a nice day for sitting on the roof with a brass cloth. Then after lunch she would visit the village.

She took her sketch book with her when she went. There was pretty church in the village with a couple of interesting gargoyles that would be fun to draw and she could possibly use the drawings later.

The mooring was not far from the road that ran between Willow Rise and Deerford and once on the road it was only minutes before she reached the first house. Granny's friend used to live there, she remembered, studying it with pleasure. It had not changed much. The thatch had been renewed recently and the woodwork painted she thought, but there had been no obvious attempt to modernise and the garden still ran wild in a riot of spring colour.

She crossed the road to give herself a bit of perspective and scribbled a small sketch, but it needed colour, she decided, looking at it critically before moving on.

It was very quiet, that warm, sleepy, after lunch, afternoon time. No one was about and she enjoyed herself wandering along, stopping every now and then to refresh her memories or admire a garden. She turned off the main road to stroll past her grandparents' house, remembering the times she had visited sometimes with her mother and then, as she grew older, on her own. She had never really been one for dolls, except here. Here she and she alone, had been allowed to play with the dolls that had belonged to her grandmother. There were three of them, not very big, perhaps ten inches tall, with smooth china heads and china hands and feet. Their painted faces were pretty, fairy-like and they had curls of soft hair. Between the extremities their stuffed cloth bodies were flexible enough to be dressed and undressed and placed in different poses.

It would be rather fun to make some dolls like that, but she'd need someone else to make the bodies. Perhaps Fali would be interested.

She was still playing with ideas as she wondered back to the main street. It seemed a long time since she had allowed herself to relax like this and she was smiling when something, perhaps a sound, perhaps a moment of discomfort made her swing around, suddenly on guard.

A car was rolling towards her, medium size, dark green with a shining grill, like teeth. Then, as she faced it, there was a roar of sound and it leapt at her, like some powerful hunting animal.

She threw herself aside fighting to keep her feet and simultaneously find enough focus to challenge the driver, who seemed to be trying to mount the pavement, oblivious to the damage it was doing to the car.

She reached for the mind in the vehicle.

Red and black, anger and despair, and then she understood that these were bound in a narrowing channel that pointed directly at her. She grappled with it, struggling to turn the channel away from her. It was not a Yareblis mind she was in, but it was under Yareblis control. Yareblis were focusing the anger and despair present in the mind, focusing them on her. Her challenge now was to break the control without breaking the mind controlled.

She held the channel in a firm grip, directing it away from her, but she couldn't do that forever. It hurt, as if she were burning. Resolutely she pushed the pain aside trying to see beyond it to what needed to be done. The threat to her was over for the moment but she felt the pain of the mind controlled and she knew she must do her utmost to free it. She knew it would hurt, and she knew too that she must contain the pain to protect the mind she wanted to free. She began to peel back the channel, weeping as her mind seemed to burn against it.

Gradually at first and then more quickly, as if the mind that had made the control was relinquishing it, the channel came apart and disappeared. As the anger and despair diffused, Marheh realised she was acquainted with this mind, but it was not until she returned to herself and saw the driver of the car, slumped in his seat, his head in his hands, that she recognised Imni's husband.

He looked up and their eyes met. Marheh recognised fear and dislike and tried to accept them without resentment. He moved and the car door began to open. She took as step back and found she was against the wall of a house. Gratefully she leaned against it. Her knees felt as if they might let her down.

Imni's husband got out of his car. He did not look at Marheh but walked around to the front of it. One wheel was balanced on the high rocky bank that edged the road. There was a dint below the shining teeth. The engine had stalled. He kicked at the tyre, bent to study the dint, put both hands flat on the bonnet and tried to push. Nothing happened.

Still without looking at Marheh he straightened, got back in his car and started the engine. Then, with a loud shriek of protest as the bumper scraped along the rocks, the car reversed into the street, paused a moment, then limped away down the hill.

Marheh let herself sag as it disappeared around a corner. Imni's husband, controlled by the Yareblis. She felt a stab of guilt. She hadn't helped. By making him hate her she'd made it easy for the Yareblis to use him. At least she'd broken the control, the memory of pain almost made her cry out, and she had not broken him in the process.

She slid down the wall until she was sitting on the pavement. There was sun and the pavement and the wall behind her were warm. She closed her eyes. It was over for the moment, but it would not be the end of it. It was good to rest, just for a moment. She couldn't stay where she was, but, just for a moment. The warmth behind and beneath her was comforting, but she should perhaps get up now.

She jumped at a light touch on her arm and a quiet voice.

"Are you alright lass?"

She opened her eyes to find a small, neat elderly man bending down to her. He wore the white, turned-around collar of a clergyman and Marheh thought she had never seen a more open, caring face.

"Yes I think so," she said, trying to push herself upright. "I had a fright and it made me a bit shaky."

"You do look a bit pale," he said, studying her kindly. "Would a cup of tea in the vicarage be a suitable restorative?"

She smiled her thanks.

"It would be lovely if you don't mind entertaining a stranger."

"It's my job," he said, offering her his hand to help her up. "I'm enjoined to entertain the stranger, but I don't think you are one."

He offered her his arm and Marheh took it gratefully. Then he guided her towards the church. She found she was a bit shaky at first but he matched his steps to hers and they went sedately through the churchyard to the vicarage beyond. As she began to recover Marheh thought they must have made a comical pair, she, a couple of inches taller than he and wearing her Silberay uniform that was the cause of such disapproval, he in his dark clerical suit, very neat but not very new.

As if he read her thoughts he said "Don't worry, the village is used to me and if I make them smile at times that's a good thing wouldn't you say?"

Marheh laughed.

"Yes indeed."

They reached the vicarage then. As he pushed open the front door he called out "Sybi dear, we have a guest, a cup of tea is needed."

A door opened at the end of the long hall and a small, plump woman appeared and stood, hands on hips, examining Marheh. She waited quietly under her scrutiny.

"I found her in the main street," the vicar explained. "She's here to take care of the threat to the village," was his next surprising comment.

"I thought she didn't look like one of your usual lame ducks."

The woman came towards Marheh, patted her arm.

"Come along lass, you look a bit peaky to me."

Marheh followed her down the hall and into the kitchen, the vicar close behind, talking all the time.

"She's had a fright. I thought at the time she'd already started work. I wanted her to know she had friends here, friends who can help although they might seem old and foolish."

Marheh turned from her enjoyment of the big, sunny kitchen.

"I never said that, or thought it."

Sybi took her wrist and led her to a chair.

"Of course you didn't lass. That's just his talk, seems he has to fill up a silence."

Marheh sat and looked at the two of them as they moved around her. They were obviously well accustomed to complementing each other for cups and saucers, a plate of bread and butter and another of biscuits, a jug of milk and a sugar bowl all appeared without fuss or need for consultation. They were much the same size, both short and stocky, both grey haired with same look of content, and so kind, with a deep unobtrusive kindness that asked nothing of the recipient.

The teapot was filled and placed on the table then they sat, one on either side of her.

"Eat up lass."

Sybi passed her the bread and butter.

"Milk?" asked the vicar, with the teapot poised.

A flow of gentle talk surrounded her as she sipped her tea and ate her bread and butter and she was content just to be there and allow them to care for her. When she put down her empty tea cup though Sybi smiled at her.

"Will you tell us a little about yourself?" she asked, while the vicar replenished her tea without being asked.

"My name is Marheh. I'm Silberay, but I think you know that. The water road is not flowing as it should and I've been asked to investigate but there is darkness pressing all around here. I think you know that too."

The vicar nodded.

"We've been doing our best, Sybi and I and there are good people here who are holding on against it, but I've been feeling as if we need some help."

"Gul has been expecting you for a week or more," Sybi said.

"Hoping, not expecting," Gul corrected her carefully.

Marheh looked from one to the other.

"I'll do what I can to help, but I don't quite understand. You're... you're not Silberay?"

"No, we're not Silberay, but our searching leads us to the same goal. We have our song too."

"And you see the water road?"

He nodded.

"Not as you do, not instinctively, but we learn to see it." He paused and Marheh saw his face become grave and still. "If we want to enough," he said almost to himself.

"And that's your job?" Marheh asked quietly. "To encourage and help those who want to?"

"That's right," Sybi spoke briskly. "And it takes all his time and energy."

She thrust a plate at Marheh.

"Have a biscuit lass. It seems as if we are going to need to keep up our strength."

Impulsively Marheh reached out her hands to them both.

"Thank you," she said and felt tears press behind her eyes. "You make me feel... very... humble. I've had the water road all my life. I've not had to strive for it."

"Not as we do," Gul said, patting her hand. "Your struggle will be different, but I'm sure there is one."

They talked for some time. Gul and Sybi explained how the threat in the darkness was affecting the life of the village, not just Willow Rise but other villages round about. Marheh told of what she had suffered in Higham's Hill and confessed her part in the actions of Imni's husband. Sybi knew who he was, Owen Mitchell, traveller in soap products for laundry and bathroom.

"A rather self-important young man," she said. "But I don't think you need blame yourself," she added.

Marheh shook her head.

"I do though. I've released him from his personal darkness for the moment, but I'm afraid he has no resources to keep it from controlling him again."

"There are so many now who fail to nurture the soul, even deny its existence," Gul said. "It's small wonder they have no defences against incursion."

Marheh nodded.

"I can sing with you against the darkness," she said. "And I will value your strength, but I'm not sure just singing will be enough."

Gul and Sybi were listening with attention and sympathy and heard what she did not say. Sybi gave her a hug.

"Of course you are afraid, you'd be foolish if you weren't"

"You will do what you can," Gul said. "And we will support you as best we can and if we fail while trying, nevertheless in that failure will be success."

There was silence for a few moments then Sybi stood up and began to gather cups and plates.

"So melodramatic you are. Foolish to talk of failure now, when we've barely begun."

Gul smiled at her.

"We won't speak of it again, but it needed to be said."

. . . .

What did he mean, Marheh wondered when she was at last back on *Day Bringer* and preparing her evening meal. What kind of success can there be in failure? She had never thought about people learning to see the water road although she supposed she should have. After all, people's minds and bodies learned, why not the soul too? She shivered a little. The water road had been given to her. What did that mean in terms of her responsibility? She longed for some company, for Nemle to scold and cosset, for Jik's loving strength. It was too hard being alone. She chopped a carrot with determination and dropped it into her saucepan. You've chosen to be alone. It's your life and anyway you're not alone. Stop feeling sorry for yourself. Look at the kindness you were given today. She gave a little snort. There was no point in whinging, better just to get on with it, supper, singing and sleep, that was the program.

She woke slowly next morning and lay drowsing for a little while trying to capture the dream that had just escaped her. It was a pleasant dream she felt sure but nothing remained of it except the lingering consciousness of warmth, warmth and love.

She pushed with her toes at the end of her bunk and felt her body awaken. Pale sunshine filled her cabin, reflected light danced on the ceiling. She swung herself out of bed and stretched more vigorously. The darkness had been pushed back a little by last night's song, that would give Sybi and Gul some respite. She would go on to Deerford and beyond. She would keep singing and she would find and vanquish the source of the dark. That was her job.

Study for 'The Three Gardeners'

Chapter Six

Haste or rhythm? She couldn't decide. Obviously they knew she was here. She could not attempt anything that depended on her being unnoticed. She stood at *Day Bringer*'s tiller progressing through the soft morning and trying to plan. They, not they, the Yareblis, she could give them a name and try to clarify what she knew of them. They were Silberay once. Seventy years ago, when Nemle was a girl they had chosen to leave rather than abide by the new law that limited the use of the discipline of the mind. Well, the law was new then, now it was seventy years old.

Nemle had told her that the Silberay had been sorry to see the twelve depart, giving up their boats and leaving the Harbour. They'd been sorry, but not anxious, after all there were still eighty odd Silberay as well as more than twenty apprentices and those who left still held Silberay values, Silberay goals, it was just in the way to attain those goals that they differed. So it was a number of years before the Silberay realised that the Yareblis had become their enemies, had contributed to the power of darkness and sought power for themselves.

No one knew quite how many Yareblis there were, but their numbers were growing and Marheh knew they were actively recruiting. In her first year as an apprentice she and Nemle had discovered a school they had established in an attempt to indoctrinate young children and train them in Yareblis ways. She and Nemle upset that project and four of the children were Silberay apprentices now, not children any more, but recruiting still went on.

The trouble was that they denied the soul and had fewer and fewer scruples about how they used the discipline of the mind. Their control of Imni's husband was a case in point.

Nemle felt that they had been aware of her, Marheh, from early in her apprenticeship because her outstanding ability could not be hidden. Nemle had drilled her rigorously and permitted Jik and Sul to challenge her too, but for all her practice Marheh knew a real Yareblis challenge would test her in ways she could not begin to imagine.

She was afraid. There was no point in denying it, at least to herself. She and Nemle had helped to care for Silberay whose minds had been damaged by the Yareblis and she thought perhaps she feared death less than the possibility of living as they did, unable to do the simplest things without help, unable to communicate except through the soul song. That was what she must hold to. There was nothing the Yareblis did or could do that would destroy that, not even if they were to kill her.

She grimaced. How melodramatic she was being. Probably the Yareblis had no interest in her except as an obstacle to whatever plans they had for the villages and since she did not really know what those might be she was not much of an obstacle. Maybe she should just keep focusing on her task for the Silberay. She knew what that was. It was becoming increasingly obvious that the water road was diminishing. Even here, near the source the level was low. She frowned, trying to work it out. Would it be better or worse further away?

Day Bringer had a draught of only two feet and she seemed to be moving reasonably well as long as Marheh concentrated on keeping her to the channel in the centre of the water road. There had been one moment when she had steered too close to the inside of a bend and felt the slight drag as the flat bottomed hull just touched the clayey bed beneath her.

As long as she could reach Deerford she could go on foot to the source. That might be best anyway. *Day Bringer* would be safer moored by the pottery than if she had to leave her where the source stream entered the water road. She could be home in two days if she boated all the daylight hours. Suddenly home seemed wholly desirable, her father's generous strength, her mother's firm kindness. They were looking forward to her coming she knew. They would not mind if she arrived a bit sooner than expected.

Almost without a conscious decision she found her hand pressing down on the throttle to increase her speed then she drew it back again, longer hours, not more speed. More speed would increase the chances of her sticking on the bottom.

Her decision made she tried then to empty her mind of worry and planning and to rest in the day and the journey, and the gentle landscape that surrounded her.

That, of course, was not as simple to do as to say. There were moments, even as much as a whole half hour, when she could forget, when the sound of bird song or the slow beating wings of a heron caught her away from herself, when a field of sheep turned their faces towards her and stared at her passing, or the simple shapes of hill and cloud together gave her a glimpse of perfect beauty. Mostly though the trouble was there waiting to snatch at her. What were they trying to do, the Yareblis? Was this all the work of one powerful individual? Were the darkness in the villages and the drying of the water road part of the same problem?

She felt handicapped by her lack of knowledge.

She did not stop for lunch but hovered in a bridge hole for a moment and ran down to grab a bit of her chocolate and later used the same trick when she needed a toilet break. As the light began to fade she started to look for a mooring only to find that she could not get in at the usual places. The water was too shallow.

She began to feel a bit desperate. She was tired and hungry and not really fit to continue into the night when boating would demand more than she had to give. When it was almost dark she came to another bridge. It was against all her training but logically there would be no one else wanting to go through. How could there be?

She eased *Day Bringer* into the narrow opening and stepped off with her centre line. It would do, and she would put a light on the roof just in case.

Ten minutes later she was moored. She stood on the path for a moment studying *Day Bringer*'s dark shape almost filling the arched opening. She would not be able to have a fire, she realised, the chimney only just fit. There was nowhere for the smoke to escape. She went below for the smaller of her two lamps, lit it and placed it carefully on the roof towards the stern, where *Day Bringer* was not actually under the bridge. It was not much, she thought, studying its brave glow from the path, but it would do as a warning.

Bread and cheese and a drink of water took the edge off her hunger and fifteen minutes later she was asleep, her last conscious thought, the comfortable realisation that she was nearly home.

She slept well and woke early, looking forward to the day and the promise it held.

As she began to move around the boat, washing, dressing, preparing breakfast, she realised there was very little movement. *Day Bringer* was barely floating, which meant the water road had dried up further during the night. Would she even be able to move on? She gulped down her breakfast and hurried through the engine checks.

When the engine was throbbing under her feet she stepped off to untie the mooring lines. Once through the bridge she should be alright, but could she actually get through. Thinking hard she began by trying to edge forward. Brown, muddy water swirled around *Day Bringer*'s propeller and she felt her straining. She tried a little reverse. That went better and she continued, increasing speed slowly until *Day Bringer* was fully clear of the bridge. Then she changed direction and pushed the throttle down hard. The bottom was soft. The worst that could happen was that she got completely stuck, but if she could get through she would have more room to manoeuvre.

The burst of speed was enough and *Day Bringer* slipped and slid through the bridge to the other side. Marheh eased back the throttle and let out the breath she was holding. If every bridge was like that would she even make it to Deerford. Then she remembered the locks, three of them, carrying the water road up twenty feet or so about an hour from the village. Going up she would be drawing water away from her destination and there was clearly little water to spare. Well it was no good worrying about it. She would find out soon enough and deal with whatever eventuated.

The day had begun cool and bright, but as she continued slowly onward the temperature began to rise and the sky to cloud over. She looked about her uneasily. The air felt heavy and still and there was no birdsong. Perhaps it might rain. It had that feel about it. Not that rain would do a great deal for the water level, but even a little might mean the difference between sticking in a lock, or more likely, in the short pound between the top two, and making it to Deerford.

By the time she reached the locks the day was well on. It had been a slow journey. Sometimes she had felt as if she was feeling her way as the channel seemed to be getting shallower and more than once she had needed to reverse *Day Bringer* off an unexpected spit of clayey silt. It was tiring too, having to concentrate so hard all the time.

As she approached the bottom lock she was surprised to see the gates open and the lock empty. At least that was one lock full of water that wouldn't be wasted but it was not the way things were usually left and it made her wary as she took *Day Bringer* slowly into the lock. Once she was established quietly in the lock she pushed her windlass into her belt, grabbed the centre line and scrambled onto the roof. From there it was not difficult to heave herself onto the lock side. Just as well, because the customary lock ladder was missing, though she could see holes where the bolts had been.

She closed one of the gates and walked all the way around the top to close the other. Stepping over the gap seemed somehow too much of a risk today.

Keeping *Day Bringer* well up to the top gate she opened the paddles carefully, just a little at first, then as the lock began to fill, she wound them all the way up and stood, leaning against the beam watching as *Day Bringer* rose slowly to the new level.

The day was still hot and heavy and even that moderate amount of exertion had made her breathe hard. Empty fields stretched on either side of her and she felt unexpectedly exposed and vulnerable in the wide landscape. "Don't be silly," she admonished herself. "The locks are part of the water road, no one can even see you, and there's no one about anyway." She firmly denied the fleeting thought that the Yareblis could see her and busied herself with pushing open the top gate to release *Day Bringer* from the lock.

The next lock was empty and waiting for her too. As before she steered *Day Bringer* carefully in and scrambled out to close the gates. Her sense of unease was increasing and she worked as fast as she could, wanting to be past the halting progress in the locks. The top lock was not much more than a hundred yards away and she could see it, too, was open and empty. It did make her progress quicker. The water between the two locks looked very shallow though and as she opened the paddles she could almost see the pound draining away into the lock.

It was very slow filling and she soon realised that she would need to raise the level in the pound if she were to be able to move *Day Bringer* into the top lock. That meant walking up there and opening the paddles. It was not very far and she enjoyed walking so she could not understand quite why she was so reluctant to leave *Day Bringer*.

There was nothing else to be done, though, if she wanted to continue her journey, so she took her out of the lock, closed the gate behind her and left her waiting in the lock mouth while she hurried up the hill to the top lock. Away from *Day Bringer*, alone on the path, she felt even more vulnerable than before and was almost running when something seemed to dart under her feet. She tripped and fell headlong, measuring her length on the grassy path. She was just getting her breath to scramble to her feet again when the attack began.

"Get into the water now!"

For an instant she did not recognise that the thought was not her own.

"Water now! Now! Now!"

She resisted, trying to block out the insistent beat of the command. Calling all her focus and strength of will she wrestled the thought out of her mind and slammed the door, but it was not enough. Something was battering away, demanding entrance, trying to break into her mind.

She gasped a little at the pain of it and tried to strengthen her defence, tried to think around the noise of the attack and find space to gather herself and decide her best action. If she could get back to *Day Bringer* she would be shielded to a degree, but if she didn't open the lock paddles then *Day Bringer* could not move on and she would be trapped.

The fifty yards up to the lock seemed impossibly far. She could see so easily where she wanted to be but her attackers were trying to force her to her knees, to keep her where she was so they could break her defence. Yard by yard she pushed herself onward, flinging herself against the attack, clawing, scratching, hitting out at the enemies who were trying to control her.

Get to the lock, release the water. That was the imperative that she must focus on. If she could block out everything but that one goal it would also keep out her enemies. The whole world seemed dark and filled with pain. She had no sense of where the attack came from or how many were beating at her defences, only that she must struggle onward.

By the time she reached the lock she hardly knew what she had to do there, but her hand grasped her windlass almost automatically and seemed to operate on the paddle as if without her willing it. She had nothing left for willing, only resisting.

The dark, empty lock seemed to draw her and she fought that too, clinging to the lock beam with mind as well as body as the water began to pour out and into the half empty pound.

As she refocused, wanting to change her goal now to making the return journey to *Day Bringer*, she left herself vulnerable for a moment. A mind thrust its way into hers. She screamed and struck at it with fire, which seemed to leap from her as if from the candle of her soul. The probing mind flinched away and she slammed up her defences against it, focused all of herself on reaching *Day Bringer* and set off at a stumbling, unsteady jog.

It helped that the way was downhill now, though it made falling more painful, and she fell more than once, tripping over nothings flung across her path, illusions of the Yareblis, made to confuse her. Everything she had learned in her twenty years of apprenticeship seemed inadequate now and only the promise of safety in *Day Bringer*, the knowledge that she was waiting for her, close now and closer, kept her moving forward, fighting with all her strength to keep that single thought.

As she grew closer and closer to safety the attack seemed to intensify. She could not see, she could scarcely feel the ground beneath her feet, but she could hear *Day Bringer*'s engine patiently throbbing as she waited to continue her journey. She reached out and her fingertips brushed the hull. For a moment her vision cleared and she launched herself across the narrow strip of water towards the gunnel.

Weak and trembling she pasted herself against the hull and rested in the gentle rocking caused by the sudden addition of her weight. Warily she relaxed her defences bit by bit as she felt the security of *Day Bringer*'s protection surrounding her. She raised her head a little to look out over the landscape. Where were they hiding? They were close enough to have seen when she was most vulnerable. It looked empty, but there were hedges and a few stunted trees.

They would be watching her still. She needed to move so they would not see how beaten she felt. She eased along the gunnel towards the back deck, her walk a poor copy of her usual confident progress. It would be alright to spend a few minutes below, that would not necessarily be interpreted as weakness because she had to wait for the water, but it could only be a few minutes. She stumbled down the steps into her cabin. Just a few minutes, to breathe deeply, to stop thinking, just to be.

She sank onto her bunk, her head in her hands, her mind empty and aching, and found the portal to her soul song offering warmth and light. For a long moment she was drawn in. Music swelled around her. It seemed like a gift of healing, but she knew she could not rest yet.

She reached for her cloak, wrapped herself in its warm green folds and went slowly, reluctantly back outside.

There was water enough now, and still coming. It was time she went forward to the lock. It would be better if she could shut off the water before moving into the lock but she was afraid to dare the path again. Slowly she steered *Day Bringer* into the current, watching all the time, feeling her way.

At the lock mouth the current was surprisingly strong. The water poured through the gate in a rush of white foam. For all her care in steering, *Day Bringer*'s hull was buffeted against the lock wall and water splashed over the prow as she moved up to the gate. Marheh dropped her cloak on the deck. She would need to be able to move quickly once *Day Bringer* was fully in the lock.

A moment of fear, a gathering of her defences and action. Leaving *Day Bringer* with a slightly forward throttle, she grabbed the centre line, scrambled onto the roof and rolled out onto the ground surrounding the lock. There was no need to think now, just act as she had planned on the short run between locks. Let down the paddle first to save *Day Bringer* being swamped, close the bottom gates, open the paddles again but slowly, waiting until *Day Bringer* was steady and the lock half full, step onto *Day Bringer*'s roof as it reached ground level to take advantage of the protection she gave.

Once there she could pause for a moment, draw breath and look around. It was a good vantage point, the top lock and the extra height as *Day Bringer* rose to the new level. At first she saw nothing but fields, dull, waiting under the grey sky, but then, far in the distance, she saw some figures. They were moving away from her and too far even to be sure how many there were, at least four, maybe five. Perhaps it wasn't them but she felt a lightening and a new energy as she swung down to the tiller to allow *Day Bringer* to gently nudge the lock gate open.

A few more minutes and she was on her way. She looked at her cloak lying in a heap on the deck and frowned wondering at her sudden need of it. Leaving the tiller for a moment, she picked it up and shook it out. That wasn't the way to treat it, dropping it on the floor. It was the special mark of her status as Silberay and she loved the way it swung around her. She draped it over her arm and moved back to the tiller again. It wasn't cold, if anything she was hot and the day still had the close, heavy feel to it, but she was nearly home and nothing mattered except that.

She stepped forward briefly to hang the cloak on its hook inside the door then settled to her steering.

Two hours later she eased *Day Bringer* up to the wharf that lay at the bottom of the garden of her home. It wasn't Silberay built. Her grandparents had made it when one of her grandmother's brothers had become Silberay and used his boat to carry for the pottery, bringing in clay and delivering finished goods. She was the third generation of her family to become Silberay. There were not many who could say that.

Suddenly she felt almost too tired to function but *Day Bringer* needed her attention before she could rest. She was just gathering her centre line ready to step off when a figure appeared on the path from the pottery. It was her brother Tep, looking uncertainly in her direction. She stepped off eagerly. Tep's face lightened when he saw her.

"I thought I caught a glimpse of something. We weren't expecting you for a week or more."

"I hurried," she said, trying to smile, but catching back tears instead.

"What is it big sister, you look tired?"

"I'm alright little brother."

She tried to sound bright and cheerful but suddenly she was sobbing. Tep reached for her and for a few moments she let herself be held then she drew back.

"Marheh the Great never cries," she told him, lifting her chin, her face wet with tears.

"Never," Tep agreed with her.

She gave a short laugh, mocking herself.

"I am tired," she admitted. "It hasn't been an easy journey."

"But you're here now. Are you coming up to the house?"

"I need to moor first, tidy up a bit, maybe even wash my face."

"Am I welcome on board?"

"Always. You know the drill. You could probably do it for yourself."

"Not quite."

She took his hand and pushed her line into it.

"Hold onto this for me."

Tep started as the rope appeared, then laughed.

"You'd think I'd be used to it by now, but I'm always surprised."

A few minutes later *Day Bringer* was tied up to the bollards on the wharf and she had guided her brother into the boat.

He had visited her before, but not since Nemle had gone and she was keen to show him the new work space. He admired it dutifully but was more interested in the pieces she had made. The three gardeners held his attention for a long time.

"I think it's the best thing you've done," he said at last. "I'll be afraid to fire it."

"I trust you." She smiled at him fondly. "It's good to see you. I thought I'd never get here. Shall we go?"

She led the way, grabbing her cloak as she passed. Once off *Day Bringer* she swung it round her and stood to be admired.

"Truly Marheh the Great," Tep teased.

She laughed and set off up the path to the house. Coming home was like being a child again, she thought later, gathered into the life and warmth in the big kitchen. She was happy to be a child just for the moment, though it would try her patience after a few days, she knew. She had been welcomed with smiles and hugs and exclamations of surprise.

They were all gathered for the evening meal, her mother and father, Tep and his wife Fali and their young sons, Fen and Tith. Her two other brothers, between her and Tep, no longer lived at home. They would visit though, while she was here and bring their wives and children. She was an aunt five times now, three nephews and two nieces, though she didn't really know any of them well. It was odd to be reminded. She didn't feel like an aunt.

She was too tired to contribute much to the conversation around the table but she was grateful for the food and warmth. After more than a month spent mostly alone, even six people seemed like a crowd, although she loved them all. She smiled reassuringly at her father when she caught his anxious gaze and managed to refuse her mother's offer of a bed in the house. It would have been nice to let herself be cared for, but she knew she needed to return to *Day Bringer.*

The opportunity came when Tep and Fali took the boys upstairs to their own quarters. She hugged her parents and parried their unspoken questions by promising to return for breakfast. Her father went with her to the wharf. The heavy, overcast day had cleared to a fine, clear night. Stars shone. They had walked in comfortable silence but as they reached the wharf her father, Sef, stopped and turned towards her. She thought for a moment he was about to question her, but he simply gathered her into a hug that was as warm and strong and sheltering as the walls of his home.

"Good night, Marheh. Sleep well."

It felt like a benediction.

"You too."

She smiled at him and stepped on board, turning to watch as he made his way back to the house. She thought he turned to look back before he went inside, but it was too dark to be sure.

Alone again Marheh let herself sag for a minute, but she knew she could not rest yet. She needed to enter the soul song, not just to sing light and uncover the dark, but to find healing for her bruised and battered mind. *Day Bringer* felt cold and dark after the warmth of the house, but she found her candle and matches in the usual place by the back door. When she had lit the candle she carried it through to the saloon and used it to light the lamp. The fire was almost out and she rebuilt it carefully before settling into the armchair, still wrapped in her cloak.

It was her mind's pain making her cold. She would be warm soon. She closed her eyes. Her breathing slowed and deepened. The image of the lamp's soft light merged into the candle flame that was her portal, then she was singing.

. . .

Just to be there had been enough, she thought, as she lit her candle again and turned out the lamp. Her own music had been weak and barely capable of melody, but other songs had lifted her and shielded her from the dark. She carried her candle to the bathroom and then the bedroom as she made her preparations for bed. There had been darkness, but Nemle had not let it near her. Nemle had been there in the song and the nurturing protection. She would feel stronger in the morning.

She slept late and when she reached the house her mother, Greya, was alone in the big kitchen.

"Fali has taken the boys to school," she said. "The men are working. We're firing tomorrow."

Marheh smiled.

"Perhaps I can work too."

"If you want to after breakfast."

There was cream and a drizzle of honey for her porridge and then bacon and eggs. When she was nearly finished eating her mother made two mugs of sperit and sat down with her.

"Do you want to talk about it?" she said.

Marheh looked up from her plate.

"Nothing to tell really. I've a job to do and it's proving to be more of a challenge than they expected, that's all."

"Are you enjoying your independence?" her mother asked, after waiting to be sure Marheh had said all she wanted.

"Mostly. I miss Nemle more than I expected to."

"You look tired and you're too thin. You've not been eating properly have you?"

Marheh reached out to pat her mother's hand.

"I am tired. The last week has not been easy and you know I've never been much of a cook, but I'm trying."

Her mother smiled.

"Alright, inquisition over, but you'll eat with us while you're here, that should set you up. How long can you stay?"

Marheh leaned her elbows on the table, sipped from her sperit and let all the different warmths soak into her.

"I'm not quite sure," she said at last. "There are things I need to do that can perhaps be best done by making Deerford my base. Higham's Hill and Willow Rise are both suffering from something. Perhaps Deerford is too. The water road itself is under attack, but I need a few days of being ordinary, working round the pottery, helping with the firing, that kind of thing, so as to get some space."

She stood up and took her plates to the sink.

"I feel a bit overwhelmed really," she finished and turned the tap on hard so the noise of it made an excuse to be silent.

Later she went down with her father and Tep and passed out the pieces she had ready for firing. They would not go in tomorrow's firing, which was for glazing the crockery that was the pottery's main product, but they would be safe in the drying room and after a few days there they would be ready for the small kiln which had finer heat control. Her father studied each piece as they spread them on the racks and his nod of acknowledgement and brief word of commendation made her cheeks burn. She had been apprenticed to him before ever she was apprenticed to the Silberay. He was her teacher, he had encouraged her to focus on sculpture, knowing that even at fifteen she had her heart set on joining the Silberay.

He was looking thoughtful as they arranged the last of her pieces on the racks and carried down some more clay for her.

"You know," he said when she reappeared after stowing the clay. "Carron Pottery has a name for good quality, hand thrown ware."

They began the walk back to the house.

"Of course."

She smiled, butted against him for a moment.

"But production generally is becoming more and more mechanised and we can't compete, don't want to compete really, so I was looking at your pieces and thinking... we might branch into a series of Marheh Caron signature pieces, a new one each year, limited edition. What do you think?"

"I'm not sure I'm good enough for that. I'm only a journeyman potter."

"Journeyman, master, apprentice even, it's not important for this. You're an artist, that's what's important. Tep is a fine craftsman. If you make the original he and I can develop a mould and put the pieces together for firing. Fali is good with colour. Perhaps in years to come your pieces will be collector's items."

Marheh laughed and ran a couple of steps as her father's enthusiasm quickened his pace.

"They'll be our pieces, not just mine, if we do it, but Tep and Fali need to have a say."

"Of course."

He stopped at the door to the pottery.

"We'll get together over lunch. Fali will be back by then." He looked at her, a twinkle in his eye. "Now are you going to show me that you can still throw a pot or are you too grand for that."

Marheh the Great straightened her spine, lifted her chin and marched ahead of him through the door.

....

She was always happy with clay in her hands and after the first failure the trick of centring came back and she worked steadily making bowls, making them match in size and shape, making them smooth and even in thickness. Tep was working beside her at another wheel and Fali was painting, and her father glazing, some bisque ware ready for tomorrow's firing.

By lunch time the quiet familiarity of the task, the small challenge of it, had given her mind space to heal and allowed her to forget for a while the larger challenge she still faced. She laughed at Tep's teasing as she took off her smock and washed up.

"You can put them all in the spoil bin if they don't meet your high standards, brother dear."

"I wouldn't be game!"

She gave him a little punch and they chased each other out of the studio and up the path to the kitchen.

By the time Fali and Sef had caught up with them they were wrestling each other around the kitchen. Tep was getting the worst of it, restrained by his desire not to hurt Marheh, who seemed to have cast off all the civilizations of maturity. Fali looked in alarm towards her mother-in-law who watched for a moment, her expression a complicated mixture of amusement and concern.

"Enough you two," she said then, not raising her voice but commanding instant obedience.

Sef smiled at Fali.

"Once a mother always a mother," he said.

Marheh was breathing hard and looking as if she did not quite know what was happening. Tep stood beside her laughing a little.

"Marheh is picking on me," he said lightly, looking at Fali.

"She'd better not do it again or she'll have me to deal with," Fali said.

"Sorry Fali. I don't know what got into me."

Sef crossed to take the end of her plait and march her to the lunch table.

"Sit down and behave yourself daughter, or…"

He left the threat hanging.

"Or what?"

"Or else!"

She laughed, then sighed a little and put her elbows on the table, her chin in her hands.

"I'm sorry, truly. I'll be sensible. It was so nice, just to lose myself in the work this morning. I didn't want to… to have to find myself again."

Fresh bread, butter, cheese, honey were already on the table. Now Greya passed them all steaming bowls of thick pumpkin soup and sat down with them to eat. Marheh could feel the weight of her attention.

"I'm alright Mother, just… you don't need to worry about me."

But there was worry in the air and for a while they ate in silence until Sef made an effort to change the mood and raised the subject he had discussed with Marheh earlier.

The others were enthusiastic and Marheh took the opportunity to mention her idea about the dolls. They would be best done with moulds too. Marheh could make the originals. Fali would love to provide delicate complexions and curls of various hues. Tep teased Marheh about a return to childhood, but was already thinking about eyes that opened and shut and china hands and feet.

When lunch was over and the others got up to leave Greya checked Marheh, putting a gentle hand firmly on her wrist.

"Stay and help me with the dishes," she said lightly, as Marheh seemed to want to go too.

She watched until the door closed behind Sef then turned back to her mother.

"Am I in trouble?"

Greya smiled.

"That was to be my question, not yours. I know you. That silly behaviour before lunch is your way of pretending everything is alright. Do you want to tell me about it?"

Marheh reached across the table to gather dirty plates and cutlery. She stood up and carried them across to the sink. She did not look at her mother.

Greya took up the remains of the bread, the cheese and the butter and moved with them to the pantry. When the table was cleared and they met at the sink the silence stretched between them.

"There isn't much to tell," Marheh said at last, taking up a tea towel. "Perhaps that is part of the trouble. I don't really know what I'm up against." She took a bowl from the drainer and polished it thoughtfully. "I've been attacked and I'm aware of darkness. I told you there was trouble in the villages and Jik has asked me to investigate the problem with the water road itself and…" She turned away with the bowls and put them carefully in the cupboard where they lived. "I'm afraid."

"That's hardly surprising," her mother said. "I'm glad you've that much sense.

Marheh laughed, choked a little and put down her tea towel to reach for her handkerchief. She blinked back tears and blew her nose before turning back to her job.

"So what are you going to do about it?" Greya asked. "Can Jik give you some help?"

"Mother! This is my first task as true Silberay I'm not about to ask for help."

"I don't see why not if you need it, but knowing you I don't expect you will, ask I mean."

"I can't," Marheh muttered, drying cutlery at speed and feeding the knives, forks and spoons into their proper places with a clatter.

Greya cleaned the last pot and let the dish water run away. She took a cloth and wiped down the table and the benches and waited until Marheh had finished her part of the job. She went to her, took the tea towel from her hands, folded it once and put it over the airing rail.

"I know you don't want to talk about it, so I won't ask any more. Just promise to let us know if we can help – alright?"

"Alright."

She gave her mother a quick kiss and went to the door.

"I might take the bus and go back to Willow Rise in the morning. I need to see someone there."

Church at Willow Rise

Chapter Seven

In the morning there was no need for the bus. The oldest of her three brothers came to collect an order and took her with him. Mek, though closest to her in age, had been more of a sparring partner than a friend when they were young, perhaps because she had been a bossy little brat. He, it had been, who first called her Marheh the Great. It had not been intended as a compliment.

She had barely seen him since she joined the Silberay. He had not been interested in the work of the pottery and had left home early to work for a delivery company. After five years he had saved enough to buy a vehicle of his own and now owned a small fleet of vans and employed three drivers. The pottery always gave him their work and he had built a reputation, along with his business, and was in demand for transporting fragile goods.

Marheh climbed into the seat beside him feeling almost shy. He was three years younger than she, which was nothing really. In fact, it felt to her now, as if he was older. He looked solid, well groomed and although he was dressed for driving rather than the office, his clothes looked expensive.

"I'd sack my drivers if they picked up a bit of skirt."

Marheh turned to him indignantly, but he was focusing on starting the van and not looking at her. He backed skilfully out of the yard and they were moving smartly along the road the next time he spoke.

"But you're not wearing one are you? Don't you think it's time you gave up this nonsense and settled down?"

Marheh drew in a big breath then bit her lip. What was the use of saying anything if that was what he thought?

"You're getting a bit long in the tooth but you're not bad looking – you could still get a husband."

"I've not completed a twenty year apprenticeship in order to 'get a husband'. I don't actually want one, especially not one like you!"

"Still the same old Marheh! Twenty years not long enough to teach you to keep your temper."

Marheh clenched her teeth to keep from reacting. When she finally thought she could speak calmly she turned to him.

"Why did you offer me a lift?"

"The Mater asked me to and I thought it might be a good chance to talk to you. You're not doing yourself any good with this Silberay business."

"Since when have you called Mother 'the Mater'?"

"Angelique suggested it. She says it sounds more suitable for a man."

"Angelique! Do you mean Nella?"

"We don't use those old nicknames any more. It's old fashioned."

"It's old fashioned… to use the soul name?"

"Old fashioned and unsuitable for a man in my position."

"Why? Does your position mean you don't have a soul any more?"

"Don't be silly!"

"What about Wilda?"

Marheh was suddenly anxious for her fourteen year old niece.

"We prefer her to be called Amanda, which is, after all, her name."

Marheh was silent for a few moments, wondering how to deal with this revelation.

"What does Mother think, and Father?"

"They still think the old way – we don't bother them about it."

Again a silence.

"Anyway, Angelique suggested we could offer you a home... you could live with us... help around the house a bit... you know... behave like a normal woman."

Marheh looked at him aghast then began to laugh.

"Poor Nella, she'd be sorry if I took up that offer. Does she hate having Silberay in the family so much? I thought it was something to be proud of."

"I knew it would be no use talking to you. You always go your own way, but you might at least dress properly when you are with the family."

Marheh found she was no longer angry but sad.

"Mek, this is my uniform," she said gently. "I wear it because I'm doing a job, but I'll try to keep out of Nella's way in future and I'll even call her Angela if that is what she prefers – I'm not sure whether I can manage Angelique."

He only grunted and the remaining few minutes of the short journey were passed in silence.

He dropped her opposite the church and drove away without acknowledging her brief word of thanks. She stood for a moment looking after the small, bright van with its painted logo 'Carron Cares'. Then she made her way into the church yard. She was going to visit Gul and Sybi but first she needed to think about Mek, her own brother who she loved, who she thought loved her. What was happening to him?

She was still thinking, perched on a flat tombstone, when Gul came out of the church.

"Marheh lass, have you come to see me?"

She nodded.

"You and Sybi if you have time to talk."

"Sybi will tell you I always have time to talk and she'll be glad to see you. Have you come from Deerford?"

She followed him to the vicarage, letting his gentle talk flow over her, responding briefly sometimes, but knowing this was his way of welcoming her and that he did not require answers just now.

It was not until the preliminaries were over and the three of them were settled around the kitchen table with cups of tea that they began to explore the reasons for her visit.

"I was attacked on the way to Deerford," she told them. "It was difficult to keep going and it left me a bit bruised, but it confirmed that there is a concentration of Yareblis hereabouts. I saw a group of people leaving… afterwards… but they were far away and I can't be sure they were involved. I need to know more, how many, where they are, what they are trying to do. At the moment I seem to be working in the dark. I thought you might be able to help me clarify some things."

"I doubt that I know any more than you do," Gul said. "We've felt the darkness, Sybi and I, and done our best to keep it at bay but more than that… I would just be guessing."

"Even your guesses would give me something to go on. I don't know how to begin, I don't understand their objective and I can't…can't find them. It's all fog and cloud."

Sybi reached out to pat her hand.

"I think you will have to expect that. You have in mind something tangible that you can get hold of and shake, don't you? But this is more nebulous and perhaps, in a way, more dangerous."

Marheh nodded.

"But there must be a physical presence somewhere, somewhere a centre where I can… direct my focus."

"Someone creating the fog and the chaos?"

"Chaos!"

"It is coming to that I think." Gul spoke slowly as if working out his thought. "While we are pre-occupied with chaos, then will come the strike for power, or dominance might be a better word."

Marheh stared into her tea cup.

"My mother suggested I ask at Silberay Harbour for help."

"And will you?"

"I don't think I can."

Gul looked at her sharply, his eyes penetrating.

"Is that true or is it pride talking?"

Marheh flushed.

"It could be pride," she admitted. "This is my first solo voyage. They gave me a job. I don't want to fail."

"If the job is bigger than they knew, there is no shame in saying so."

Marheh shook her head.

"I need to know more. It wouldn't be easy for help to come. It would have to be really needed."

She put her hands over her face. She couldn't ask for help, she couldn't. She could feel Gul and Sybi's sympathetic gaze then heard Sybi's voice quiet, unemphatic but nonetheless piercing.

"Your failure would affect us all. You won't let pride get in the way if help is needed."

Marheh was silent. She wanted to cry out that she **was** asking for help, she was asking them and they were not giving it, but she refrained. She understood with part of herself that what they had said was help, even if it was something she did not want to hear. She had acted alone out of pride too many times in the past, and come to grief because of it. There had to be a balance though, you couldn't play for safety all the time or nothing would ever get done and this was her job.

She looked up, looked from Sybi to Gul as they sat quietly waiting with her.

"My brother drove me here," she said unexpectedly. "He wants me to give up this nonsense. My own brother."

"That must have been hard."

"It makes me more determined to find out what is going on. He doesn't even use his soul name any more. You're right. It does feel like chaos."

She sat up straighter. Her brothers would have recognized Marheh the Great.

"I think I have to find the path in and through by myself because that is my gift and what I'm trained for, after that you will help me and the Silberay know where I am."

Gul took one hand and Sybi the other, then their own hands were joined and the three sat for a moment linked by more than the clasp of hands. Then Marheh released herself gently and stood up.

"Thank you for the tea and the ... affection and support..."

She heard Sybi say quietly "It's love really."

"I don't really know what I ought to do, but you've shown me I can't just sit here not doing it, and that you are strong, like an anchor and between you here, and Nemle at the Harbour, I can't stray out of reach."

She grinned then.

"Listen to me pontificate! I'll shut up and be off, but thank you."

They hugged her and let her go, back through the church yard and into the church to sit for a while alone and come to terms with the plan that had edged into her mind. Just by being who she was she could draw them to her, to attack and challenge her. Out and about she was a target so out and about she would be, and watch carefully with the hope of ducking the arrow and glimpsing the archer.

Thinking too much about what she planned was not helpful really. She had to be doing. She would show herself around the village then take the bus onto Higham's Hill and do the same. Tomorrow she would bring a sketch pad, always a good excuse for lingering and looking.

Waiting for the bus was quite a good excuse too, she thought later as she stood by the bus stop looking forward to home and *Day Bringer*. She had wandered around Willow Rise and Higham's Hill without incident, even braving the shop at Higham's Hill and buying herself a little box of coloured pencils. She had attracted a few curious glances and overheard a few unfavourable comments but nothing she could not shrug off.

There were a couple of others waiting for the bus and they were joined by a third whom Marheh recognised. It was Blethan's neighbour, Mrs Tarrant. Marheh felt her animosity and moved a little aside, but it was not enough to suit Mrs Tarrant who drew in her skirts and circled around her. Marheh could hear herself being described as a thief, how else, after all could she have obtained the bus fare, or perhaps she was waiting to cadge a lift, in which case she was a beggar. She tried to shut herself away from the poisonous words but Amelia Tarrant meant to be overheard.

When the bus came Marheh allowed the others to get on first although by rights she headed the small queue. For a moment she thought the driver was about to go off without her, but realised her mistake when he grunted a greeting and took her money. Mrs Tarrant's poison had made her defensive. She would have liked a seat by herself but there wasn't one, so she moved towards the back of the bus, sat beside the face that looked the least unwelcoming, and tried to disappear.

The bus jogged its way around Higham's Hill and Marheh began to relax as people got off and on and she was forgotten. The next village was Lowcroft and she wondered whether she should visit it too, but not today. Today she had done enough. The bus gathered speed as it left Higham's Hill and took the main road for Lowcroft. The surrounding fields were bathed in a soft afternoon glow. The sky was a clear pale blue. It would have been good to be standing at *Day Bringer*'s tiller and moving slowly through the landscape but this, more tumultuous passage, was pleasant enough.

They had reached the top of a long hill and started down when Marheh became aware of a disturbance at the front of the bus. Looking forward she could see nothing untoward but the sense of agitation grew and she began to focus her mind, hoping to discover the cause. Then the bus began to weave back and forth across the road, all the time gathering speed. There were murmurs of dismay from round about. She needed to hold on to keep her seat. The driver, there was something wrong with the driver. Marheh reached out to his mind, just gently. Perhaps he was ill, but perhaps there was Yareblis interference.

As soon as she reached him she understood that he was fighting an attempt at control. His sense of responsibility to his passengers was giving him strength but it was nearly overcome. It was all he could do to wrench the bus back onto the road when the Yareblis control tried to send it off into a ditch.

Marheh pushed her mind against the attacker, trying to protect the bus driver. She felt the attacker turn on her and understood that this exposure of herself was what had been wanted all along. Someone had known she could not refuse her help and that her action would leave her vulnerable. There was no time to wonder any more though, for she was fighting now, for her mind if not her life.

It was not a single attacker any longer. She was being wrung like a rag between two contorted entities she barely recognised as minds.

She screamed and twisted, pulling herself close and tight. They sent her flying then, a ball spinning and falling through spears of ice. The ice was of their making. She gave herself warmth and wings and flew at them like a striking eagle, plummeting down from the height where they had thrown her. The ice melted running in rivulets of fire towards them. She pursued them, skimming over the heat, powerful and impervious.

Suddenly they left her. She heard herself shriek, anger, pain and exultation mingled, then she was falling, drifting. Almost reluctantly she took possession of herself, let go the power she had discovered and returned to her body.

The bus, she found, was stationary now, and she the centre of a hostile crowd with Amelia Tarrant at the fore.

"She did it. She bewitched the driver," Marheh heard her say. She tried to shake her head, moved her lips in rebuttal, but all her strength had drained away.

"She looks pretty harmless," a man's voice. "Now't to be upset over."

"She's one of those water gypsies," another woman. "You can't trust them."

"She were in some kind of trance just now."

It was her seat companion.

"Frozen like."

"See, I told you." Amelia Tarrant, in triumphant vindication. "She was putting a curse on the driver."

Marheh still could not find her voice but looked from face to face, curious, hostile, afraid, even sympathetic, but all staring at her. She closed her eyes and concentrated on the few, simple things that were all she could manage, her hands grasping the seat in front, feeling the firm, smooth surface of the seat that supported her, her feet in their well-worn boots resting on the bus floor.

Was she really a fighting eagle? Where had that come from? Don't think about that now. This is a different kind of trouble.

"Leave the lass alone." It was the bus driver's voice, gruff and tired. "We're way behind schedule. If you all get back to your seats we'll get on."

Marheh opened her eyes, met those of the driver. His face was grey with weariness from his own struggle, but there was strength and determination there too.

"I don't know what got at me," he said, and Marheh knew he was speaking mostly to her. "But it wasn't her. I know that. Now let's get on."

There were a few protests with Amelia Tarrant's voice shrill and loud demanding Marheh be put off the bus, but most passengers just wanted to get home and hustled her to her seat without heeding her demands.

By the time they reached Lowcroft it was almost as if nothing had happened and in the telling of the adventure to those waiting passengers demanding an explanation for the lateness of the bus, Marheh was forgotten.

Another twenty minutes to Deerford was time enough for Marheh to collect herself, though she still felt drained of energy. She did not dare explore what had happened here, where she was vulnerable, but tried to keep enough focus to offer protection for the driver should it be needed. She longed for home and *Day Bringer* and safety, and even more for Nemle or Jik or Kel, another Silberay to help her make sense of the astonishing power she had discovered within herself.

She left the bus in the centre of Deerford. As she passed him the driver spoke.

"Thank you lass. It were you drove them off, I think."

Marheh turned in surprise, a smile lit her face.

"You were doing a good job by yourself."

The warmth of recognition went with her as she walked to the pottery. It was not all darkness in the villages, surprising bursts of light shone through.

When she reached home her mother was there to greet her. Greya held her at arms length for a moment, studying her face then she gave her a little shake.

"Go and wash your hands. There'll be food in the kitchen when you're ready."

Marheh leaned in to kiss her and went to do as she was told. She felt as if she was once again a troublesome ten year old, but obedience was restful sometimes.

In the kitchen there were no questions, just a large fresh loaf, a wedge of cheese and a steaming mug of sperit. When she had taken the edge off her hunger, she sighed and looked gratefully at her mother.

"Stay there."

Greya disappeared and came back a moment later with a hair brush.

Marheh, still with the ten year old in mind, gave a little gurgle of laughter.

"Am I to be spanked?"

Greya shook the brush with mock ferocity.

"Little scruff that you were, and are. Your hair is a disgrace."

She stood behind Marheh and began to undo the plait and then to brush Marheh's hair, long, smooth strokes. Marheh felt all the day's tensions flowing away. She closed her eyes.

The silence lasted until the brushing was done and Greya gathered the strands for plaiting.

"My daughter with grey in her hair," she said rather sadly. "Where did the years go?"

"And I'm still a trouble to you," Marheh said, bracing against the small tugs as the plait was reformed.

"No you're not," Greya said, then sighed a little. "At least, not in important ways."

She tied off the end of the plait and Marheh swung around to look at her.

"Mek thinks I should leave the Silberay," she said, testing.

Greya's face fell into sadness.

"You know then. He's the one I worry about, but it's no good saying anything. He just pretends to agree with me and goes his own way – or rather Nella's way."

"Apparently Nella suggested giving me a home. I could help around the house and start behaving like a proper woman."

Greya gave a shout of laughter.

"Little does she know what she would be taking on."

Marheh pouted. "Don't you think I could do it?"

Greya gave her a hug.

"Go along. Go down to that boat of yours and put yourself to bed for a bit. Supper won't be until seven so you've time for a nap."

When she was on *Day Bringer* she was most truly herself, Marheh thought, as she made her way down into her cabin. It was nice to be the daughter of the house and be looked after sometimes, but it was better to take up the responsibility her Silberay training laid on her. She wouldn't go to bed, though a nap would be nice, more important was to make sense of the day.

She went through to the saloon, made up the fire a little, then sank into the armchair. For a few minutes she drew on thoughts of Nemle, holding her in her mind, picturing her face, austere, stern even sometimes, but looking at her with loving wisdom. Then she reached for her journal.

Today something happened that I can't explain, she wrote. *I was so filled with strength and power that I became something other. It was both terrifying and exhilarating and I need to understand it. If I can't understand it I can't know whether I'm breaking the law and if I'm not breaking the law then I need to understand it to be able to call it to me again.*

I had wings and I made fire.

She stopped and looked at what she had written. I had wings and I made fire, she told herself, not quite believing it. But I didn't really. It was just an illusion. She picked up her pen again. *An illusion,* she wrote. *The Yareblis believed it and fled. I believed it, but I made it.* Again she stopped. There was surely nothing wrong in making an illusion for a right purpose. The Yareblis made illusions, and left them as traps for the unwary. She shuddered, remembering as if it were yesterday, how she had been caught in an illusion that made her believe her hands had been cut in half by her mooring rope.

She had been young then and needed Nemle's help to be free of it. She had learned since then, learned to recognise and see through these traps, but she had never heard that Silberay made them.

She covered her face with her hands. Oh Nemle, I need you. Silberay and Yareblis were the same. If Yareblis could make illusions then it followed that Silberay could, only they never had. Was that on purpose or did they not know it was possible? It had saved her today, the illusion she had made, and she didn't even know how she had done it. It had come to her in need and fear and she had not hesitated to use it. She had been acting on behalf of someone else, and that was her job.

She sighed and closed her journal. She could not share her experience with anyone, but she could sing with them. There was time before supper.

The singing refreshed her as nothing else could and she felt much more like herself as she made her way up the path to the house. She was a little late and when she entered the kitchen it was filled with family. They were all there, Mek with Nella and Wilda and her middle brother Bol with his wife and two children as well as the usual residents. She had been told of their coming but the events of the day had pushed it from her mind. Now it seemed too much to bear. She wanted to turn and run but she pulled herself together, pasted a kind of smile on her face, and stepped forward into the throng.

A wash of talk, taking the pressure off and then a girl's clear, high voice sounded above it all.

"Aunt Mary you have ink on your chin."

Marheh felt them look at her but before she could react another child's voice, puzzled and demanding.

"Who is Aunt Mary?"

Marheh laughed then and picked up five year old Tith to give him a grateful hug.

"I'm Aunt Mary," she told him quietly. "But I'm Marheh too and I like that better."

"So do I," Tith nodded.

Tep strolled across to claim his son and suddenly everything was alright. She had her place here as well as with the Silberay. She grinned ruefully at Tep.

"I suppose I do have ink on my chin."

Tep looked at her gravely.

"You do, but it suits you."

Supper was a crowded, noisy affair but with so many she found she did not need to talk much. The children were excited and demanding attention, the other adults had everyday affairs to talk about and exclaim over. A polite question or two were directed her way but Nella and Mek dominated the conversation. It seemed that a company Mek did occasional work for was buying land in the district of Lowcroft. There were plans for building an exclusive community. Nella was determined that she and Mek would buy there.

"The selection process is quite rigorous," she said, "But Mek has been promised a place if we want one. Of course it will be expensive but worth it."

Marheh listened without commenting as Nella explained how there would be facilities like a swimming pool and a recreational and social space for residents. It would be fenced too, which would make it safe from undesirables.

"It sounds horrible," Bol said, when the paean of praise was ended. "I'd rather live in a village, where you get all sorts of people."

"I haven't agreed to go yet," Mek said. "It's basically a company project, for their executives and employees, but it's a compliment to have been asked and Angelique is keen."

"And I am too Daddy."

Mek smiled fondly at his daughter.

"And W... Amanda is too."

There was a moment of stunned silence as the adults present registered Mek's choice not to use Wilda's soul name and the children worked out whom he was talking about. It was Bol, always closest to Mek as they were growing up, who succeeded in putting the question for which they all wanted an answer. Mek looked uncomfortable but he spoke firmly.

"We have decided we want to be called by our real names. We're grown adults, these nicknames belong to childhood."

"But..."

Just that one word from Greya before she pressed her lips firmly together.

"I'm sorry Mother-in-Law." Nella picked up the silence smoothly. "I know you like the old ways but nobody believes all that nonsense about soul names nowadays and I can't pretend any longer, even for you."

Again silence.

Greya turned to look at Sef who rested one hand over hers.

"We will try to understand if that's the way you feel, but you're wrong to say that nobody believes in the value of the soul name. I do and so does Greya, and Marheh lives her belief."

Perhaps it was the mention of her name that made Nella flare up angrily, at least Marheh thought so.

"Exactly my point! You are so proud of her, and what is she except a lonely, deluded middle aged woman, soon to be a lonely, deluded old woman unless she changes her ways. Look at her, dressed like a man, can't even make the effort to wash her face before going into company. She's so pleased with herself she can't even see how she shames the family. We even offered her a home and she just laughed. It's not fair that she should be associated with us. If the company looked into Malcolm's background and found her they'd probably withdraw the offer of land at Lowcroft Heights."

She ran down into silence. Even the children were quiet, not really understanding but aware of anger and pain.

Marheh was concentrating on her breathing, slow and even, not wanting to reveal her feelings. She had known Nella did not like her but not this depth of anger. It hurt. In the silence she wondered briefly whether the whole family felt the same way, but rejected the idea at once. Then she felt Fali beside her, heard her draw in her breath.

"I'm proud to be part of Marheh's family," she said quietly, then stopped as everyone turned to look at her.

"I admire what she does and the way she gives herself," she went on, red-faced but determined. "The others think they can't say that because she belongs to them, but I can."

Talk broke out as she finished. Marheh let it swirl around her not trusting herself to speak. Tep gave Fali a hug and they both turned to smile at Marheh and draw her into their warmth.

"I can understand if she doesn't like me," Marheh said. "But how can what I am, what I do, damage her?"

"I think perhaps she's jealous," Fali said. "You're strong and independent. You've chosen your own way and followed your vision for yourself."

Marheh shook her head, not disagreeing, but not quite understanding either. She looked across the room to where Mek, Nella and Wilda stood talking to her parents.

"It looks as if they are going," she said. "Do I say anything?"

"Nothing," Tep said firmly.

Marheh gave him a little push.

"Alright brother dear."

Bol and his family came across to them then, to exchange hugs and say their goodbyes also. His three year old held up her arms for Marheh to pick her up, giggled and gave her a sloppy kiss.

"M'auntie," she said as Marheh cuddled her. She stroked Marheh's cheek with one small, sticky hand. "M'auntie," she said again.

"Come on scallywag." Bol held out his arms for her. "Time to go home to bed."

Tith and Fali took their boys upstairs and Marheh was left alone with her parents. The big kitchen seemed a different place, quiet now with shadowy corners. There was plenty of clearing up to do though. Marheh began to gather dirty dishes from the table. Greya filled the sink. Sef cleared away the rubbish, then he and Marheh picked up tea towels. The silence between them was warm and restful.

When the work was done Greya gave Marheh a hug and said goodnight. Marheh thought she had aged ten years this one evening.

"I'm alright mother, just sad for Mek and Wilda."

"And Nella," Greya said. "Be sad for Nella too."

"I'll try."

She turned to say goodnight to Sef but he shook his head.

"I'm coming down with you." He turned to Greya. "I won't be long. I'll just see this daughter or ours safely home."

It's worse for them, Marheh thought as she got ready for bed. It had hurt to be described as lonely and deluded but it couldn't touch her for long. Mek had rejected the teaching, the values and beliefs of his parents and that must be a constant pain.

She washed her face, cleaned her teeth and brushed out her plait. Imagine wanting to live behind a fence. Never mind how luxurious the facilities, it would be like being in prison. It was the sort of thing the Yareblis might go in for. She stopped in the act of picking up her nightdress. The sort of thing the Yareblis might go in for, she said aloud. She pulled on her nightdress and got into bed. Tomorrow's task was laid out for her. Tomorrow she would go looking for Lowcroft Heights.

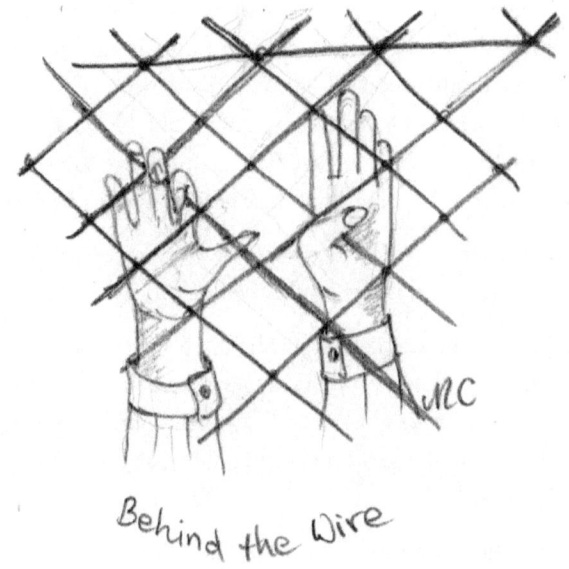

Behind the Wire

Chapter Eight

You had to expect changeable weather in spring. She let the noise of the storm wash over her and pulled up her blankets, grateful for the cocoon of warmth, snug in her bunk. It was still the middle of the night. She could see nothing, not even the shape of her window that usually revealed itself as a different kind of darkness. It might help the water levels, she thought drowsily, as the storm settled in to steady, beating rain. The noise of it on the roof began to recede into the background as sleep took her again. Then a new noise stirred her to wakefulness. It was the creak of a rope under strain. It came again, not much of a sound but one she was trained to be alert to. The bollards of the wharf had less give than her usual mooring pins. Perhaps she had tied up too tightly. She ought to go out and look, but it was still raining hard and her bed was so comfortable. It was no good though. She couldn't rest now she had thought of possible harm to *Day Bringer*.

She got out of bed and fumbled her way to the window. Perhaps there was a little bit of lighter gray now. There was no point in lighting her candle, it would just spoil her night vision. What would she put on? Her cloak would keep her dry but she wanted to be able to move quickly and once it was wet it would take ages to dry. She thought for a moment then pulled off her nightdress. **She** would dry more easily than any of her clothes.

She grinned to herself as she pushed open the doors to the back deck. Wouldn't Nella feel justified if she could see her now!

It was like plunging into a cold shower. She gave a little gasp and a shiver as the rain struck her bare skin. It would be good to yell and make a dance on the back deck, but better to get on with loosening the mooring lines. The water had risen surprisingly fast. She bent to her task, struggling a little with the straining, wet ropes.

When she had finished she stood and stretched, lifted her face to the rain. You had to give yourself to it. Accept the wet and the cold. She danced a few little steps, beating a rhythm on the wood of the wharf. The she spun around twice her arms wide, her face uplifted, before jumping back onto *Day Bringer* and descending once more to the warm darkness.

Sleep would be impossible now, for a while at least, but she could sing. She lit her candle and rubbed herself dry, then, wrapped in her dressing gown, she went out to the saloon, made up the fire, and settled herself in the armchair. The rain still beat steadily on the roof, heightening her sense of being enclosed. She sighed a little, snuggled her gown closer around her, drew up her legs so her bare feet were tucked underneath her and gave herself to the soul song.

It was still raining when she emerged, stiff and disoriented and stumbled back to bed.

The world seemed quite different when she woke again. Light was reflected from every damp surface. The sun was not long risen and still held the soft, golden look of early morning. Marheh stretched luxuriously. Had she really gone dancing about naked in the rain? A smile spread over her face. Scandalous! Suddenly she was filled with energy. She flung back the covers and hurried into her clothes.

Lowcroft this morning. She needed to refresh her memory of where it was in relation to the water road. If she went there by bus perhaps she could explore around it on foot and make her way home via the water road. She spread out her chart and studied it carefully, then went for the little sketch map Jik had sent her. It looked as if she might be able to visit the source of the water road as well, though after last night's rain the levels would not be a problem for a while.

She packed a small sketch book and the coloured pencils she had bought into her small back pack and made her way up to the house, confident that her mother would be happy to give her food to take for her lunch.

Fali and the boys were just about to set off for school but there was time for a quick hug and a brief discussion about the picture Tith had drawn for his home work. Then she was alone with Greya. Her mother gave her a long look and she blushed.

"What have you been up to?"

"What makes you think I've been up to anything?"

"I've known you a long time. You haven't changed." She gave her a kiss. "But I should remember that you're grown up and it's none of my business."

Marheh laughed.

"It was nothing really wicked. I just went dancing about in the rain last night."

"Well it seems to have done you as much good as a night's sleep."

Marheh grinned and slid into the place that had been laid for her at the table.

"Am I the last? Have you eaten?"

"Yes and no. I thought I'd wait for you. Sef and Tep were keen to see how the firing went."

Marheh nodded.

It was always an anxious time, opening the kiln after a big firing, even though they were confident of their skills, a mistake could cost dearly.

Greya put a plate of porridge in front of Marheh and sat down with her own breakfast.

"You have plans for the day?"

Marheh decorated her porridge with milk and honey.

"I'm going to visit Lowcroft. I'm curious about Lowcroft Heights."

Greya looked sharply at her.

"Because of Mek?"

"Partly."

Marheh ate a couple of spoonfuls of porridge.

"You know I don't remember even visiting Lowcroft as a girl. It's so close. Why didn't we go there?"

"Thirty years ago it was only an estate, Lowcroft, and a small church. It's only in the last twenty years that the shire acquired land there and built housing. Then the bus service started going that way. There's no school. The children travel to Higham's Hill. No jobs either."

Marheh nodded slowly.

"There doesn't appear to be a shop there. I suppose that's why I've never visited from the boat. It's not very close to the water road, right on the edge of my chart."

"I'm sure you would have explored over the estate when you were a girl. You were always off on some expedition of your own, especially when I wanted you to mind the boys."

Marheh grimaced and polished off her porridge. She stood up with her plate.

"I know I was a selfish little brat at times." She picked up her mother's plate and took them to the sink. "Stay there why don't you? I'll cook the eggs."

Greya laughed.

"No thank you. I like mine edible. You can do the dishes."

Marheh heaved a melodramatic sigh then laughed and acquiesced.

An hour later she was waiting at the bus stop in the centre of Deerford. She'd some sandwiches and a piece of fruit as well as her sketching things and felt herself ready for anything. One or two people recognised her and greeted her as they passed on the way to the shops. She was aware of some curious glances from the three other prospective bus passengers but nothing like the hostility Amelia Tarrant had shown her. She took pleasure in the bright morning and felt positive about the action she was taking after her long period of indecision.

Lowcroft wasn't a bad little place, she decided, strolling around it in the sunshine. She had been the only person to alight here, though there had been a good half dozen waiting to leave for Higham's Hill. It was very quiet; a couple of young mothers with prams and an old man in his garden were the sole evidences of occupancy. The big old house of the estate was sitting firm and gracious in the midst of the newer houses, mostly semi-detached of formal design, set in good sized gardens. There were three short rows of terraces as well, presenting bland, unassuming faces to the world. She could see no sign of any building to indicate the beginnings of Lowcroft Heights, but then, Mek had said 'in the district of'. She wandered around the churchyard and looked at the headstones, no new graves and only half a dozen surnames amongst the old ones. She couldn't remember ever having been there before, but she knew she would have avoided what must have looked like a private estate in her youthful expeditions. The land around was another matter. When she had seen enough of Lowcroft she set off confidently towards the special place that she now knew was the source of the water road.

For about half an hour she walked uphill along an old bridle path then the path crossed what looked to be a new gravel road. She hesitated, trying to remember her map. There was no road just here, unless she was badly off course. The sound of a laboring engine reached her and she stepped into the shadow of a clump of trees and watched as a truck with a load of timber joists made its way clumsily past her, strewing stones and dust in its wake.

Impulsively she turned to follow it. The dust and gravel made for uncomfortable walking but she persisted. The truck looked to have been carrying building materials and she was curious about any building that might be going on near here.

The countryside was high and open on one side of the road, with a view over fields and even an occasional glimpse of water that might, just possibly be the water road. On the other side were trees, scattered over a steep, rocky hillside. She looked up into the trees and wondered whether it would be better to scramble along with some cover. The sound of another engine behind her made the decision easy and she climbed up off the road as another truck came by, panting a little at the gradient.

She decided to continue keeping to the higher ground and the cover. If this were Lowcroft Heights she was not at all sure what her reception would be if she approached openly. As quietly as she could, she followed the dust raised by the trucks, moving from tree to tree, going carefully, conscious that a sprained ankle could keep her anchored all night.

At last she reached a place where she could look down over the wide circle at the end of the road. The two trucks were there and several men were busy unloading. It all looked very orderly and the men were talking and joking as they worked, but there was a new, high wire fence and from her vantage point, Marheh could see that it stretched around an enormous area of land. It seemed to her that it might even stretch as far as the water road itself.

She sat down on a rock and took out her lunch. If this was Lowcroft Heights it was a very big operation. Could the Yareblis have grown strong enough to control this? Were they involved at all, or was it just her imagination that this prospective development seemed to reflect Yareblis values? She watched thoughtfully while the unloading progressed, barely tasting the egg sandwich Greya had provided for her.

There was not much to see inside the fence, no actual buildings at least, though she could count what looked to be foundations for five separate structures. There were several big piles of lumber, partly covered by tarpaulins and a large piece of machinery that looked like some kind of earth moving equipment. It looked as if the road was being extended into the enclosure; a wide red gash scarred the fields.

She finished her lunch and watched the trucks depart, then stood up cautiously. If she was right in her geography, then the source of the water road was likely to be inside the gates that were now being closed behind the trucks. Whether the project was the work of the Yareblis or of some unscrupulous developer, or both, their action was illegal. The Silberay owned the narrow wedge of land that carried the source stream. It was considered too important to the water road to be left to chance to preserve it from the tractors and bulldozers of the everyday world.

There was no way she could approach the gates unseen. There were still a couple of men at the site, and now that the trucks had gone she realized that there was also a caravan, the door of which stood open. Presumably that meant someone was living there. Quietly she moved back the way she had come. She had to find out more, but better if she appeared to have been innocently following the road that crossed the bridle path.

When she knew she could not be seen from the gates, she made her way down to the road and walked back to the site, trying, as she went, to make up some story about why she was there.

When she reached the gates she stood openly looking through them, then she reached for the bolt that held them closed.

"Hey! What do you think you're doing?"

A man stood up from where he had been fastening a tarpaulin over the newly delivered timber. She put on her best smile.

"I've just been following the road. I was sure there was a public footpath up here somewhere."

She gestured towards where she thought the water road would be.

"I need to get over there. Could I go this way?"

The man came towards her.

"This is all private property. You can't come through here."

He did not speak aggressively, but then he did not need to, he was twice her size and the gate was still closed.

"I can't see why not. What harm could I do? If I have to go back, or around, it will be miles out of my way."

"Way to where? There's no where to walk to around here."

"Well there was when I was a girl. I used to walk all over here from my home in Deerford. I don't believe you've any right to keep me out."

Again she fumbled with the bolt, pushed a little at the gate.

"Stop that!"

He held the gate against her.

"This is a construction site. We're talking safety regulations. You can't come in."

"Why not?"

She leaned against the gate. She could make him let her in if she entered his mind. She shouldn't do it, but she could. How important was it that she visit the source? Surely she already knew what had happened. The Silberay land must have been taken in illegally and, knowingly or unknowingly, the source stream bulldozed. It was not enough to guess though. She had to know for sure. She smiled at him again.

"Please let me go through. If I can't go this way it will be dark before I get home."

"Not my problem lady."

She nudged a little feeler into his mind. It was a Yareblis mind and he didn't seem to know she was there.

"Please let me through," her mind whispered to his.

He seemed to be studying her.

"What was it again that you wanted?" he asked.

"To come through the gate, so I can walk across the fields to my home."

"It's against regulations," he said, sliding back the bolt and opening the gate just enough so that she could slip through.

"I'm very grateful."

"Take care now."

"I will."

She began to make her way towards the red gash, looking back briefly to smile her thanks. She went to continue and found her way barred by another man. This one looked her up and down knowingly and she caught her breath. This one understood something, at least, of who she was. Well she need have no qualms then about entering his mind. She looked up at him. He too was large, tall and broad with small eyes and very little chin. He reached out and grabbed her by the arm. Looking down, she noticed he had quite long and carefully manicured finger nails.

"Let go my arm," she said quietly, preparing to use her mind to reinforce her request should it be necessary.

He smiled a little, moist red lips parting briefly before, surprisingly, he released her.

"Looking for something?" he asked.

"Just going home."

"Ah!" he said and she felt for the first time a stab of fear. Then he stood back to let her pass. She looked up uncertainly and wished she hadn't as she met the hard, narrow, blue gaze. It felt as if she was doing what he wanted, yet he was not in her mind, she knew that. She stumbled a little at her first step and he reached out to steady her.

"Mustn't keep you," he said, mocking her.

She walked carefully past him and along the new red path, her back straight, her chin up. It was an effort of will to keep from running. She felt as if she might be attacked from behind at any moment.

But nothing happened.

Gradually her tension eased. She no longer felt eyes boring into her back. She had gone below the crest of the hill and risked a glance back the way she had come. Nothing. She relaxed a little, walking on with something closer to her usual steady, swinging pace. These fields had been beautiful once. She remembered trees, long wild grasses and flowers; yellow flowers, pink, red and white. There had been butterflies and bees and bird song. How there was the red dirt piled and bare flattened squares.

Now the landscape was so changed she barely recognized it, yet there were still hints, flashes of insight that guided her towards the place she had once known so well. Close to the fence she found it in the end, nearly as far from the gate as she could be. The great over-hanging rock was still there and the central stone but around was no bubbling spring. The sides of the pool had been mashed down so that the water was no longer contained, but spread uselessly into mud. The narrow stream that had led to the water road had been so churned up, trampled over, that its bed was barely visible and it seemed mostly chance that any found its way beyond the fence.

She stood sad and silent, unaware of the tears that mourned the loss of beauty and the destruction of memory. There was nothing she could do alone though. She would have to get word to Jik. She smiled ruefully. She had resisted so hard when Greya, Sybi and Gul had encouraged her to ask for help and now she had no choice. She leaned down to touch one of the muddy pools at her feet, cupped her hands to scoop up some of the thick, clouded mixture. She wanted to croon over it, love it a little into wholeness. She held it for a few moments before letting it dribble slowly back. Mud clung to her fingers.

After a few more minutes she rubbed her hands on her trousers, and took a good look at the fence. It was quite an obstacle, but she had no intention of going back to the gate. New and shiny, made of wire mesh, it was higher than she could comfortably reach. Angry, pointed twists of wire finished the top. She found a bit of rock to sit on while she considered the problem.

Going over it looked to be impossible unless she had something to climb on. It was low to the ground too, no going under it either.

She looked along the fence in both directions, walked hopefully towards a tree that turned out to be yards from where she needed it, then walked back to the source rock. There was a way, there must be. Too preoccupied to watch her feet, she stepped into a muddy pool and felt her boot sink until the mud covered it. Cross with herself, she stepped back feeling the mud suck at her boot. Clammy dampness seeped into her trouser leg. The depth of the mud meant that she had got dirty almost to her knee.

She stood and studied the ground, wondering where to step, then realised that the soft mud was actually the bed of the stream and it extended under the fence. Slowly she walked alongside it till she stood beside the fence. How deep and how soft was it here? Holding onto the fence she lowered her already filthy boot into the mud. It was soft right to her knee. It would be a horrible job, but perhaps she could dig her way out.

She stood and looked at the mud, bent and felt for the lower edge of the fence. It would be possible if she could dig away the mud.

There was no way she could keep clean. Though she began by kneeling beside it and scooping it with her hands, she found that it soon filled again with sludgy water. Obviously she was not going to be able to clear a passage, but perhaps she could push her way through. Her hands stopped working of their own accord as she understood that would mean putting her head into the horrible, custard consistency, not just her head, her face, eyes, mouth, nose – she couldn't do it.

It's that or go back to the gate and beg to be let out. It would just be like swimming really, but what if she got stuck with her head under. She would drown. She took a deep breath to calm herself and think around the problem. Anything would be better than going back to the gate. Well, no, drowning wouldn't be, but she could minimize the risk if she thought it through.

Carefully she lowered herself to sit in the mud then she pushed her legs out under the fence. Deliberately she closed her mind to the cold damp seeping into her clothes and concentrated on her strategy. She couldn't decide whether head first or head last would be best but by pressing her body close to the fence she could use her legs to feel for potential obstacles on the other side. Slipping and sliding in the mud, she began to feel the bed of the stream like a trough around her.

Then she realised that her body was keeping back some of the sludge and that decided her. She would go head first on her back. Perhaps that would mean less mud and the use of her arms to pull her through. Again and again she rehearsed the moves in her head until she became aware that she was procrastinating, putting off the moment when she must act.

She tucked her plait into her tunic and turned to sit with her back to the fence. Sliding her body away from the wire she lay down in the mud. She found that her own bulk was acting as a plug and the sludge moved away a little behind her. Carefully she reached her hands back to feel for the edge of the wire, moved until she could feel it against the top of her head. Then she let her head drop back until she could feel the edge of the fence on her forehead, just below her hair line. Mud soaked into her hair and seemed to lap her face. She clutched the wire. One sharp, downwards pull. She could do it, she could. She took a deep breath and closed her eyes, then opened them again for one last look at the sky. A brief admonition against cowardice and another deep breath, then she gripped the fence and pulled herself down.

A short, endless struggle as she pulled with her arms and pushed with her legs and felt the mud ooze around her head and face then she was through and lifting her head to breathe again. Mud dripped from her face as she clung to the fence panting, not able to breathe through her nose. She snorted and mud spattered. She managed to loosen her grip on the wire and wipe ineffectually at her eyes. Then she wriggled and pulled and pushed until at last her body and her legs had followed her head and she was free of the enclosure.

Euphoria carried her a short distance but it was not long before discomfort made itself felt. Her clothes were clammy and heavy with mud, her boots seemed leaden. One cheek was beginning to sting. There was still a long way to go. When she reached the water road, where the water was clearer, she could at least wash her face and hands. As she plodded along she tried to distract herself by thinking about what she had learned. It seemed very little, given what it was costing her. Still she had established something, had at least determined what was starving the water road. It seemed now though, that this was only a small part of what was wrong.

This project, Lowcroft Heights, was Yareblis inspired and influenced. They were increasing their power in the community and challenging the Silberay by their treatment of the source. They cannot have expected to remain undetected for long and clearly they had been anticipating the arrival of someone like her. What were they preparing for?

There were too many unanswerable questions and she was too tired and uncomfortable to ponder them any longer. At least she could look forward to warmth and kindness when she reached home. She was reminded of her younger, rebellious self, struggling back to *Day Bringer*, damp and defeated and fearful of Nemle's disapproval. She had received warmth and kindness then too, though she had not expected it.

By the time she reached the pottery and stumbled up the path to the house she had become an automaton, no thought, no feeling, just one foot after the other, after the other, after the other. Then she was trying to pull herself together, to enter as if all she wanted was a bath. Perhaps it was all she wanted. She held the door frame and straightened her shoulders. She was home, she was fine, she had succeeded. It was enough to support her as she opened the door and went into the kitchen.

This was a scene of peaceful domesticity. The two boys were home from school. Fen sat at the table with some homework and Tith was crawling around the floor pushing his model cars ahead of him. Greya was beating a mixture of something in a big bowl and laughing at a comment of Tep's, peeling potatoes beside her.

For a moment no one noticed her arrival, then Tith ran one of his cars into her muddy boot and looked up.

"M...Marheh?"

He stood up and backed away from her, clutching his car.

"Yes, it is Marheh." She tried to reassure him. "I'm a bit dirty."

"A bit dirty!"

Greya stared at her for a moment then went into action.

"Fen you run upstairs and get my old dressing gown, the blue one. Tep and Tith go and run a bath. Marheh, into the laundry with you and take off everything."

Marheh laughed, a little hysterically.

"Yes Mama."

Tep grinned at her and set off up the stairs with the two boys. Greya escorted Marheh into the laundry and stripped her of her clothes with a mother's practiced efficiency.

"What have you been doing?"

Marheh opened her mouth to reply.

"No, I don't want to know. You'll have to borrow some of my things while I get these clean. I'll hear all about it after you've bathed."

There was a knock on the laundry door and a hand appeared dangling the old blue dressing gown.

"Thank you darling."

Greya took it and thrust it at Marheh.

"Go on up. The bath will be filling. Take as long as you want. I'll look after things here."

Marheh sighed and wriggled into the dressing gown.

"Thank you." She bent to kiss her mother. "Sorry to be such a nuisance."

Greya took the edges of the dressing gown and wrapped them over each other. Then she reached for the belt and tied it firmly around Marheh's waist.

"You've a nasty scratch on your cheek. Make sure you wash it well."

Tep was sitting on the toilet seat watching over the bath with Tith on his lap. Aromatic steam was rising from the water that nearly filled the big tub.

"Your towels Madame," he said, indicating two big yellow towels folded over the rail. "I put some of Fali's bath salts in for you. She won't mind. I'll get her some more."

"Kind of you both." Marheh grinned at him.

He stood up, setting Tith down on the floor.

"Come on young man. We had better let your aunt have her bath or Grandma will be cross with us too."

Tith studied Marheh solemnly for a moment.

"Are you naughty?" he asked at last.

"Very naughty." Tep scooped him up. "Grandma probably gave her a big paddy whack."

He whisked out the door and shut it behind him before Marheh could respond. She took a half step towards the door then stopped as weariness engulfed her. Untying Greya's neat bow, she let the dressing gown fall to the floor, eased herself into the warm scented water and closed her eyes. Bliss!

She lay and drowsed, thinking of nothing for perhaps half an hour. Then there was a tap on the door.

"Don't fall asleep in here," Greya's voice came to her. "I've put out some clothes on my bed. Supper in half an hour."

Marheh roused herself enough to call out her thanks then set to work to wash rather than soak. The water turned black in minutes so she let out the plug and finished off with a shower that became cooler and cooler as she stood under it. Finally, with one towel, turban like around her head and the other wrapping her body, she scurried across the hall to her parents' room to don the clothes Greya had found for her. These were too wide and too short and she felt very odd in a skirt, but she was covered and comfortable, except for her feet.

She went downstairs again at last to find them all waiting for her.

Summoning a smile from somewhere she pirouetted into the kitchen, making her skirt swing about her.

"What do you think?"

She stood posing for them.

"Sit down and stop showing off," said Greya. "Fali's brought down her slippers for you."

"Yes Mama. Thank you Fali. Coming home is very salutary." She thrust her feet into the slippers and sat in her place. "Just when I think I've grown up, I discover that I haven't at all."

There was a bit of a laugh at this then they settled to eat Greya's lamb casserole with dumplings. Apple pie and custard followed and Marheh began to relax. Warmth and safety, no responsibilities, no wonder she felt like a child again. Of course the responsibilities were waiting for her and she would pick them up again soon, but just now she could forget them. She looked down the table and met her mother's eyes. She might have spoken, but Fen, having polished off his pudding, was eagerly asking for seconds and the moment was lost.

Only when the clearing up was done and they were relaxing with mugs of sperit did Sef say;

"Am I to understand you had an adventure today, daughter of mine?"

"You could call it that I suppose. I did have to make a fairly unorthodox exit from a building site." She smiled across at Greya. "Hence the mud."

"Marheh was naughty," Tith informed him importantly.

"Was she now!"

"You didn't see her Grandpa," said Fen. "She was muddy all over, even her hair, and all her clothes."

"Oh dear," said Sef. "But I don't think she was really naughty. I think she was working."

"Thank you Father for that vote of confidence."

She looked around at them all.

"What do you know about this place that Mek wants to live in? Lowcroft Heights? I think I found it today. It's only a building site at the moment, but it's a huge enclosure. Already there's a high fence and guards at the entrance. And they've enclosed Silberay land. I ought to telephone Jik and tell him if you don't mind me using the phone."

A telephone at the Harbour was a fairly new innovation, but it was handy sometimes to be able to ring, not that she was very experienced at using it, but her father helped her to navigate the intricacies of operators, connections and numbers and she was able to speak to Jik and report what she had learned from her day's explorations.

That done, weariness dropped over her, a covering she could no longer hold back. When she appeared again to the family, her face was white, her eyes large charcoal smudges. She looked at her mother.

"Please may I be excused?"

The words came unbidden out of childhood.

"You take her Sef," Greya said. "Make sure she gets home safely."

Her father was already on his feet.

When she got there *Day Bringer* was cold and dark. The fire was out, the lamp unlit. She was too tired to care. Her borrowed garments were easily shed. She slipped naked beneath the blankets and slept and slept.

My armchair

Chapter Nine

It was late when she woke and later still when she got up. She might have a lazy day, or at least a day of quiet, ordinary activity. She'd done no cleaning for a while and she knew Greya would want to be invited to see the modifications that had been made to *Day Bringer* for her. All the family would, but it was Greya who would notice her housekeeping.

After she had dressed and made up the fire she went up to the house to issue an invitation to Sef and Greya. She hoped there might still be breakfast on offer and she was not disappointed.

"You're spoiling me Mother … It's very nice."

Greya smiled and reached up to cup Marheh's face between both hands.

"It doesn't happen often. Have you put something on that scratch?"

Marheh shook her head.

"It could do with a bit of mercurochrome. I'll have a go at it after breakfast."

The mercurochrome stung and left a bright pink stripe down her cheek.

"You're not likely to start a new fashion," Fali said, coming back from walking the boys to school.

"You think not?" Marheh laughed.

"Better a pink stripe than an infection," Greya said.

The three women laughed together then went their separate ways. Marheh went back to *Day Bringer* to clean and tidy and make a batch of biscuits so she would have something to offer her parents when they visited.

The chores left her mind free to consider her next moves. She had done what she had been asked. She had discovered the cause of the problem of the water levels but it did not seem right to move on while the Yareblis were active and trying to establish some kind of power base. Gul and Sybi were depending on her too. It might be worth going to see them again, or Mrs Armstrong, Blethan. They might have an idea about Lowcroft Heights, or at least the connections to enable them to find out.

Jik had promised to give her love to Nemle so she would understand why she had not sung yesterday. It had to be a priority today though. Taking meals with the family was lovely but it did seem to use up a lot of time.

Cleaning did too and she regretted past neglect as she dusted and polished, dug grime out of odd corners, wiped down sooty walls and finally addressed the brass. Luckily she did not have a whole house to take care of. She was reminded of Mek and Nella's offer of a home. How she would hate it, being their housekeeper. That's what they wanted of her. Someone who conformed to their ideas of what a woman should be like. Her parents had never expected that of her and she didn't need to consider anyone else.

At last *Day Bringer* looked as smart as she could make her. It was worth the effort and she knew she should do it more often but there was always something more interesting beckoning her away from the paths of righteousness – if that is what housekeeping could be said to be. She made up the fire and gathered the big heap of laundry she had been saving for her mother's washing machine. That really was a treat. Hand-washing everything in *Day Bringer*'s little bath was the thing she liked least about her life.

Greya came to meet her as she stumbled up the path with it. She took the laundry bag, leaving Marheh with an armful of linen and towels.

"Just remind me how the washing machine works," Marheh said. "I'll do it myself."

"You've got about three loads here. You've been saving it up I suppose."

"You're not to do it mother. You're doing enough for me."

Greya only smiled.

The day continued in quiet domesticity until it was time for afternoon tea and the visit of her parents. Marheh stepped onto the wharf to greet them and guide them on board. They were both accustomed to the strangeness of disappearing into the water dimension and indeed had lived long enough with the knowledge of its presence that they could catch a glimpse of *Day Bringer* without Marheh's help. Greya carried Marheh's clothes from the day before, clean and pressed.

It was a happy visit. Everyone was on their best behaviour and Marheh enjoyed offering hospitality. Her biscuits had turned out well and *Day Bringer* was looking her best. Greya sat in the armchair and Sef at the table with Marheh hovering between them until she felt relaxed enough to push the footstool so that it made a triangle and she could sit too. With part of her mind she noticed and thought it odd that she should be self-conscious entertaining her parents when she wasn't at other times, but soon enough she forgot herself.

Sef had been particularly interested in her new workspace and Greya had applauded the extra light that came in with the opening up of the saloon.

"And *Day Bringer* is all yours now," she said. "It seems odd to be visiting and not to see Nemle."

"I miss her very much," Marheh admitted. "More than I expected I would really."

"You were very important to her. She always seemed to understand you very well."

"She set out to love me when I became her apprentice and she never stopped, even when I behaved badly."

She paused, felt her cheeks warm a little and knew she was blushing.

"And you, of all people, will not be surprised to know that sometimes I did behave badly."

Greya smiled at her.

"There were never any half measures with you. When you were little you could be an angel all day then suddenly, for no apparent reason, the devil got into you."

"And you didn't stop loving me either."

Marheh looked from one to the other.

"I was only thinking the other day how lucky I am to have you."

"We feel lucky too," Sef said.

A comfortable silence fell until Marheh stood up to offer more sperit or another biscuit.

"I think it's time we went really," Sef said. "It has been good to visit and see your home. Now when you go we can picture you here and feel happy about you."

When they had gone she washed up the few dishes then settled to the soul song. It did not go well and she was conscious of darkness and distractions, but she did manage a few moments of light and music. What she really wanted was direction, but that was elusive and needed more work than she felt capable of. She seemed to have lost her focus.

Sighing a little she made her way up to the house for supper. It was all too hard sometimes.

At the door she breathed deeply, stretched and stood straighter. Pull yourself together. You've no reason to feel miserable.

Sounds of talk, a little laughter reached her through the door.

Stop feeling sorry for yourself.

She'd never minded being alone before. Why should she feel lonely now with the family all around, welcoming and loving? Of course she had always had Nemle before, wise and loving and her own in a way that the family no longer was. She had prided herself on the way she had cared for Nemle's physical needs in the last few years of their time together and never acknowledged, not really, that Nemle's loving care of her had never stopped and had supported her in ways she was unaware of until they were no longer there.

"Grow up," she admonished herself and pushed open the door.

"Here she is!" Fali's smile welcomed her, the two little boys ran up for hugs and from across the room Sef's eyes met hers with steady, warm affection.

Back on *Day Bringer* after the meal and the bedtime stories and the quiet sharing of every day events she tried to make sense of it in her journal.

This was the life she had chosen, the life she had trained for, the life she wanted. She had the support and affection of her family, most of them anyway, and the respect of the Silberay, some of whom loved her too. So why was she so unsettled? She couldn't decide on any single reason, but she knew that a balance of discipline and action would be her best cure.

Before she closed her journal she made a list;

> *visit Gul and Sybi,*
> *visit Blethan,*
> *look for places where people were hurting,*
> *spend extra time with the soul song,*
> *invite Fali to visit Day Bringer and work on doll's heads,*
> *go back to the fence and look at the source to see what could be done there.*

Just doing that made her feel more positive and this time when she entered the soul song there was music and light and the accompanying harmonies of other Silberay. There was darkness too, hovering at the edges, but she understood that this was not the time to push out and back, this was the time to consolidate. She went to bed feeling as if she had made progress.

Next morning saw her back on the bus soon after breakfast. She'd not done much as yet to help Gul and Sybi, but perhaps her thoughts about Lowcroft Heights would be useful. The building site was far enough away that most people would know little about it. Probably that was part of the plan. The longer things went unnoticed the harder it would be to make changes. She looked out the window and watched the landscape in its spring colours. The sun was shining too and the only clouds were high and white.

There were passengers waiting at Lowcroft but Marheh carefully avoided looking at them. She preferred to remain unnoticed if possible. Then a child's high voice spoke her name.

"Marheh, Mummy it's Marheh!"

It was Rebah.

Marheh smiled at her and looked up to where Imni was making her way towards her.

"I want to sit next to Marheh, Mummy."

"Why don't I sit down and you can sit on my lap. That way we can both sit next to Marheh."

When they were settled Rebah looked at Marheh with a hint of disapproval.

"Why aren't you on your boat? You said you would come back."

"I've got some work to do just now," Marheh told her. "I will come back on the boat, I promise." She smiled. "You're a long way from home."

"We came in Daddy's car. We're going to see Nother Granny. Daddy's gone to look at a place."

"Owen wants to move," Imni explained. "He's taken against our house and he's been offered an option on a place at a new development."

"Lowcroft Heights?"

"You've heard of it? What's it like?"

"It's barely started, nothing but mud surrounded by a big fence." Marheh chose her words carefully. "It's hard to tell what it will be like at this stage."

"The way Owen speaks I thought there was a mansion all ready for us to step into. I don't want to move."

"I don't want to move." Rebah's little murmur sounded sad.

Marheh saw Imni's arms tighten around her.

"If we must go we'll just have to make the best of it. There might be some other children living near who you can play with."

"But no water," Rebah said. "No boats."

"No boats," Marheh agreed.

"Have you seen another boat?" Marheh asked the question casually not wanting to reveal how much the answer mattered. Another boat would perhaps mean help and support.

Rebah nodded.

"I waved, but he didn't see me because I was in my tree house."

"That must be fun – a tree house!"

Marheh turned the conversation and it remained with tree houses for the rest of the journey to Willow Rise.

It seemed Rebah and Imni were getting off there too. Marheh followed them down the steps and they stood together watching the bus out of sight.

"Nother Granny lives in Willow Rise, does she? I wonder if she knows my friends."

"She is a very old friend of my mother's. Mother died before Rebah was born so she offered to be another grandma. We don't see as much of her as we would like, do we sweetheart?"

"Nother Granny tells me stories and we have special biccies."

"That sounds lovely," Marheh said. "You have fun with Nother Granny."

She watched them out of sight along the high street. Rebah turned to wave every twenty yards or so and Marheh was ready to wave back. The thought of Rebah living under Yareblis influence gave her another pressing reason to investigate Lowcroft Heights. She was torn, wondering whether to warn Imni of the possible dangers, or wait until she had more concrete evidence or perhaps a plan for derailing the project altogether.

At last she turned towards the church and the vicarage where Gul and Sybi lived. Even as she approached the house she felt anxious. There seemed to be a heaviness, a weariness about the place, that suggested it was under siege. It was hard to walk up the path to the front door and harder still to force her hand to lift the knocker.

As she waited she tried to prepare her mind for the possibility of assault. It seemed to be ages before she heard a noise on the other side of the door. Then instead of a wide, welcoming opening, it opened only a crack and Marheh saw a chain pull tight. She was welcome though, for Sybi's face lit up when she recognised her visitor. The chain was quickly unfastened and she was hurried inside. It saddened Marheh to see the door bolted and the chain fastened again before Sybi guided her along the passage to the kitchen.

It was filled with warmth and light and should have been a delightful place to be. Gul sat at the table in an old wooden chair with a high back and smooth, polished arms. Last time Marheh had seen him in this chair he had been comfortable, filling it and radiating the geniality that he had displayed at their first meeting. Now he seemed to have shrunk and the miasma of grey that emanated from him overshadowed all the warmth and the light.

Marheh turned to Sybi.

"How long?"

"Two days." Sybi's voice broke. "He came home the day before yesterday and he could hardly speak. He seemed to be in pain, but he couldn't tell me. At first he seemed to be struggling but now… now he…"

Marheh did not hesitate.

"It will help if you touch him, let him feel your love," she said, pulling up a chair to sit opposite him, their knees almost touching.

She took a deep breath and closed her eyes. There was no time to waste. If Gul had been battling alone for two days he must be nearly spent, if he was not already overwhelmed.

Carefully she sought his mind, trying to balance her own need for defence with the need to rescue and release Gul. Yareblis had become so skilled at this invasion of the mind, skilled and ruthless in a way Silberay would never be as long as the use of this discipline was so hedged around with restrictions. She caught herself back from these thoughts. Later she could look at them again, now she must focus.

It was like entering an arena where two gladiators were imprisoned in a fight to the death. There would be no mercy and no giving in. The Yareblis mind was stronger but the stubborn defence of the other was taking its toll and both combatants were near the end of their strength. Just the presence of another mind was enough to tip the balance and as it became aware of her the Yareblis mind attempted to flee, but Gul would not let go. Marheh was not sure whether he would not, or could not, but it gave her the opportunity to act. Quick and incisive, a surgeon wielding a scalpel, she found the malign, distorted segment of the Yareblis mind that enabled perception of the water dimension and wrenched it clear.

No longer able to maintain a presence in another mind, Gul's invader disappeared, leaving Marheh to withdraw, carrying the excised part, painfully aware of its corrosive poison leaching into her own mind. As she returned to herself she had a momentary vision of her hands burned black, the flesh eaten almost to the bone.

The lingering horror of that glimpse remained with her as she sat in the bright kitchen and watched as Gul emerged from his long battle. The knowledge of what she carried shadowed her pleasure in Sybi's joy, but held also a terrible temptation. Could she take that thing she carried into her own mind, gain its ability without being tainted by its poison? In her heart she knew she could not, yet she wanted the extra power.

Gul's eyes were still closed, but his voice when he spoke was strong and urgent.

"Put it on the fire now."

Marheh and Sybi both started. Marheh felt a flash of anger. How dare he tell her what to do! She would keep it, take it into herself. She was strong. She would not let it twist her. It is twisting you already. It was as if Gul's voice spoke in her head, or was it Nemle's voice she heard. Deliberately she pictured herself opening the fire door in Sybi's stove, taking the thing she carried and thrusting it in, far in so the fire bit her hands, trying to welcome the cleansing, cauterising pain of it.

The child in her cried out for comfort, but she resolutely denied that voice. The pain in her mind would heal, the poison had burned away and she had learned something – at least so she hoped.

There was a sound from Gul, something between a sigh and a grunt, and his eyes slowly opened. Sybi took his hand, kissed it and held it to her cheek. The tears she had not shed before now ran unheeded. Marheh blinked back tears of her own, recognising the love that flowed between them and acknowledging that her own life choice made this closeness something she would never know.

Gul looked across at her and spoke his thanks. His look of gratitude and affection meant more than any words. Sybi went to put the kettle on for sperit and Marheh and Gul sat in comfortable silence, weary but content for the moment just to be.

"I think," Marheh said hesitantly when the mugs were almost empty and something like normality had returned to the sunny kitchen. "I think we should … sing … It will complete the healing. That's what we call it. Perhaps you have a different name for it."

"We understand sing," Sybi said.

Gul nodded.

"But perhaps we need to talk first," he said. "You perhaps came to visit with a purpose?"

Marheh looked surprised for a moment then nodded.

"Lowcroft Heights," she said. "What do you know of it?"

"Lowcroft Heights," Gul repeated. "That was the subject of my research too."

"And you were stopped," Marheh said slowly. "That confirms there is something wrong about it. What made you investigate?"

"One of my parishioners farms land near by. He was worried by the great fence next to his property. He thought perhaps they might be building a new prison or some high security defence project. I thought we would have been told if that was the case, but when I tried to look into it for him I found so much secrecy it provoked my interest."

"Why should there be so much secrecy if there is nothing wrong?" Marheh said. "Something to be hidden. They have enclosed land belonging to the Silberay. I know that. I have seen it. But that alone is not enough."

"What made you look in that direction?" Sybi asked her.

"Something my brother said first of all. He has been offered the option of purchasing there. It seems that the property is to be exclusive, enclosed, rather luxurious… it sounded like Yareblis values at work. I went there and saw how the land has been enclosed… I had to escape under the fence."

"It just sounds like development to me," Sybi said bluntly. "I don't suppose either of you checked with the estate agent in Deerford. If it is to be so exclusive they will already be starting to advertise I should think."

Marheh shook her head.

"I didn't of course. It didn't occur to me. Silberay don't own land individually. But I just got the impression from my brother that it is to be by invitation only."

"I'm not doubting that you and Gul have stumbled into something that someone is hoping to keep hidden, and obviously it is associated with Lowcroft Heights, but I can't believe that the greed of some developer is causing the darkness we are aware of. There has to be something else."

"I thought at first it was a direct challenge to the Silberay because of the damage to the water road, but it seems like more that that now."

"It is about power," Gul said. "A place like that has power over the people that live there. It changes their values, or encourages wrong values already held."

"And that is how the Yareblis work." Marheh nodded agreement. "They make use of pride and greed and self importance, so perhaps this development is being encouraged by them so they can build a community of people they can use."

"Hardly a community!" Sybi's voice was dry.

"No, the opposite really, but I don't know a word for that."

Sybi stood up and looked from Gul to Marheh.

"What you two need now is food. Gul hasn't eaten for two days and Marheh looks ready to drop. My loaf is ready for the oven and there is soup that just needs heating. Why don't you two do your singing while I get it ready?"

They would not sing without her though so they waited while she arranged oven and stove top to her liking then settled down together.

This was different music than Marheh was used to. Silberay song was golden and filled with light, spun thread weaving cloth of gold, spread against the dark or reaching out to enfold and transmute it. Now she was conscious of earth colours, reds, browns, ochres singing together, sturdy and determined. This song did not reach out in the same way as Silberay song, but it felt solid and grounded, in a way that even Nemle's song had not.

They were not together long, but Marheh knew herself to have been touched and supported in a new way. She wondered whether, now her ears were opened, she might find this song beneath her own more often. She understood that her song had offered them something too and was glad.

The food was very welcome then and Sybi insisted they kept away from discussion of Lowcroft Heights while they ate. Since that was the subject uppermost in their minds it was not so easy, but each had questions about the others that could be explored. Marheh found herself encouraged to talk of her life with Nemle and the new challenges presented by life alone. She in her turn listened while Gul and Sybi spoke of their life and work.

It had been a sensible suggestion of Sybi's and they returned to consideration of Lowcroft Heights with new focus. Marheh wondered whether perhaps the enclosure of Silberay land was a mistake, drawing attention to the planned development before it was ready. She was aware that Jik was planning to take legal action on behalf of the Silberay and perhaps that would be of some use, but the attacks on her and on Gul were clear warnings that their interest in the project was unwelcome.

"It's the secrecy I don't understand," Gul said at length. "If it was just a development such as your brother described, then Sybi's thought about the estate agent would make sense, but as it is…"

"I'm wondering whether they plan it for training and recruiting." Marheh spoke slowly working out her thought. "If they perhaps were targeting people whose values they could use and manipulate, and mixing with them Yareblis who need to develop their skills. They wouldn't advertise at first because the idea of being chosen and exclusive would appeal to the people they are interested in."

She put her head in her hands.

"I'm worried about the families especially if there are children – they would be hoping to recruit from them I think."

"We can let your Harbour Master take care of the legal challenge, but if they are wanting secrecy then I think our action should be to publicise," Sybi said. "Once our communities are talking about it, we might begin to see some light on the whole development."

It was a beginning, an action they could take that could conceivably make a difference, or at least bring the dark things to light.

"Like cockroaches scuttling about when their hiding place is uncovered," Sybi said.

Marheh laughed at that, though she was still uneasy. Nothing they had thought of seemed reason enough for the attacks on her that had begun before she knew anything about Lowcroft Heights.

She stood up and stretched.

"I think it's time I went. Thank you for the talk and the food and everything."

Sybi gave her a hug.

"Thank you for what you did for us."

"And for what you are doing," Gul said, taking both her hands in his. "Be careful Marheh."

He squeezed her hands and let them go.

"I will."

The mouth of the tunnel

Chapter Ten

She had plenty to think about on the bus ride home and after a brief greeting to her mother she went down to *Day Bringer* to spend time with her journal. Then she pulled on her smock and took up some clay letting her hands explore ideas while her mind rested.

She had built up a ball of clay thinking she might play with dolls' heads but what emerged was a portrait of Nemle. When she realised she put her head down on her folded arms and gave in to tears.

How she missed her.

Nemle would have known how to heal her mind of the pain from the Yareblis poison. Nemle would have helped her to understand what she was seeing and hearing in the landscape around her. She sat up and wiped her eyes. Nemle would have known she was feeling sorry for herself and made her face it. She put the little head to one side. Nemle could look at her for a bit and keep her disciplined.

She packed away her tools and her smock and went out to the well deck. She had been so preoccupied with the day's activities that she had barely acknowledged the spring sunshine, the clear blue sky, the natural world that was normally such an important part of her life.

Now she stood drinking in the landscape, the glow of late afternoon light, the brightness and the shadows that seemed to add emphasis to everything. On her right was the pottery. The path through the garden was still sunlit but the buildings were softly shaded now. Only the tall kiln and the chimneys of the house caught the light. Ahead was the mouth of a tunnel, above it the road into Deerford. The reflection made the arch into a perfect circle, dark against the warm sunlit bricks of the bridge. Opposite the pottery, to her left, rose a glowing field, the grass an impossible green. Patches of wild flowers shone yellow, white and pink and two black and white cows grazed peacefully. A hedge covered in pink may blossom trimmed the crest of the small hill and served to hide the road. She stretched, breathed deeply and let the peace of it wash through her.

Nothing was left of the sunshine but a rose-coloured glow behind the pottery when she finally came back to herself. She shivered a little and went back inside, taking a moment to warm herself at the fire, and make sure it would last while she was eating with the family. Then she went through to the back, swung her cloak around her shoulders and made her way up to the house for supper.

That night singing was at first difficult and painful, yet it was good pain, if there could be such a thing. She felt herself gently held within the pain, and after the first anguished moments, understood that what hurt was the cleansing, the washing away of the last remnants of the Yareblis poison. Then came the gold and the delight and she knew she was whole again.

It was hard to come back to the empty darkness after that. The warmth of the fire was comforting, but not like the warmth of Nemle's love.

She had never expected to be lonely. It seemed like a weakness somehow, as if she had failed some kind of test. She took refuge in habit. The regular night time tasks, banking the fire so it would last until morning, brushing out her plait and re-doing it, washing her face and hands, cleaning her teeth.

At last she was in bed, warm and snug, but sleep would not come.

In order to discipline her thought, she set herself to remembering the source of the water road as she had known it as a child. Carefully she built a picture to replace the picture of devastation she had found the previous

127

day.

At first it was not easy. She was tempted to indulge instead in empty longings for comfort and company, but gradually the picture took hold of her. She knelt on the grassy bank and watched the bubbles emerging from the depths. She dabbled her fingers in the cold water. The underneath of the cavernous rock that partly sheltered the pool was damp and chill. Moss grew there and she stretched up to touch it. She felt herself twelve again, bare brown legs under a faded cotton dress. The sturdy scuffed boots were too cumbersome for the bright day and she sat down to take them off and dip her toes in the refreshing chill. There was sun on the island rock, her island. She gave herself a little run up to make the jump, gripping the warm stone with her toes as she landed, her arms wide for balance. One little toe had been scuffed against the stone and a bead of blood welled up. She lowered herself to the rock and sat with both feet in the water until they were numb with cold then drew them out onto the sun warmed stone.

When she awoke the dream memory was still with her. She would go back there today and see if she could understand more clearly what had been done.

She felt light and happy as she set out, the twelve-year-old Marheh still with her. She remembered the guilty pleasure in escaping the ever present little brothers, the joy in the prospect of exploration and adventure. The day matched her mood, a light breeze, sunshine, small white puffs of cloud moving slowly above. The water road danced beside her. It seemed high and healthy today. She stepped out vigorously, a song pulsing in her veins and threatening to burst forth to join the birds that were expressing their delight in the day from the trees and hedges that lined her way.

As she drew nearer the stream that came from the source her steps slowed a little. She was not going to that special place of delight that had been her refuge in childhood, but to a scene of destruction. She did not want to think of it and she would not, not until she had to. Deliberately she returned to the memory of what it had been.

Soon enough she came to the place where the stream flowed under the path and into the water road. The water seemed clearer. She thought she remembered a cloud of yellow mud, but there was no cloud blossoming from beneath the path today. A tangle of bushes masked the entrance and she pushed through them to stand at the stream's edge and look into the water. It was running quite freely here, perhaps things were not as bad as they had seemed.

She turned to climb beside the stream. At first she made her way between trees that rose almost from the water's edge. She knew she was in the right place, yet it puzzled her. Of course she had been almost blinded by mud when she had struggled along here two days ago, but it seemed healthy now, and it had not then.

Ahead of her the water spread out into a small, dark pool, and above the pool it splashed and chattered through rocks. She sat down abruptly on a sun splashed stone at the water's edge. This was how it should be, this was the place the twelve year old had known, but it was not the place it had been the day before yesterday. Had she made a mistake? She had approached from the opposite direction then, had walked through a landscape of devastation. Perhaps she had misremembered and what she had found before was not the water road at all.

She tried to persuade herself that she had been wrong, but she could not really believe it. This was the source stream, but so was the other. She stood up and continued to follow the water course. There was only one way to find out.

The little stream wandered in and out amongst rocks and she followed it for perhaps another hundred yards before she reached the fence and stood pressed against it to stare, amazed and puzzled, at the source. It was behind the fence, she had been right about that. It was surrounded by the work of machines bullying the landscape into some form of submission, but the source itself was already recovering. Where there had been heaps of dirt with dying foliage buried in them there were now grassy hillocks with small shrubs sprouting new leaves. Two or three young saplings grew beside the big overhanging rock and the rock beneath was again an island.

She looked down at her feet and there, where she had struggled in the mud, the water flowed swift and clear beneath the fence. She closed her eyes, opened them again. Nothing changed, unless perhaps to move closer to her childhood memory picture.

She stood for a long time wondering at the regeneration, her mind filled with speculation and unanswerable questions. The long walk back to *Day*

Bringer and the pottery went past almost unnoticed as she wrestled with what she had seen. Everything about the water road seemed to confirm that the regeneration was real, but the dryness had been real too. Perhaps if she knew more about how the source had been created she might understand what she had happened. She was not aware of having done anything other than report what she had found. Had Jik and the old ones at the Harbour like Nemle, had they been able to use what she had told them to rebuild? It seemed too easy, but perhaps not easy for them.

It was mid-afternoon when she arrived back at *Day Bringer* aware of hunger and weariness. The levels were perfect. She made a point of noticing as she approached and stepped on board. She didn't want to go up to the house. She couldn't talk to them about what she had seen and it was too fresh in her mind for her to put it aside. She would go through to the saloon, fix herself something to eat and take out her journal. Perhaps writing it down would help her make sense of it, or at least enable her to leave it behind.

She stopped for a few moments in her cabin, changing her boots for slippers, then made her way through to the saloon. As she reached the galley and looked across she thought for one startled moment that there was an intruder, but the dark shape in the armchair resolved itself into the welcome presence of her Uncle Jik.

"Did I frighten you? I'm sorry."

"Just for a moment until I knew who it was." She started towards him. "Is something wrong? Is it Nemle?"

Jik smiled.

"I suppose in a way you could say it was Nemle, but there's nothing wrong with her. It's you. I think she would have set out herself if I hadn't agreed to come."

"How did you get here? Where's *Autumn Wind*?"

"You don't think the Harbour Master has time to go boating, do you?"

Marheh made a face at him and reached for the kettle.

"I took the bus to Cuddes, the train to Featherstone, another train to Bartelford and a bus to Deerford." He made it sound like a marathon journey then grinned at her. "So I hope you're worth it."

"You can't think how glad I am to see you."

She spooned the dried berries and spices into mugs and dived into a cupboard to bring out the last of the biscuits she had made.

"So much has happened that I don't understand. I've so needed to talk about it."

"But you're all right?"

She felt his scrutiny.

"Nemle was sure you were in danger, hurting perhaps."

She prepared the sperit and took it to him without answering. He waited until she had brought the plate of biscuits and her own drink and settled herself on the footstool facing him.

"And Nemle is usually right, especially when it relates to her beloved apprentice."

Marheh felt tears come and blinked hard.

"I miss her so much."

She looked up at Jik.

"There have been times… She would have listened to me and comforted me and…"

Jik reached out to lightly touch the half healed wound on Marheh's cheek. "And doctored you too. How did you come by that?"

"That was getting under the fence," she said, and once started out it all came.

Jik listened without saying much, just once or twice a question for elucidation. She told him how she had explored and found Lowcroft Heights and the source, and about that day's discoveries. The only thing she did not speak of was the help she had given the bus driver.

"So was it the old ones at the harbour who fixed it?" she asked at the end of her tale. "That was all I could think of."

Jik reached out and touched her arm then stood up.

"Let's go and sit at the table. You're not an apprentice now. You don't need to be sitting at my feet."

Marheh laughed and stood up with him.

"But I am your niece. Can't I sit at my uncle's feet?"

Jik gave her a hug.

"We've just done the 'uncle' bit, now we'll be Silberay."

He waited while Marheh slid into her place then sat down opposite her. She looked at him expectantly.

"It was not the old ones who fixed it," he said. "You did."

"Don't be silly! I didn't do anything."

"I think you did."

He was silent for a moment, looking at her, forming his thoughts into the appropriate words.

"Marheh already you know things, understand things that some Silberay never know. You and Nemle together were a wonderful partnership and Nemle was the perfect mentor for you. You've grown with her and past her and that is how it should be and how she wanted it to be."

He paused again.

"So why the lecture?"

"Is it sounding like a lecture? That's not what I wanted."

He put a hand over hers, holding it still.

"The water road was made with blood, struggle and imagination. Sila and the others gave themselves to it, their lives, their passion for people and the land. You know that."

Marheh nodded remembering the small, private graduation ceremony that had preceded the public celebration at the Gathering.

She and Nemle had sat quietly together in a special place at the Harbour. A small arm of the water road had been brought up to some wide, shallow steps. Trees grew around it giving shelter and privacy. There was a comfortable seat at the top of the steps and for a time they had sat there without speaking. Nemle had suggested she think back over the years of her apprenticeship. There was good and bad and it was not always easy remembering. When that was done it was time to envision the future, both together imagining the water road and her contribution to the life and people it touched. It was like a promise.

Then Nemle had helped her to undress. She had gone naked into the water where she made a small cut in the pad of the first finger of her left hand. The bubble of blood had bloomed for a moment then disappeared, but she had crouched in the water, her arms spread across the surface, until the cold drove her out.

"Blood, struggle and imagination," she said at last, echoing his words.

"You've just told me about all three," Jik said. "The struggle, the effort of finding the source, confronting the enemy and finding the courage to escape under the fence, the blood..." He touched her cheek again where it still sported its mercurochrome stripe. "I'm sure that bled and no doubt you washed it off into the water road."

Marheh nodded slowly.

"And the conscious, disciplined imagining."

"It was remembering really."

"And lucky for the Silberay that you had the remembering to build on, most would not have."

"It seems too easy really, to have rebuilt without knowing what I was doing."

"But it wasn't easy, was it?"

Marheh thought back over the story of the past few days she had just related.

No it had not been easy. She had needed the discipline Nemle had instilled in her. She had hurt in several unexpected ways and struggled to regain equilibrium. It had not been easy, but she had succeeded.

A little surge of pride resulted in a straighter spine, a lifted chin. Jik smiled at the emergence of Marheh the Great. He leaned back and lifted his mug, saluting her. She laughed, enjoying his commendation, her face alight with pleasure. Then she was suddenly serious again.

"If I had known enough to do it consciously, would I still have been able to?"

Jik shook his head.

"I don't know, you've gone beyond my experience, but I expect you will find out sooner or later… One thing I do know… the struggle and the blood must be real and the imagination willed and disciplined, not just day dreaming."

He sat back then, sipping at the last of his sperit and leaving his words for her to think about.

She was silent for a long time and when she did speak it was to change the subject, ask after Nemle and the work at the Harbour and tease him about the rigors of his journey to Deerford. She got up and made more sperit for them both and they finished the biscuits. He was happy to follow her lead knowing he had said enough.

Later they sang together before going up to the house for supper. Singing was often unexpected and his presence with her added a new harmony.

Over supper they discussed Lowcroft Heights and what it might mean to the villages round about, as well as to the Silberay. It was something that even five year old Tith could have an opinion about.

"I live here," he told them all emphatically as Fali and Tep took him and his brother upstairs.

"Which is just as it should be," Jik said and wished them both good night and goodbye.

He would need to be on the first bus if he were to get back to the Harbour at a reasonable hour.

He it was who escorted Marheh down the path to *Day Bringer* that evening.

"I don't think there will be much problem getting the fence removed. Our title to the land is very clear. The lawyers will handle that. The development itself is likely to be more of a challenge though." He gave her a hug. "I think you need to move on for a while at least."

"But…"

"But?"

"If I do that I feel as if I will be letting Gul and Sybi down. This is as important to them as it is to us, perhaps more important, because they live here all the time."

"I'm not suggesting you abandon them, you couldn't, but I think you need to give yourself some space for thinking and some distance."

Marheh looked as if she disagreed with him, though she said nothing. He took her by the arms and gave her a gentle shake.

"Let Gul and Sybi start the publicity campaign – people know them. Let the Yareblis think you have accomplished what you were sent to do and continue on your way for a week or two. You'll be needed more later. Take time to build up your strength and prepare."

Slowly she nodded.

"That makes sense I suppose. I wish I could explain to them though."

"Write them a note. I'm sure Tep or Fali would post it for you.

"Alright." She looked up at him. "And Jik ... Thanks for coming."

As she made her quiet preparations for bed she realised that Jik's suggestion had helped her, that she was looking forward to moving on. She thought perhaps she would be less lonely away from the family and the constant reminder of the life she had turned her back on.

It wasn't them. They loved her and applauded her life choice. It was her own feelings that had surprised her and put her off balance. The things she had encountered had not helped either. As she pulled the blankets up around her and snuggled into the warm darkness she felt a little surge of pleasure and anticipation.

She was up early enough to walk with Jik to the bus stop, to send messages of love to Nemle and wave as the bus bore him away. Back at the pottery she had time to breakfast with them all and explain her sudden departure.

When she took up her letter for Gul and Sybi she was all ready to go. There was a spring in her step and a little rush of adrenalin that made her feel alive again. Her mother put the letter carefully with the other mail and she and Sef went with her back to the mooring. She started the engine and untied the lines before stepping off for brief goodbye hugs. Then she was away.

Ten minutes later she had negotiated the short tunnel and emerged into the sunlight. It felt like freedom and for a moment she felt guilty. Freedom, to be away from family and those who loved her? Then she shrugged off the thought. She loved them too and if they needed her she would be there, but this was the life she needed to live if she were to become who she was meant to be.

The weather looked to be set fair for the next few days and she would make the most of it. An extra hour or two of boating today and tomorrow, would bring her to a favourite mooring, a place where *Day Bringer* could lie in the sun, and she could sit and gaze at a wide landscape of fields on the far side of the water road, or step off and explore the little wood that lay beside her. The bluebells would probably be finished now but there were other flowers and the trees themselves flaunting their new leaves.

The slow, steady progress was good for thinking too, not the worried, anxious questioning of the last week or so, but a more positive, constructive assessment of what had been and what might be to come. How good of Jik to visit. How sensible his advice. How encouraging his confidence in her.

The two days of boating had an almost dreamlike quality after recent exertions. There were no locks and the water road curved gently between low hills and across wide plains. She was in deep country now, remote and peaceful. Sometimes she passed a farm house, rich red bricks glowing in the sun, a curl of smoke from a chimney suggesting activity within. Early or late she saw long lines of cows making their way to milking. Perhaps she saw half a dozen people during the time, individuals for the most part, tending an animal, walking across a field or a garden, working in a vegetable patch. She thought about these gentle, unhurried activities and wondered whether these too were vulnerable to the Yareblis quest for power.

The mooring, when she reached it, was as she remembered. The last time she had been here was with Nemle of course. It had been a favourite of hers too and they had stayed several days while Nemle spent time in the woods gathering plants and barks that she used in her medicines. Marheh had not been trusted with this task but was sent off to gather dandelions. The roots and leaves could be used and the plant was easily identified. Nemle had tried to interest Marheh in her craft and she had, perforce, learned a little, but it soon became evident that her interests were not in that direction. She was very happy to draw the specimens Nemle collected though and eight years ago they had completed a project that drew together all Nemle's extensive knowledge of the use of plants for medicines, tonics and tisanes. Marheh's drawings had been an important addition and they had both been delighted when *Nemle's Herbal* found a publisher. Nemle had raised seedlings too, in pallets on *Day Bringer*'s roof. Marheh had been expected to help care for them since they provided part of their livelihood. She was not sorry to be rid of them.

She arrived in the late afternoon and settled in with quiet contentment. There was time for a walk in the woods to gather fuel before the light began to fade. She cut and broke it into the short lengths that were necessary for her stove and stacked it neatly on the back deck. Then she wrapped herself in her cloak and sat in the well deck to watch as the sun set.

There were no theatrics tonight, no fiery clouds, no shafts of gold piercing through, instead the pale, pearly sky faintly pink, the gradual leaching of colour, the gradual cessation of sound and movement. She heard the busy, going to bed, activity of the birds in the wood behind her then this faded. An arrow of dark shapes streamed across the sky, flying home. The water road darkened and a ring of ripples spread where a fish reached for a surface morsel.

At last when it was almost too dark to see, she stood up and stretched and made her way back inside. She wouldn't bother with a fire tonight. It was not really cold. Sperit would be nice, but water would do, and a supper of bread and cheese. Then she would sing. Peace had washed her through and through and her song would take it and change it and give it back three fold.

Tenfold, she thought sleepily, when the song ended and she was making her way to bed. Not because of anything she had done except that she had been there, a conduit for the song of others, so many others who loved the land, the people and the one person present in the land.

The next few days she spent happily moored. There was time to play with her clay until she found a doll's head that pleased her. She worked at modelling some of the animal figures and groups that were her bread and butter and she worked at the disciplines. In particular, she tried to understand the illusion she had created in protecting the bus driver. She wondered briefly why she had not spoken of it to Jik but somehow she knew he could not have helped her. It was something that belonged to her alone and she had to come to terms with it herself.

Her journal recorded her thoughts and her experiments.

She had experienced the illusions left by the Yareblis to play on a person's hidden fears. She knew how to see through these traps, but she had never tried to understand how they were made. It had to be related to the discipline of the mind, but she had never practised this alone, always it had been mind against mind for training or in self-defence.

At first she thought she might be able to leave an illusion that would be an experience of peace. She had found such peace here that it seemed something she might build upon, but though she could recreate for herself the peace of that first evening by disciplined remembering, she could not believe that she was placing anything outside herself.

"I can't tell," she wrote. *"I feel peace but would anyone else and if they did would it be the peace from my illusion or the peace of the place itself."*

Then she thought perhaps it might be better to try for some other feeling, but what? Pleasure – but some people, the Yareblis, took pleasure in that which hurt others. Happiness – but mostly people did not hide their happiness. No wonder the Silberay did not encourage the making of illusion. Yet what was the water road itself but a kind of illusion.

In the end she moved away from emotions and decided to work on something a little more tangible, an illusion of warmth. Once, one of the Yareblis had created an illusion that made her feel cold. She remembered how Nemle had had to stop her from building up the fire to dangerous heat. An illusion of warmth might be manageable and it would be a pleasant, comforting thing.

Two things kept her struggling with the possibility, the knowledge that she had done it once, created the fire that melted the Yareblis ice, and the stubborn refusal to believe that the Yareblis could do something she could not. She had stopped thinking about the legality of it – she could revisit that should she succeed.

It had to begin with imagining, the same sort of disciplined imagining she had unwittingly used to repair the source, but then she had to put the fruit of her imagination outside herself, leave it here where it might be experienced by another.

In some ways it was not so very different from what she did with her clay. The sculptures she made were the fruit of her imagining as well as of her years of disciplined practice in seeing and understanding. And had she not done something similar when she disposed of the power she had taken from the Yareblis who was fighting with Gul? She imagined herself making a nice little fire in a little brazier. That part was not so difficult and she rather enjoyed making sure she had every detail correct. The hard part came when she tried to remove it from her mind and give it life of its own.

She tried imagining the recipient of her created warmth, thinking of walkers in winter, of the Travellers she had made friends with in the first year of her apprenticeship and of farm workers out with their animals in all weathers. Perhaps the animals themselves would appreciate it too and the pictures of cows and rabbits and moles gathered around her brazier made her smile. Would a passing Silberay, rugged up against the weather, linger a little? Would she ever know?

She spent just over a week at the mooring and each day she practised using her mind, though she was never quite sure if she succeeded. Then one morning she woke knowing she had to return to Deerford.

It did not seem to be an urgent demand but there was no possibility of ignoring it. She made herself and *Day Bringer* ready for departure then lingered to create her brazier yet again and leave it, with faith and hope, on the bank next to her mooring.

She needed to continue on to the next turning place about half an hour ahead. As she travelled back past the mooring she seemed to feel a drift of warm air but she was aware that the wish may well have led to the thought, especially since the day was not cold in any case.

Two days of steady boating and she was back at the pottery. As she emerged from the tunnel she was surprised to see another boat moored, then delighted when she recognised *Storm Cloud*. Kel emerged at the sound of *Day Bringer*'s engine and helped her to tie up against him, since the mooring was not long enough for two boats.

She couldn't help grinning. This must have been the boat Rebah saw and Kel, who lived on it, was her particular friend amongst the Silberay.

When *Day Bringer* was secure he gave her a hug and drew her into *Storm Cloud* where the kettle was boiling and a big pot of soup sat warming on the edge of the stove. There was no need for words. Her response to his hug was more than enough to tell him how glad she was to see him. He filled bowls and made sperit and they sat at the table to eat.

Six years older than she, Kel had given her much needed support through the sometimes turbulent early years of her apprenticeship. He was kind and steady and she knew he cared for her.

"Did Jik sent you?" she asked, once the edge was off her hunger. "This wasn't your assigned route was it?"

"He told me he'd given you a job. I think he was feeling guilty that he may have made your first solo voyage more of a challenge than it needed to be."

"He's been here. Did you know? He came on the train, but he didn't say anything about sending you."

"Perhaps he was not sure how you'd react." Kel smiled at her.

"You mean he's sent you to baby sit!" Marheh's indignation was mostly feigned. "When did you get here? Have you been up to the house?"

"About three hours ago and no, I'm not sure they know I'm here, and it's many years since I met them."

"Tep probably knows … my brother … he can see something of the water road."

She paused, remembering why she had returned.

"Did you call me?"

Kel shook his head.

"I expected you to be here when I arrived. I hadn't started to think about what to do if you didn't come."

Marheh grimaced.

"Someone or something called me, perhaps not intentionally. There are things going on all around this area. Jik ordered me away to get some space from it, but we both knew I would have to come back." She propped her chin on her hands and sighed. "A lot has happened. There are things I don't understand. Things have happened to me and I've done things…"

She looked across at him. "I've lots to tell you, but I think I'd better go up to the house first. Will you come with me?"

They finished eating and washed up then Marheh led the way up the path.

"Mother is Greya, father Sef, brother Tep, brother's wife Fali," she filled him in as they went. "Probably it will just be mother in the kitchen at the moment. The others will be working."

Kel was only half listening, but he took in the essentials.

"Are you worried about them?" he asked.

She stopped in her tracks, looked back at him.

"I suppose I am." She sounded surprised. "I don't know why I should be."

She set off again a little faster and a minute later she was showing him into the kitchen.

"Mother, you remember Kel?"

Greya turned around from the bench where she had been working. A range of emotions was revealed in her face but the predominant one seemed to be relief.

"Mother, what's wrong?" Marheh cut across Greya's greeting to Kel.

"Mek's disappeared. His secretary has been trying to contact him for a couple of days. She can't raise Nella either and Wilda hasn't been at school."

Marheh threw a glance at Kel then drew her mother across to sit at the table. Kel came to sit too.

"Sef's been trying to find him," Greya said. "In fact he's out now, visiting some of the people he works for. He visited the house after the secretary called, but there was no one there and no sign that they were planning a trip."

Marheh reached for Greya's hand and held it.

"He wouldn't neglect the business, it's too important to him but what if he's got into debt or done something illegal and he's just left it all behind?"

"Mek wouldn't do that mother."

"Wouldn't he? Now that Nella has persuaded him to deny his soul name and turn his back on the things we value there's no telling what he'd do."

Marheh shook her head.

"That's not Mek. He might not value the same things we do but he does value his good business reputation and he loves Nella and Wilda. He wants the best for them."

"Then where are they... all of them?"

Greya was struggling to contain her feelings.

"When did you last see him?" Kel asked.

"He came to pick up a delivery four days ago. He didn't stay, just popped in to say hello while Tep was finishing the last bit of packing."

"And he seemed alright then?" Marheh asked.

"Very pleased with life, I thought and..." Greya's face showed her remembering. "He said he still wanted to be Mek when we were alone. It made me happy."

She covered her face with her hands for a moment then looked up at Marheh.

"Something has happened to him hasn't it?"

Marheh chose her words carefully.

"It does seem as if they are in some kind of trouble. I can't help wondering about Lowcroft Heights. Has there been any more said about that?"

"Wilda came in after school last week to get some clay she wanted for a school project. She was full of it. Apparently Mek had taken them to visit the site and there is to be some kind of tour of inspection that she is looking forward to."

"Mek has definitely decided to go ahead then?"

"It seems so."

Marheh stood up and walked around to give her mother a hug.

"I know it is no use saying don't worry. I know there are things to be worried about... that's why I'm here."

Greya clung to her for a moment then let her go and stood up.

"No sense in giving in to worry... it doesn't help feed the family." She turned to Kel. "Will you eat with us this evening? You'll be very welcome."

Kel glanced at Marheh who nodded.

"Thank you," he said. "I will enjoy that."

Marheh was reluctant to leave Greya but she needed to be alone on *Day Bringer* to listen to the landscape and make her own investigations in her own way into who might have called her.

She was very quiet as she walked down to the mooring but she knew Kel understood. As they parted she arranged to meet him again to walk up to supper then she made her way across *Storm Cloud* and onto *Day Bringer*. Once in the saloon she stood for a few minutes allowing *Day Bringer* to nourish her then she sat on the footstool as she had done so often as an apprentice, back straight, hands loosely resting on her lap, not wanting to be too comfortable now when there was work to do.

She emerged from her disciplines with a weight of desolation pressing around her. The darkness had increased and she could not sing it back with any confidence that her song would last. She knew Kel had been singing too and was grateful for the sturdy reliable bass he provided. He couldn't really help her though, not help her enter the darkness and discover the cause. His skills did not lie in that direction she knew. The responsibility of her own skills seemed too heavy for her to carry despite, her time of respite. A weight of fear clung about her, dragging her down, but this challenge was not something she could sidestep.

She had to force herself to consider a strategy because she knew Kel would have questions, would want to help. He would have experienced the darkness when they sang and would be holding himself ready to do what ever she felt was best.

She couldn't decide. Perhaps another visit to Gul and Sybi would be useful, but perhaps better if she went again to Lowcroft Heights. She was convinced that was part of the problem, but not the whole of it, only a symptom. Somewhere there was a mind behind what was happening and she had yet to discover that.

She thought of Mek and wondered where he fitted in all this. Nella might have gone willingly anywhere she thought she would be admired and appreciated. Was that their fault? The family? Had they let her feel left out of their closeness? Perhaps they had been too casual in their treatment of her, let her feel that she was not quite one of them? Were she and Wilda and Mek even now guests of the Yareblis? Guests, or prisoners?

She was still struggling with a plan of action when it was time to go up to the house. She stopped on *Storm Cloud* and waited for Kel to come out and join her. He looked at her sympathetically.

"There is a weight of sadness about."

She nodded and headed up the path without speaking.

At supper she was noisy, bright with a volley of brittle talk. She played with her nephews and had them laughing and shrieking at her fooling. Kel was looking at her in surprise and the other adults with a mixture of concern and disapproval. In the end Greya said her name, firm and kind, bringing her down from where ever she had escaped to. She covered her face with her hands for a moment, drew in a deep breath and apologised.

She listened while Sef spoke of his fruitless expeditions and the others discussed possibilities. Everyone was very kind to her, not commenting on her silence, not even looking at her with expectation, yet she wanted to shout at them.

"I can't do anything, you're asking too much of me."

But she knew what they hoped and she knew they were right. This was her problem. It was what her long apprenticeship was about. She had no choice but engage with the Yareblis because she was the other side of them. She pushed herself away from the table a little too roughly and felt a rush of anger at their surprised glances.

"I think I can find him," she said, pushing out the words. "At any rate I'll do my best."

Once she was committed the weight lifted a little. Marheh the Great emerged to help her disguise her fear, but she found it hard to meet Greya's eyes, full of concern for her as well as fear for her son and his family.

She left then, refusing all offers to see her back to *Day Bringer*, needing to be alone to come to terms with the commitment she had just made. It meant entering the darkness. She was afraid of that, but there were other dangers that she had less control over, physical danger when the work of her mind left her body vulnerable, danger that her mind might be lost in the struggle. It was no good dwelling on it though, better to work out a plan of action and start work. She still didn't even know who had called her since it wasn't Kel. Perhaps it was Sybi or Gul. She didn't know whether their skills, developed from a different direction, would include that ability. She could go and see them though, tomorrow. That would be a starting point - and she could ask Kel to go with her, introduce him, perhaps encourage him to offer them protection.

She felt him board *Storm Cloud* and knew she should go to him, reassure him and tell him what she planned. He was too kind to her sometimes, letting her get away with bad behaviour because he was a bit in awe of her abilities. She would have to share her weaknesses with him if she was to change that though, and that was too confronting for the present.

Perhaps he knew her better than she realised she decided when she had said goodnight to him and gone to her bed. He had made her feel more positive about everything without denying the danger or down playing the part she had to play. She had been on the edge of patronising him. A bit uncomfortable she rolled over and pulled blankets closer. Tomorrow she would tell him about making the illusion and ask him to help her uncover how she had done it. She could trust him to believe her and take her seriously.

Wilda's Unicorn

Chapter Eleven

Next day when they got off the bus they walked a little around Willow Rise. Marheh pointed out some of the places she remembered from childhood and Kel listened and watched and sympathised without saying very much.

They met Gul coming out of his church. Marheh thought he looked tired but he greeted her warmly and urged them both to go with him to home and Sybi.

"So you're another one," he said, looking up at Kel, who had shortened his long stride to suit his companion. "We certainly need you – and I think Marheh does too although perhaps she won't admit it."

Marheh, a few steps ahead, looked back to grin at him and make a face.

"I know, I'm arrogant and too independent. I've been told so since I was ten years old. Don't rub it in!"

They both laughed with her then.

"How's the publicity campaign going?"

She dropped back to walk beside them.

"Well it seems to have got people talking," Gul said. "But I'll let Sybi tell you about it. She is the one doing all the work."

They reached the vicarage then and Gul pushed open the door, calling to Sybi as he did so. Marheh was reminded of her first visit, but Gul's warm benevolence seemed somehow diminished, his energy lessened.

Sybi, on the other hand, was just the same and welcomed them warmly into her kitchen, giving Marheh a hug and taking Kel's outstretched hand in both of hers. Marheh saw though that she was especially careful of Gul and caught the anxious concern that lay behind all her kindness and expressions of pleasure in their arrival. She busied herself with preparations for morning tea, refusing Marheh's help but letting Kel pass plates and cups.

Marheh sat beside Gul and took his hand.

"What's the matter?" she asked quietly.

He shook his head.

"Just tired. The darkness weighs and I can't seem to get above it."

She squeezed his hand and released it to take the tea Kel was holding out to her. Later she would ask him again, she decided, in case she could help him.

"Did you get my note?" she asked, when they were all sitting around the table. "I hope you didn't think I was deserting you."

"No, but I'm glad you're back," Sybi said. "People are starting to question Lowcroft Heights. There has been quite a lot of talk, but now it's as if Willow Rise has become a target."

"Willow Rise," Marheh asked, "or you and Gul?"

"I don't think they have homed in on Sybi and me yet, but there is a lot of gratuitous nastiness. Things I never thought to see in Willow Rise – vandalism in the church yard and in people's gardens, fighting and drunkenness, hate slogans painted on walls."

"He feels he has failed," Sybi said. "These are his people and he thinks he has not cared for them enough."

"Which is nonsense of course," Marheh said. "But understandable."

"These are good people," Gul said. "People who care about the village and the feeling of community we have here."

"There are degrees of goodness though don't you think," Kel offered. "And sometimes good behaviour is just a matter of expedience. The Yareblis use that."

Marheh nodded.

"They can manipulate people's values if they're not thought through."

"It just seems so unlikely," Sybi said angrily. "Why here? I know not everyone cares about the things we value but it's cities where the power struggles happen. Who would want a power base in a village? What possible reason could there be for destroying what we have."

"There is really no point in 'why us'." Gul's voice was dispirited. "It's happening and we have to do what we can to stop it."

"There's no harm in trying to understand why, it might help find out who," Kel said.

"We know who – it's the Yareblis," Marheh said.

"In general we know, but not in particular. Isn't that part of the problem? At the moment the enemy is come kind of nebulous darkness. There is nothing to focus on."

Marheh looked at Kel. When would she learn? He may not have her ability with the disciplines but he had his own wisdom.

"What do you think we should do?" she asked, trying for humility.

Kel laughed at her.

"What would you suggest?"

Gul and Sybi smiled at them both.

"I think we should, sing, I think you call it, together," Gul said. "That might throw some light on our particular darkness."

"And if it doesn't we will still be sustained by it," Kel agreed.

It was, Marheh thought when the song was ended, as if together they were building a raft of light that was all they had to cling to in the midst of a dark, devouring storm at sea. They were all exhausted with the struggle, yet in a strange way Kel was right and they were sustained by it too. As well, it revealed to Marheh how alone they were. Their four melodies sang contrapuntally and that was all she heard, no harmony from other souls, no distant music stretching across the darkness. She shivered a little. No wonder Gul was so weary. She looked across at him and he smiled.

They rested quietly together for a time and then Marheh and Kel stood up to go.

"We won't be far away," Marheh said. "A message to the pottery at Deerford will always find me."

There were hugs and farewells and a quiet walk back to the bus stop.

"Gul is really tired," Marheh said as they waited. "I think he has been fighting the darkness for longer than I knew."

Kel nodded.

"They're both of them strong though."

"I don't know. I'm worried about them – Gul especially. I feel as if I should stay and help them, but I know my job is to find out where the darkness is coming from. That's even more important than finding Mek." She turned to Kel. "You could be with them though – they need you more than I do."

"I rather doubt that."

"Don't be silly. I'm pleased you're here, but I don't need you."

"Jik and Nemle seem to think otherwise."

"They still think I need a baby-sitter."

Marheh couldn't keep still. She took a few steps away then whirled back.

"You don't have my skills, but you could be a real support to Gul and Sybi."

"And not to you?"

"Of course to me, but I don't need you – they do."

Kel watched her without replying. His face was under careful control, but his eyes revealed amused affection.

"And don't patronise me," she snapped. "You'd be best staying with them, helping them, and then I won't have to worry about any of you. I could concentrate on what's important."

Kel looked at her for a moment, amusement and affection now eclipsed.

"Very well," he said. "If that is what Madame requires."

He made a small movement in her direction then turned and walked quietly away.

Marheh stared after him.

"Kel…" but she said it quietly and perhaps he did not hear because he gave no sign.

She took a couple of steps as if to pursue him, but then the bus appeared at the end of the street.

"Kel…"

She covered her mouth with her hands. He was doing what she wanted wasn't he?

The bus drew up and she got on and found a seat. Kel was best where he was. She would get off at Lowcroft and explore the village a bit more, perhaps walk along to Lowcroft Heights and see what progress had been made. She would listen to the landscape and see if she could pinpoint the source of the darkness. She straightened her shoulders and lifted her chin and stared out the window, trying to persuade herself that she had been acting sensibly in sending Kel back to Gul and Sybi, but feeling both guilty and desolate.

When the bus stopped in Lowcroft village she got off. She was the only person to do so and she was alone in the street as she stood and watched it disappear down the road. Even when it had gone completely she still stood staring after it wondering what on earth she was doing. At last she turned and made her way towards the little church hoping it might offer somewhere to sit and think.

She found it locked, with a shabby, handwritten notice informing her that there was a service of morning prayer once a month on the first Sunday and evensong on the third Sunday, and instructing her to call on the verger in Meadow Road if she wanted a key or to arrange a wedding.

She did not want to visit the verger, but since there was a bench seat in the little porch she sat down, tucked her feet up under her and tried to think.

She had to apologise to Kel, acknowledge her fault to herself first. It was no good even thinking about the disciplines until she had done that, and then to Kel himself when next she saw him.

"I'm sorry Kel," she whispered, thinking about his guarded expression as he reacted to her rudeness. She held her apology and her thought of him together for a few moments then sighed and tried to plan what she should do next.

For ten minutes or so she sat and built her focus. No point in wallowing in guilt. Better to get on with the job. Then she took herself for a careful, listening walk through the village. There was so little of it that she was done in half an hour and nothing had changed since her last visit, only, since the day was not as nice, the mothers with prams and the old gardener were indoors. She got no sense that darkness threatened here, although there was a kind of greyness that signalled some kind of malaise.

Not enough people care, she thought. They are comfortable, kindly but a bit insular. They don't want to know about other needs or other challenges. It makes it very easy for the Yareblis to infiltrate. Of course, since there was little resistance there was little need for the kind of massing darkness that threatened Willow Rise. Perhaps she had been wrong to leave there, but there was still Lowcroft Heights.

She set out to walk with attention along the bridle path to the new road. The day, which had begun with the kind of morning redness that warned shepherds of squalls ahead, was now demonstrating the truth of that old saying. The wind had strengthened and clouds raced across the sky in layers of different greys. She thought rain was on its way, but perhaps not yet. When she reached the road, she climbed above it and into the woods, feeling, for the first time, a little anxious about the wind that bent the trees and even broke off small branches.

It was easier not to think, otherwise the sense of failure that pursued her could prevent any action at all. Even the thought of the success she had had at the source could not lift her spirits. It had not, after all, been anything she had consciously done. She was no nearer finding the enemy or the reason for the darkness. She had not been able to help Gul and Sybi and she had been rude to Kel.

Her legs carried her onwards through the trees, progress became a battle with the elements and she seized the opportunity to fight almost with relief, since it prevented her from thinking.

By the time she reached the viewpoint above the entrance to Lowcroft Heights she was windblown and exhausted. She leant against the trunk of a tree, finding a little respite from the wind as she pressed against it. Lowcroft Heights was spread out below her. Construction had obviously proceeded since her previous visit and there were now five structures in different stages of completion emerging from the sad landscape of destruction.

Most of the work was happening close to the entrance. She could see figures moving and the wind carried snatches of sound; shouts, hammering and the rumble of an engine. Two men in overalls were battling with a tarpaulin that billowed wildly, two more were anchoring a long ladder, as another came carefully down off the skeleton of a roof. It was just a construction site. What was she doing here? She sagged against the tree and let herself slide down the trunk to the ground.

The fury of the wind seemed to increase. Leaves and twigs flew past and the sky grew blacker. She pulled her legs closer to her chest and made herself as small as she could. Her back was pressed against the tree trunk and she could feel tremors as the wind gusted. Below her the tarpaulin was torn away and the five men raced for the truck that stood in the entrance, rocking as the wind hit it. They all piled in, the last one wrestling the door closed.

Marheh watched, wondering whether they were planning to leave or just taking shelter. She was beginning to feel, not comfortable exactly, but more accustomed to the tumult around her and thus able to think about what she was seeing.

Very carefully she let her mind reach to touch those in the truck. It had to be a feather touch, she knew she should not be doing it at all by rights, but she had to know whether Yareblis were at work in them. At least they were all together and distracted by the weather so her approach was less likely to be noticed. Of course if they actually were Yareblis then she had no chance of remaining unobserved, but she thought it unlikely. Yareblis would be controlling the work not doing it. These men were just what they seemed, construction workers doing a job they were paid for.

She eased back from them and continued to study the site. There had been Yareblis there. The man who had appeared from the caravan had recognised her and she him, but the caravan was no longer in view. Was it gone altogether, or just moved somewhere she could not see? Perhaps all their efforts were now directed at Willow Rise – after all Lowcroft Heights was able to proceed without them.

She was just preparing herself to listen to the landscape and sing a little when the wind eased suddenly and big drops began to fall. In a moment she was engulfed in a deluge that seemed as if flood gates had opened above her. The trees were little or no protection and in a few moments she was wet to the skin. There would be no benefit in moving, so she tried to lose herself in listening, but there seemed to be some kind of barrier. She could hear nothing but the rain with all its different music as it drummed on the road, gathered and gushed in runnels and pelted the new leaves around and above her. She could not move into the landscape in the way she was accustomed to, letting it speak to her of its health and well being.

Well it was not healthy. They had slashed and cut and dug and destroyed, but she should have, at least, been able to hear the pain.

The rain had eased a little, becoming now a steady, relentless down pour. She heard the truck start up. Obviously the workmen had decided it was time to leave, as it backed slowly through the open gate and began to make its way carefully down the road. She watched it out of sight then looked back to the gate, still standing open like an invitation. She ought really to investigate. She couldn't get any wetter though she was loath to leave the protection of the trees even if it was only illusory.

Carefully she stood up, trying to ignore the way this made new chills run into the few, comparatively dry places beneath her clothes. She could see no further movement from the site, only the rain splashing into the spreading puddles that were already appearing. She began to make her way slowly down to the road then across to the gate. By now she had abandoned herself to the cold and damp. It made enduring easier. She stood by the gate looking and listening, then lifted her face to the rain. Still the landscape seemed to reject her attempts to listen to it. She stepped inside the gate and was immediately drowned in the sound of its pain. Involuntarily she went to step back then held herself steady. If she could do nothing else, she could at least listen.

Her warm tears mingled with the cold rain as she heard the cries of the dying landscape. The destruction had gone deep into the land without care or respect.

Sadly she wandered through the rain, reaching down sometimes to touch a half buried branch, or a struggling patch of willow herb, or a few damp green blades of grass. It was so much worse than when she had come through before, not so much what she could see, but what she could feel. She would have to work to understand.

Determined now, she made her way across to the half made structures, dark and sad in the rain. Close to she could make out the size of rooms, the spaces for windows and doors, the vaunting ambition of it all. She sat on a floor joist and tried to take it in, tried to imagine her brother Mek in such an environment. Where was he? Wasn't she supposed to be finding him and Nella and Wilda? Was she getting side-tracked or was this part of the finding?

She was cold all through. It would be better if she kept moving and made the best use of her opportunity for exploration and kept herself warm at the same time, well, warmer anyway. She wasn't even sure why she was here anymore. Without much hope she made her way around all five structures, looking and listening, wondering about the depth of sadness she had found. She was just making her way back to the gate when something bright caught her eye.

At first she thought it was just a trick of the light reflecting off a drop of water, but it kept drawing her attention until she knew she must go to investigate. It was on the ground, almost under the floor joists at the corner of one of the constructions and as she went closer she saw that it was indeed a small object made of some bright metal. It was amazing that it had not been covered, or washed away in the deluge.

She bent to pick it up and discovered that it was a small, round medallion tangled in a chain. She held it out for the rain to wash clean. As the surface of the medallion was revealed she realised that she recognised it. It was silver and on it was embossed a delicate, prancing unicorn. She had given it to Wilda for her tenth birthday, spending more than she could easily afford because it was a pretty thing and Wilda had reached double figures and had a passion for unicorns.

She turned it over and over in her hands. Wilda at least had been here, which probably meant the others had too, but there was no one here now. She pushed the little trinket into her pocket. It was nice to think Wilda still wore it, and could again. Where were they? What could have happened to them from here? Had she looked everywhere? Of course she had, but she stood and scanned the site again.

The five partially completed homes made a wide curve with their backs to the gate and since there were no walls in place she could see through them pretty well to the flattened muddy space beyond. No doubt more building would commence when the first were closer to completion. There was no possible hiding place. She might as well go home and get dry and warm. The state she was in they might not even let her on the bus, but she would hope for the best.

She had to stand all the way so as not to spoil the seats, but she didn't mind that and the bus was at least warm. She was not the only damp passenger and the windows were all fogged up so she could not see out. To pass the journey she let her mind drift over her fellow passengers. Most were women with shopping bags. She did not recognise anyone. Did they know what was happening around them or were they too pre-occupied with getting through the day. The bus driver had recognised her. She thought that was probably why he had let her on, the state she was in. His raised eyebrows and the wink he gave her made her smile. Fortunately there was no repetition of the happenings of the last journey she had made with him. She knew she was too tired to cope.

The rain had eased to a fine mist by the time they reached her stop in Deerford. It hardly seemed to matter she was still so wet. She wished she could go straight to the comfort of *Day Bringer*. She did not want questions. She was too tired for explanations. On the other hand a proper bath… and Greya would be hurt if she saw her. Getting to the mooring without going through the pottery meant a longer walk.

When she reached home the decision was made for her for there was one of Mek's vans parked in the street by the front gate.

It did not necessarily mean Mek himself, but it would be unusual for one of his drivers to come here. She went through the gate around to the back and pushed open the kitchen door, suddenly eager and lifted from her weariness for the moment.

The kitchen was warm and bright after the grey outdoors and for an instant she saw a smiling family tableau, Sef and Greya, Mek, Nella and Wilda talking and laughing around the table. A moment later they had turned towards her and the picture separated into parts. Sef stood up, a look of concern replacing his smile. Greya spoke her name. Mek and Nella exchanged looks that commented unfavourably on her dishevelled state. Wilda darted a sharp, scornful glance at her.

"Goodness, is that Aunt Mary," she said. "I thought it was a tramp."

Marheh felt anger rise within her. How dare they sit here and mock when it was her efforts to find them that got her into this state, fruitless efforts it now appeared. She pressed her lips together to prevent the angry words escaping. When she thought she could speak without it becoming an attack she said "I've been out looking for you and it is raining outside. We were worried. Where were you?"

"Looking for us! How kind!"

Nella gave her a sweet, false smile.

Marheh wanted to slap her face. She took a step forward then noticed that Nella was holding a buttered scone.

"That flashy silk shirt would look better with butter down the front," she thought and pushed into Nella's mind.

It was only a moment but Nella, a frightened look on her face had raised the hand with the scone and turned it towards her shirt before Marheh realised what she was doing. Appalled at her loss of control she pulled herself up and was about to leave Nella's mind when she recognised that hers was not the only control working there.

Nella... under Yareblis control? Somehow it was not surprising. She would have few defences against them. If she was careful perhaps she could remove it without Nella being aware, only she was so tired. She could not turn aside though, not now she knew. Sharpening her focus she eased herself around the Yareblis control and took it into her own mind. She was ready for the pain of it, but it still came as a shock how much it hurt.

The others saw only that she paled, as if she might faint, then walked steadily towards the stove, opened the fire door and threw something in. She turned back to them then and tried to smile as if nothing had happened.

"Mother I'd love a bath..." she began as reaction set in and she began to shiver uncontrollably.

Greya was beside her in a moment, only pausing to reprimand Wilda who was giggling.

"It's Aunt Mary... she looked like some kind of zombie." She began to mimic the careful steps that had taken Marheh to the stove.

"That is enough Wilda!" Marheh heard her father say as Greya shepherded her out to the stairs.

It was easier to let Greya run the bath and strip off her wet clothes than to protest her independence and there was something comforting about being mothered as if she were a child again. Greya sat on the lid of the toilet and watched as she eased herself into the hot water. She closed her eyes to hold back the tears that threatened now the need for effort was over for the moment.

A comfortable silence fell between them. Marheh felt all her knots beginning to untangle. She opened her eyes to smile at Greya.

"In the pocket of my trousers," she said. "A little chain... it belongs to Wilda. I found it at Lowcroft Heights."

Greya nodded but did not move. A little more silence while Marheh felt the warmth reaching all the way to her bones.

"Did they say where they were?" she asked next.

Greya shook her head.

"An unexpected opportunity for a holiday."

Marheh thought for a minute or two.

"Perhaps they were all taken to where they could be more easily... influenced... by the enemy."

Greya looked at her sharply.

"Meaning?"

"I'm not supposed to say – you're not Silberay – it's just…"

Greya waited.

"Nella had been invaded. Perhaps Mek and Wilda have too. I need to check." More silence. "I lost my temper and nearly did something to Nella that could have had me grounded for years," Marheh confessed at last.

Greya nodded. "Nella can be very provoking." She stood up and picked up a big towel. "If you're warm you can get out now." She held the towel open, ready to wrap around her. "When you're out I'll go and get a dressing gown."

The fluffy towel was warm, like Grey's hug. Greya gathered up Marheh's wet clothes, felt in the pocket for the little chain and placed it carefully on the edge of the basin.

"Back in a minute," she said, leaving Marheh to dry herself.

A bit later, warm, dry and demurely dressing-gowned, she was shepherded back into the kitchen by Greya. A chair was placed for her near the stove and she sat with her back to the heat and her hair spread out from its plait to dry.

The others were still sitting around the table with Sef, although it seemed to Marheh that they were not happy to be there. Greya left her and went to join them and Marheh suddenly realised that this was deliberate, a way of giving her the opportunity to check on Wilda and Mek. How much did Greya understand, she wondered, watching her mother gathering up the conversation to exclude her. She could speculate about that later. Now she had better take the opportunity offered.

She closed her eyes, prepared herself and carefully slid into Wilda's mind.

She and Mek both carried a Yareblis control as Nella had. Marheh took them into herself before getting up to dispose of them in the stove. Then she walked towards the table feeling in her dressing gown pocket for the medallion and chain. She held it out to Wilda.

"I think this is yours."

Wilda's face brightened. "Thanks Aunt Mary. I thought I'd lost it."

Marheh smiled, satisfied that none of them knew what had been done to them, or what she had done. She looked from one to the other around the table.

"Will you excuse me? I'm going to find some dry clothes and perhaps have a little lie down. I'm glad you're safe."

"Safe! Of course we're safe," Nella said.

Wilda giggled, but she was holding out the chain for her father to fasten around her neck.

Mek looked a little uncomfortable. "I'm sorry you had the bother of looking for us," he muttered.

Marheh only smiled and let herself out the door, shaking her head to refuse her father's move to escort her.

It was still softly drizzling, a light misty rain. Her feet were bare and she chose the wet, grassy verge to walk on rather than the gravel path. All she wanted now was to be alone on *Day Bringer*. Crossing *Storm Cloud*'s bow reminded her of another obligation, but it would have to wait. Thinking, discipline, discipline, she forced herself to get dressed and make up the fire. Then she knew she had to eat something. Deciding what, given her meagre supplies, was nearly her undoing, but there was the heel of a loaf and an egg and she could grate a bit of cheese over the whole. Perhaps she was almost coping – and the thought as well as the food heartened her.

It was a pity she had no way to analyse the controls she had removed. If she had been thinking straight, if it had not hurt so much, perhaps she could have found out what the controls had been placed to do before she destroyed them.

She went into her workroom and pulled on her smock. She needed to think, but if she didn't have something to do with her hands she could easily fall asleep. She began to wedge a piece of clay, taking pleasure in the rhythmic pummelling she was giving it, slice it, slap it together, press it down, over and over again.

The three of them, all with a Yareblis control, was it just coincidence that they were her family or was it planned to target her. The enemy would not necessarily know the control was gone until the planned action did not happen. They had been at Lowcroft Heights, Wilda's chain proved that, but did they even know? Why hadn't Wilda asked where she had found it? That would have been a natural question.

She cut off a piece of the wedged clay and put the rest back in its airtight container, a wet rag over it to prevent it drying out.

The acquisition of power was the ultimate purpose of any Yareblis' action, but she could not grasp the reason behind Lowcroft Heights. How would it enhance their power? She formed her clay into a ball then pressed it flat. She had no real purpose in mind but as she played with it a shape evolved. There was one body, or if there were more they were so closely pressed together they seemed to be one – anguished faces on heads that twisted away from the body, parts of hands or arms thrusting or clenching. It was just a sketch, not a finished work and she would not keep it, but she stood back to stare and wonder whether it had anything to tell her.

Then she felt the boat move and realised Kel had returned to *Storm Cloud*. A final, long stare and she squashed the clay into a ball again and returned it to the bin. Mending fences with Kel was her priority now. She dragged her smock over her head and let it fall. Kel had put up with her and supported her since she was first apprenticed. He had helped Nemle extricate her from the consequences of her impulsive actions and believed in her when she had been accused of misusing her ability. She caught her bottom lip between her teeth. He had come at Jik's suggestion to help her and she had, more or less, told him he didn't have the skill. She felt herself redden. How arrogant she had been.

She walked back through her work space and out to the bow. Drawing a deep breath she crossed to *Storm Cloud* and knocked on the roof, tentatively at first, then more firmly. She felt the boat move and knew Kel was coming through. Normally he would have just called a welcome, normally he wouldn't come to confront her. She covered her face with her hands then let them drop to her sides again.

The door opened and he stood at the foot of the steps looking up at her. She backed away a little as he slid back the roof hatch and came outside. His face was unreadable. Now she looked up at him. It made it easier somehow.

"I'm really sorry Kel."

There was a moment of silence as he studied her face. She was reminded of her father and put her hands behind her back, feeling a child again, but she did not look away. Then Kel smiled.

"Well I'm glad you're sorry, because it hurt, but it's alright really."

She smiled back, relieved.

"Shall I go down on my knees?" she offered.

He laughed.

"Now that I would like to see!"

Quick as a flash she was down, her hands clasped under her chin, her eyes wide and penitent.

"Idiot!"

He reached down and pulled her into a hug.

Inside she wouldn't let him give her the armchair, though he offered it.

"You're too big to be comfortable on the footstool," she said, then grinned. "And it is the penitent's place after all."

She did let him make her sperit though and very welcome it was.

There was an easy silence for a while as they sipped their drinks and relaxed in the knowledge of friendship renewed.

"Did you get caught in the rain?" Kel asked at length.

Marheh laughed.

"Did I ever! Properly punished I was. I suppose you were dry and comfortable with Gul and Sybi."

"They welcomed me back very kindly and fed me lunch and let me think they were glad to have me."

Marheh looked into her mug then back at Kel.

"I'm glad to have you too."

"I know. I expect I over reacted. You were very likely right to send me back."

"Of course I was right – I'm always right." She laughed. "In my own opinion anyway."

She finished her drink and put the mug on the floor beside her.

"I'm worried about them. Somehow they seem to have become a target. There's no real darkness at Lowcroft and though Lowcroft Heights is filled with pain there is no struggle there."

"Willow Rise is where the resistance is, so it is drawing the attack."

"That's what I thought too. Did anything happen while you were there?"

"I sang so they could sleep without the blackness invading their dreams. They needed that."

Marheh looked startled.

"Their home does not protect them like *Day Bringer* and *Storm Cloud* protect us?"

"It seems not. Gul thought perhaps they might be better to move into the church. Their kind of song is strong there."

"That makes sense. I wish we could get more sense of where the attack is coming from though. I just seem to be stumbling around in the dark."

"Is there news of your brother?"

"I forgot you wouldn't know. They're back. They all had Yareblis controls in place, even Wilda."

"You've dealt with them?"

"Yes."

He studied her in silence for a moment. She shifted uncomfortably under his gaze.

"What?"

"You've had to do quite a lot of that recently haven't you?"

"A fair bit – but it's one of the things I do."

"I know, and it's not something I can help with but…"

"But?"

"Always in the past you've had Nemle…" He hesitated again as she drew herself up to protest that she was perfectly capable without Nemle. "I just wondered whether there is a chance that you might still harbour some of the poison."

She opened her mouth to protest then closed it again. What he had said made sense. She knew she had been touchy, had had more trouble with her temper than usual and was finding focusing on anything very hard. Nemle had always helped the healing needed from past encounters.

She sighed.

"Have I been so difficult?"

"Not so much difficult as troubled."

"It could be, I suppose, but if it is I'm not sure what to do about it. I've always thought it was the singing that healed me afterwards, not Nemle."

"I expect you're right, but hasn't your singing had a different focus too, lately?"

She nodded and wrapped her arms around herself as if she was cold.

"It always hurts so much," she said. "I thought I'd learned how to accept that."

She remembered the image of her burnt hand that had come to her after she released Gul. She didn't see the look of compassion Kel gave her.

"I didn't realise it hurt you, though I know it makes you tired."

"There's not much point in talking about it really ... only I'm glad you understand."

"Would it help if we were to sing now do you think?"

She didn't answer for a few moments but then she nodded.

"Only could we be on *Day Bringer*? I need to be on *Day Bringer*."

Kel stood up and lifted her to her feet.

"Come on," he said.

. . . .

It was good singing, strengthening, but the light of it had shown her that Kel was right and there were places festering within her, remnants of Yareblis poison. Recognising it was good, helpful, because she could guard against its influence, but ridding herself of it was going to need deep and painful cleansing that she did not think she was capable of right now.

"You were right," she told Kel. "There is poison and ..." She paused, reluctant to speak her need. "I think I will need your help to be rid of it."

Kel smiled at her.

"Do you know, I think that might be the first time I've ever heard you ask for help. Of course I will help if I can."

Marheh grimaced.

"My besetting sin, arrogance – no doubt that's why the poison lingered."

Kel looked a question.

"It's hard not to want power. I try to tell myself it is for good purposes, but that's where the Yareblis began – by wanting power for good purposes. I try to be grateful for the pain that surrounds it, because that seems to begin the humbling process."

Kel took her hands. "I think you're too hard on yourself."

She shook her head but did not elaborate.

"Can we do this now?" she asked instead. "I was thinking to wait until we're rested but I don't think I can rest until it's done."

"Of course we can. What do you want me to do?"

"It's a matter of burning away the poison, cauterising the places where it has taken hold."

She felt his hands tighten their grip but he said nothing.

"I can make the tool but I know I don't have the resolution to apply it properly."

"I might not either."

"Yes you will. It's not as bad as it sounds, not like a burn to the body. The healing begins immediately and the pain doesn't last long."

"Tell me what to do?"

"I'll open my mind to you. I'll make the tool and give it to you to use. Take your time and search out every tiniest place. I won't have the strength to repeat the exercise."

She felt his hands tremble and managed a little grin.

"Steady hands please."

He took a long breath and let it out.

"Steady hands it is."

….

Like all the Silberay Kel had practised the discipline of the mind and could use it against the Yareblis, but his skills were no more than average. Nothing he had so far experienced could have prepared him for being drawn into Marheh's mind.

Once there he knew her. Knew the mixture of feelings that accompanied this exposure of herself, this nakedness. The trust she was placing in him was overwhelming. She was so vulnerable and yet so strong as she prepared the white hot wand for him to apply. He could see the festering places that disfigured her and wanted now to act to make her whole again.

She gave him the tool and he felt its heat, then she laid herself out for him.

Somehow he managed to shut away the awareness of her anguish and focus on the healing he could see happening with each touch. He did not hurry, though he wanted the task over, but took care to examine every inch of the quivering, exposed mind. When he was satisfied he understood she wanted him to place the wand in the water road to complete the healing.

When it was done and he had left her mind clean and whole he was exhausted but he could think only of her. She lay slumped in the arm chair. She was unnaturally pale, but relaxed as if in a deep sleep. There was something childlike about her posture of complete abandonment. He sat on the footstool, his arms around his knees, and watched anxiously as her colour began to return and she stirred a little.

He stood and bent to pick her up, thinking to carry her to her cabin, but when he gathered her in his arms she cuddled in to him with a little sigh and he knew he couldn't leave her. Instead he sat himself in the armchair so that she rested on his lap, her head against his chest, and held her close.

He had known Marheh since she was twenty, just a girl; impulsive, head strong, independent, courageous. He had admired her then and been in awe of her ability. Now the woman she had become had revealed herself to him, had given him the gift of her trust and he knew that he loved her. He watched the slight movement of her breathing for a few minutes then closed his eyes to enter the soul song. That, at least, was something he could do for her.

….

It was Tep's voice, a little hesitant, calling her name, that brought them back.

It was almost dark and *Day Bringer* was full of shadows. Marheh reached for Kel's hand and held it briefly against her cheek before pushing herself to her feet. She went out to the bow and called to him across *Storm Cloud's* stern.

"I'm here Tep. What's wrong?"

"Nothing really, only Mother insists on waiting supper for you and we're all starving," he finished plaintively.

Kel had come out to stand beside her and now he responded easily, cutting off the rather sharp response he knew Marheh was about to give.

"I'm sorry," he said. "We were working and the job took longer than expected."

"I knew it would be something like that, but Mother was anxious."

"For goodness sake! I'm grown up now, let me get on with it!" The words wanted to make themselves heard, but she managed to prevent them escaping and followed Tep and Kel with studied meekness up the path to the house.

Permission to view

Chapter Twelve

It was not until the next morning that Marheh felt rational enough to examine the events of the previous evening. She had gone to supper in an extraordinarily bad temper and the effort of keeping it hidden had only increased it. Of course she had not been able to conceal it from these people who knew her so well and most of them had been humouring her all evening. Only her father had offered to put her across his knee if she didn't snap out of it. She couldn't blame it on Yareblis influence either for that was gone thanks to Kel.

If she had stripped off her skin as well as all her clothes she couldn't have revealed more of herself to Kel. She didn't know how to deal with that. He had been generous in his dealings with her always and last night he had been strong and loving too. Waking in his arms, surrounded by his loving song had aroused feelings she didn't want to acknowledge. She wondered now how she would have behaved without Tep's interruption. She felt herself grow warm and knew she was blushing.

Silberay chose not to enjoy physical love, but that did not mean they couldn't. It wasn't wrong. She had put it aside as something that was not for her, way back in her twenties, when an unscrupulous man had almost seduced her. She had not thought of Daniel for years, but his touch and his kisses had awakened her body to sensual pleasure.

Poor Daniel had not been so unscrupulous in the end and he had paid for it dearly. A tremor ran through her as she remembered the feel of his mouth on her breasts, then, without her willing it, his mouth became Kel's mouth. She gave a little whimper then covered her face with her hands. No and no and no.

She had a job to do. Right or wrong, these feelings would only get in the way. Silberay chose to be celibate because anything else would compromise the work they did. But she was better at the work. Surely there was room for both? Being better just meant a greater responsibility to the work, that's what Nemle would have said. She made a face, and didn't she have a responsibility to Kel as well. His choice had been made. Here she was again, arrogant and self centred, thinking she had only to offer herself and she would be taken.

Resolutely she pushed her thoughts aside and tried to forget them in the business of getting up, of morning chores, but there was still the challenge of meeting Kel after all he had done for her, after all she had revealed. He made it easy for her though, greeting her with the same warm smile, the same affectionate hug, so that she felt ashamed that she had not trusted him enough.

After breakfast they sat for a while talking with Sef and Greya. Marheh told them a bit more about what had been happening, apologising for her bad temper and admitting that she was finding it difficult to know what to do for the best.

"There is darkness everywhere, I've been attacked more than once, Sybi and Gul seem to be under siege and I can't seem to get a grip on any of it. Everything I've done is just reaction to something they have done and I don't know who *they* are."

"I know you've been focusing on Lowcroft Heights," Sef said. "But that almost seems more like a symptom than the disease itself."

Marheh put her head in her hands.

"I know, but I can't see past it."

"What about Higham's Hill?" Kel asked. Wasn't that where your troubles began?"

Marheh looked sharply at him then thought back over what she had just related.

"I suppose it was really, but it's just another village. Blethan woke them up and I had no trouble there when I went back on the bus."

"But you were attacked after you left there."

"I can't see why you have to make yourself so visible," Greya said. "Surely it's asking for trouble."

"I hoped someone might reveal themselves."

"It helped you to meet Blethan and Gul and Sybi and it has shown someone you're here, but maybe it is time to change your strategy. It isn't essential to wear Silberay uniform is it?" Sef asked.

"It's all I have."

"That's easily fixed if you want it to be," Greya said. "Is there any reason why you and Kel couldn't go about together looking like an ordinary couple?"

Marheh couldn't answer. She felt herself grow red, much more and she would spontaneously combust. Why was her body behaving like this? She and Kel, an ordinary couple, loving the ordinary, extraordinary way that ordinary couples did!

"You could pretend to be house hunting," Greya suggested.

Marheh could feel her mother watching her and speculating. She tried to frame some kind of reply then heard Kel speak.

"It mightn't be a bad idea. Worth a try anyway. That way we could even visit the Estate Agent here in Deerford and get some orders to view, find out if he knows anything about Lowcroft Heights."

Slowly her blush subsided and she found herself able to re-enter the conversation.

"And poke about a bit in Higham's Hill too," she said. "I think you might be right that I've overlooked something there."

With Marheh's agreement, Greya immediately became practical.

"Sef, why don't you take Kel upstairs and see if there's a tie and a jacket that would do for him?"

As they left she turned to study Marheh.

"You'll be a bit more of a problem. Nothing of mine will fit you properly and you're a bit taller than Fali."

"Perhaps we should ask Nella. I'm sure she'd be happy to see me respectable."

"Be sensible. Shoes might be difficult. You'll need stockings and a girdle."

"Oh mother no!"

"Oh Marheh yes. If you're going to do it, you need to do it properly."

"But a girdle!"

"Well a suspender belt then if you prefer. You need something to keep the stockings up."

"I've changed my mind. This is not a good idea."

"What's not a good idea?" Fali spoke from the doorway.

"Ah good, just the person! We need to make Marheh into an ordinary woman."

"Why? I like her being extraordinary."

"Just temporarily," Greya explained. "So she can be less visible while she investigates."

"Only mother says it means stockings," Marheh groaned. "I'm sure men invented them to keep women in subjection."

Fali laughed.

"If you want to be ordinary it does mean stockings. Think of it as disguise. Come on up to our place. I'm sure I'll have something that will do."

Marheh and Greya followed her out and up the staircase that led to Tep and Fali's part of the house.

"You have made this nice," Marheh said as they emerged onto the wide landing where Fali had put a little writing desk by the long narrow window. "I haven't been up here since I left home."

"It's a nice spot to write letters in the afternoon, and Fen can do his homework here if he needs to be quiet."

She led them down a short passage and opened the door to her bedroom, holding it wide for them to enter.

"So much space," Marheh said, looking around with interest. "I'd nearly forgotten what a real bedroom looks like."

"It's a lovely room," Fali said. "Big enough for both of us and a real refuge if we need it." She turned to smile at Greya. "Does this sound like procrastination to you?"

Greya laughed.

"Indeed it does."

"Let's see what I can find," Fali said studying Marheh. "You're a bit taller than I am, but... "

She whirled around and plunged into a drawer.

"Take your things off and put these on to start with."

She tossed a pair of stockings onto her bed and handed Marheh a suspender belt.

"I'll spoil them," Marheh said, backing away.

"Nothing to spoil," Fali said. "If you ladder the stockings you can buy me a new pair... now come on," she was choking back laughter. "Be a good girl and do as you're told."

"It's not funny," Marheh growled, but laughter broke through. She began to undress while Fali fossicked in her wardrobe, every so often turning to consult with Greya.

She was still undoing her boots when Fali drew out a plain, narrow blue skirt and a pale blue blouse patterned with small blue flowers.

"This was always a mistake," Fali said, holding it up. "I'm not tall enough. Every time I put it on I wish I hadn't."

"I can't wear that," Marheh said, looking up.

"Why not?" Greya said. "I think it will look rather nice on you."

"I'll look like... like..."

"Like what?"

Silence.

"Like a woman," Marheh muttered at last.

"You are a woman," Greya said, going to her. "So that's alright."

But it wasn't alright, not really, Marheh thought. In her Silberay uniform gender was irrelevant. She didn't want to reveal the woman, especially not to Kel. Why ever had she agreed to this?

"Think of it as play acting," Greya said. "Then you'll be alright, much less visible than you are in your uniform, just like everyone else."

She pushed Marheh gently to sit on the edge of the bed and knelt to take off her boots. By the time her feet were bare she had recovered her equilibrium. She bent to help Greya to her feet.

"I'm sorry mother. I was just being silly."

Only all the time she was taking off her tunic and her trousers something inside was crying "I don't want to do this". She picked up the suspender belt and looked at it, saw how it fastened, held it around her waist.

"Here, let me fasten it for you," Fali said, coming to her rescue. "It goes under your knickers."

In the end Marheh let them dress her, moving obediently to facilitate the fastening of zips and the doing up of buttons. Greya cinched her waist with a wide blue belt and Fali brushed out her hair and piled it on top of her head. She even allowed Fali to make up her eyes and mouth, but she rebelled when presented with a pair of neat, navy blue court shoes with two inch heels.

"I can't wear those."

"Why ever not?"

"I won't be able to walk."

"Of course you will. These are not very high and you certainly can't wear your boots."

When the transformation was complete Fali led her to the long mirror set into one of the wardrobe doors. Marheh stared at her reflection in silence. The woman in the mirror was someone she didn't know, didn't particularly want to know, a slim, elegant stranger.

"No one will recognise me," she said at last. "I don't recognise myself."

"You look lovely," Fali said, tweaking the collar of the blouse so it sat better and fastening a string of blue beads around her neck. "I know you wanted to look ordinary, but I don't think you can."

Marheh swung away from the mirror so suddenly that Fali was nearly knocked over.

"I'm sorry," she said, reaching out to hug her sister-in-law. "You've been so good and generous, but I just hate it."

"Of course you do," Fali said, recovering from the hug. "It isn't you – but it is the disguise you wanted. Come on, let's go downstairs. You can practice walking."

"Head up," Greya said as they approached the kitchen door.

"I'll introduce you," said Fali. "Who do you want to be?"

Marheh stopped suddenly on the bottom step.

"Kathleen," she said slowly, remembering a long ago time when she had pretended to be Kathleen. She straightened, lifted her chin. "Introduce me as Kathleen Mackenzie."

Fali pushed open the kitchen door and went in. Sef and Kel were both there sitting at the table talking. Kel appeared to be reasonably at home in his borrowed jacket and tie. He stood up quickly as the three women entered.

"Father, Kel, could I introduce you to a friend of mine, this is Kathleen Mackenzie."

"Pleased to meet you Miss Mackenzie," said Kel, going towards her with his hand held out. Marheh took his hand, smiled and murmured something inaudible.

Sef snorted.

"Butter wouldn't melt in her mouth. What have they done to you

173

daughter?"

Fali laughed.

"We tried to make her ordinary, but it didn't work."

Kel looked at Sef then back at Marheh.

"You've certainly made her unrecognisable." He offered her his arm with a little bow. "May I escort you on a house hunting expedition, ma'am?"

Marheh grinned at him.

"They've gone to so much trouble it would be a shame to waste it, and the sooner we get on with it the sooner I can get back into my boots and trousers."

They all laughed.

"Just a minute," Greya said as they made for the door. "You've forgotten something."

She disappeared through the door and they heard her on the stairs. A few minutes later she was back, a small black box in her hand.

"You'll need this," she said taking out a plain gold ring. "It was your grandmother's. It would have been yours already if you had chosen to marry."

Marheh took it and put it on the fourth finger of her left hand. It was just a little tight.

Sef stood up.

"Better if you are not seen coming from here. Why don't I get the car out and drop you near the church? You can stroll along to the estate agent from there."

It seemed like a good idea so they thanked him and followed him out to the garage.

Fifteen minutes later they were standing together outside the church watching him drive sedately away.

Kel turned to Marheh.

"Well Mrs ... Mackenzie was it? What now?"

"You're asking me!"

Marheh looked up at him and batted her eyelashes.

"Yes, I'm asking you. Somewhere under all that finery is the Marheh I know and love, who usually has a pretty good idea of what to do."

"I think all this 'finery' has affected my brain," she said, holding onto his arm and taking her left foot out of her shoe so she could wriggle her toes. "My shoes hurt."

Kel patted her hand and bent over her solicitously.

"Now Kathleen dear, wasn't the plan to go and visit the estate agent and see if we can find our new home?"

Marheh gave his arm a little pinch and put her shoe back on.

"Yes dear. You're quite right dear."

Arm in arm they began to walk towards the High St, Kel still solicitously inclined towards her.

"If you don't behave yourself I'll tell your mother of you," he said.

Marheh laughed.

"And she'll tell my father and he'll take me into the study and…"

Kel stopped walking and waited. Marheh took a deep breath.

"Sorry Kenneth dear, it's just that I'm rather apprehensive and that always makes me behave badly."

Kel gave her arm a gentle squeeze and they walked on.

It was not far to the High St and the little row of shops that bordered the green. The estate agent had an office in one corner of the Post Office. It was a very small agency and a rather plumb, very eager young man seemed to have responsibility for this and the post office counter. Marheh couldn't help wondering about him and whether the heightened enthusiasm he displayed when he learned they were interested in buying a house was just what it seemed.

"We're from the North," Kel was saying. "But my wife is finding the climate rather trying."

"You do too, dear," Marheh murmured.

"We like this area and hope to find something that will suit us, to buy or perhaps a long lease."

Marheh stopped paying attention to the words and considered the young man. His enthusiasm did seem rather exaggerated, even inappropriate, but that did not necessarily mean more than that he was inexperienced and anxious to impress. She was tempted to probe a little, but she had no real reason for doing so. She did not think he was Yareblis, they did not seem capable of such an innocent emotion as enthusiasm, but he would be a very easy target for control.

Then Kel was taking possession of a key with a large label attached and a scrap of paper with a scribbled map.

"Thank you Mr Bumstead, that will suit very well," he said. "We will walk around to see this one and by the time we return your superior will have arrived to take us to one or two other properties." Kel turned to Marheh. "Will that suit do you think, my dear?"

Marheh smiled and nodded and let Kel lead her out.

"Turn left and then left again," the young man called as they reached the door.

Marheh had no need of the map, though they made a point of glancing at it from time to time. The house, when they reached it, was completely empty. It was a nice little house, sunny and warm, but not, of course, for them. Marheh would have liked to sit down and take her shoes off.

"Why don't we want this one?" Kel asked.

"We might want it, but it isn't quite what we had in mind," Marheh said. "The dining room is a little bit small and your study has a northern aspect which makes it rather dreary."

"I see," said Kel. "Well, I suppose I had better explore and see if you're telling lies. Do you want to come?"

Marheh grinned at him.

"Why not?"

She stepped forward then stopped, hobbled by the narrow skirt.

"I hate these clothes, how do other women bear it?"

Kel offered her his arm ceremoniously and they progressed slowly through the house.

Twenty minutes seemed to be long enough to pretend to view. Kel locked the door again and they headed back to the estate agent.

"Did you ever regret not having... that?" Marheh asked as they walked away.

"No," Kel said. "Never that... occasionally other things perhaps, but *Storm Cloud* is all the home I ever wanted."

Marheh nodded.

"Yes I'm the same. Even at the beginning, when I was unhappy and fighting with Nemle, I loved *Day Bringer*. It still feels strange to be on her without Nemle though."

"I remember being quite lonely at times, especially in the first few months after Sul retired, but it passes."

"I suppose it will. I do miss her though, more than I ever expected to."

They reached the door of the Post Office and stopped to assume the appropriate characters.

"It isn't quite right somehow," Marheh said as they entered. "Though I suppose it might do – but perhaps we will see something we like better."

"Yes," said Kel. "After all we've hardly begun."

Mr Bumstead came eagerly forward to meet them and listen to Kel's grave repetition of Marheh's suggestion. Then he took the key and went to knock at the door of the inner office.

"This is Miss Dee," he told them as they entered.

The woman standing behind the desk seemed slightly unreal to Marheh. She wore a dark suit, a jacket and narrow skirt that fit her like a second skin. Her light hair was short and carefully held in place so that it seemed glued to her head. Her face was skilfully made up, only the red smile was too red and did not reach the hard blue eyes. Marheh listened to the introduction and murmured an appropriate response then turned to look adoringly at Kel while he outlined their requirements. The woman was unguarded at the moment, thinking them of no account, but Marheh did not want to meet her eyes in case they saw through her disguise. This woman was Yareblis. At last she had found one. It was even worth the stockings.

Kel was doing a good job. She wondered whether he had realised the woman's nature. It was not fair to leave it all to him, but that was the character she had assumed.

"You must tell Miss Dee how much we liked Higham's Hill," she said to him now. "We came through it on the bus."

"Of course Kathleen."

He drew her arm through his and patted her hand reassuringly. Yes, Marheh thought, he knows.

Another few minutes and it was arranged. Miss Dee would spend the afternoon taking them in her car to see a house and a cottage in Higham's Hill, a cottage in Lowcroft and a new development that might interest them just outside Lowcroft. Perhaps, it was suggested, they might like to take lunch at the pub before they began as Miss Dee had one or two thing to arrange.

The pub was not busy and they were able to acquire some cheese sandwiches, a beer for Kel and cider for Marheh. More importantly they were able to compare notes and plan their strategy. Marheh would be very sweet, very spoilt and very fussy. Kel would be adoring but not entirely uncritical.

"Do you have any more of that stuff for your mouth?" Kel asked her when they had finished their lunch. "You've eaten it off. Probably you should put it on again if you can."

"It's called lipstick," Marheh said. "Even I know that." She opened the little clutch purse Fali had given her to carry. "I suppose there might be some in here."

There was a lipstick and a small powder compact with a mirror. Marheh applied both, hoping she looked as if she knew what she was doing. Kel gave her a little nod of approval when she finished.

"Very nice," he said, knowing he was asking for trouble.

Marheh blew him a kiss.

"Next time I'll land one on your cheek and then you'll be sorry!"

"Are we ready to go Mrs Mackenzie," he said, standing up and offering her his arm.

Miss Dee was all ready for them when they arrived back. Her car was parked outside the agency and several keys dangled their tags from her hands.

"Perhaps you would sit in front, Mr Mackenzie," she said. "There is more room in front."

"Oh but I want you to sit next to me," Marheh said in her best little girl voice. "You don't mind darling, do you? I'll be lonely without you."

"As you please," said Miss Dee, clearly displeased.

She took them to two properties in Higham's Hill. The first of them was in the same little row as Blethan's house and Marheh wondered whether she would be recognisable in her present attire. She was beginning to enjoy herself.

"Oh it is a dear little house, don't you think darling, but perhaps a little small," she said after ten minutes of wandering. "The bathroom is much nicer than the one in the Deerford house, but I just can't imagine our furniture here."

Miss Dee led them back to her car.

"Perhaps you'll find this next one more to your liking. It is a little older of course but very well built and quite roomy."

This was quite expansive of Miss Dee and Marheh responded graciously.

"You're being so kind isn't she K...Ken dear. I'm sure we will find something we like."

When they were again sitting side by side in the back seat Kel gave Marheh a little warning pinch, to which she responded with a demure smile and an adoring look.

They saw the cottage in Higham's Hill and the one in Lowcroft but nothing was quite right.

"Such lovely places, and all with different things to recommend them, but... well, perhaps we could just think about them for a bit."

"Are you sure darling... I thought that second place at Higham's Hill might have suited us, and you did like the kitchen."

"But the bathroom was a bit small."

Marheh whittered on for a bit longer as they stood in the little front garden of the cottage at Lowcroft. Then she felt an almost uncontrollable urge to cover her mouth with her hands. For an instant she hesitated realising that Miss Dee was trying to control her, then she understood that if she wanted to maintain her anonymity she would have to pretend to be controlled.

She clapped both hands across her mouth and left them there.

"I've one more place to show you," Miss Dee said to Kel before turning her attention back to Marheh and directing her to drop her hands back to her sides.

Marheh obeyed the suggestion and turned to Kel.

"I've been talking too much. Are you cross with me darling?"

As they got into the car again she began to realise the difficulty of the balancing act she was trying to perform. To accept the directions of the control without accepting the control itself meant disciplining her own will to comply with the will of the other without losing her awareness of that other and to manage the discomfort of holding the control away from herself.

It was not too hard while they were in the car. Miss Dee had enough to concentrate on with driving. All Marheh was being told to do was to keep silent and her sense of humour asserted that she could hardly blame Miss Dee for that. She took Kel's hand, moved closer to him and rested her head on his shoulder. Then, as Marheh had guessed they would, they arrived at Lowcroft Heights. They sat in the car and watched the workmen while Miss Dee extolled the amenities they could expect to enjoy.

Marheh was still being instructed not to speak and Kel was looking anxiously at her while attempting to respond to Miss Dee's information. Then, when they were to get out and visit the site, Marheh was told to stay in the car.

"I'm a bit tired darling," she said plaintively. "You go."

She looked at him, willing him to over-ride her. He did, taking her by the arm and almost lifting her out, but she could see that he did not understand what was happening.

Once out of the car and walking across to the most advanced of the buildings Miss Dee left her alone for a bit, but then she began to test what she perceived to be her control over Marheh. She walked her into a wall and then over to flirt with one of the workmen. Kel reacted angrily to this bit of bad behaviour and marched her away. Then, thank goodness, she could let him know what was going on. Knowing, he was able to minimise the effects of Miss Dee's efforts at control, catching her when she tripped over her own feet, remonstrating with her when she stamped in temper and catching her wrist when she attempted to slap his face.

After this last he apologised profusely to Miss Dee and begged to be taken back to Deerford as his wife was unwell. Miss Dee ordered Marheh into the next room to stand in a corner with her face to the wall. Marheh went with a wry inward acknowledgement that this treatment as not inappropriate for the spoilt, doll wife she was pretending to be.

She could hear Miss Dee remonstrating with Kel as he attempted to go after her, and also hear her sales pitch. If she were to be believed Lowcroft Heights would be heaven, gates and all. Kel rumbled in response and refused to be side-tracked. He had to find his wife. She was not herself. Marheh was instructed to return, to apologise and plead to be allowed to live there at Lowcroft Heights. She could not quite manage tears, but she butted her face into Kel's chest and hoped that Miss Dee would not notice. In the back of her mind she was aware that she was beginning to enjoy herself and tried to remind herself of the need for caution. This charade was intended to help them make progress in finding out what was going on and she needed to focus on that.

At last Kel was able to persuade Miss Dee that they would give serious consideration to purchasing at Lowcroft Heights and insist that she drive them back to Deerford. Marheh was very glad of his tight grip on her upper arm since Miss Dee was enjoying herself instructing her to trip over, to run back to talk to the workmen, to bite Kel's hand, to stand still, to speed up, to drop to all fours, all of which he was able to prevent with quite natural displays of annoyance and concern.

It was not until Kel had thrust her into the car and got in beside her that

Miss Dee stopped tormenting Marheh with instructions and she was able to sit quietly as they were driven back to the office in Deerford. Kel promised they would return after they had been in touch with the bank and got an opinion on the worth of their present home. Then they said goodbye, Kel still keeping firm hold of Marheh, fortunately, for they were barely out the door when she was instructed to run back.

At last they were out of sight of the office and she could relax.

"You are just pretending I assume?" Kel asked. "I was beginning to be worried."

"So was I!" Marheh grimaced.

"Do you think you've convinced her that she has planted a control?" Kel asked. "Won't she realise that you don't have it?"

"But I do have it," Marheh said. "I'm holding it separate, but I want to look at it before I destroy it."

"Marheh!"

"It's alright. It isn't a very strong one. It doesn't hurt much."

"You never cease to amaze me," Kel said. "And here I was thinking you were just a spoilt brat."

Marheh grinned at him.

"I was just starting to enjoy myself. It would be good to get home now though. Do you think they would let us use the telephone at the pub to call father?"

Half an hour later they were back at the pottery. Marheh badly wanted to resume her proper clothing but the control she was holding was nagging at her too. She wanted to examine it. She wanted to be rid of it. She wanted the protection of Kel's song while she did this. She wanted Kel. That thought slipped in with the others but she pushed it away to deal with later, when her other needs were resolved.

Leaving Sef to make her apologies to the family she and Kel went straight down the garden to the mooring. Kel came with her onto *Day Bringer* and they sat at the table opposite each other.

"You just want me to sing?" Kel asked.

Marheh nodded.

"I don't know whether I can do this, or what I might find if I manage it. It might be like opening Pandora's box. Your song will contain the damage."

He took her hands and began to create his portal, the warm, smooth, glowing heart of a tree.

When she knew he had entered his song Marheh set herself to look at the control she held. They took different forms, these Yareblis controls, but always appeared to her as some kind of container. There had been containers as big as a dam wall that had cracked with her tears. There had once been a tiny bottle leaking poison. What she held now appeared as a small box, a little drawer like a match box.

She bent her mind to it, putting aside without too much difficulty the small hurt it caused her. It was quite ordinary looking, inconsequential, a drab grey, like a pebble, easily overlooked. In the past she would have taken it and put it in the fire, now she intended to open it. The moment of fear was put aside too. She had to know.

Cautiously she pushed at the inner box exposing first a tiny crack, then a little more and a little more until she could see what it held. Fitting neatly inside was something that looked like a dark, coarse sponge. It had a faint sheen that suggested dampness. She touched the surface lightly and yelped as it stung her. Then she was bombarded with commands and sensations so that it was like a huge, deafening noise made up of a multitude of other noises, indistinguishable from the whole. She pushed the box closed and the noise died down a little. She wanted to try to identify some of the sounds that made it. Cautiously she let her mind listen for certain notes, tones, colours. At first, even with the box closed, it was too confusing, but gradually she became more attuned, began to identify a range of dark emotions and became aware of coldness, such cold that it almost burned.

When her focus began to fray and she realized it would be dangerous to continue, she withdrew her mind from it and put it away from her, then took it and put it in the fire.

As soon as it had gone, she became aware once more of Kel's song surrounding her. She returned to sit opposite him and put her hands again in his. Then she found her own portal and let the candle flame lead her into song with him.

It was a song unlike any she had ever experienced, beginning so gently, a tender exploration of each other's music, now unison, now harmony, sometimes even discord resolving into sweetness. Then tenderness became warmth and passion and an explosion of glory. The song ended at last, inevitably, the glory dwindled to tenderness again and finished on a sigh. Marheh understood it had bound them together for the rest of their lives.

They looked at each other across the table then Kel stood up and drew her into his arms. For a while they stood holding each other then Kel moved to the armchair and pulled her onto his lap. Until now they had not spoken, but this movement broke the spell of silence that had held them.

"Kel," Marheh said.

It was almost a question. She knew that some few Silberay found a soul friend, there were stories of Sila and her soul friend Lor, but it was a rare privilege and one she could not believe she deserved.

"Marheh," Kel said.

His was not a question. It had long seemed to him inevitable that he should become Marheh's soul friend.

She cuddled against him for a time, tired and contented, but they were expected at supper and she needed to get out of her borrowed plumage. There were things to do, plans to discuss. She needed to talk about the control, to try and make sense of what it had shown her.

"Kel," she said again, but this time without the questions.

He smiled at her.

"Marheh," he said. "You have a dirty face."

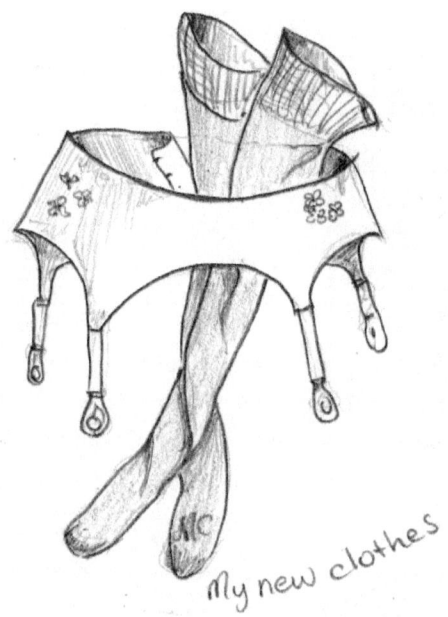

My new clothes

Chapter Thirteen

It was almost a relief to climb off Kel's lap and head for the bathroom after all the emotion. She turned at the doorway to grin and put her tongue out at him before making for the washbasin. She studied her face in the little mirror. She must have cried at some point because the stuff Fali had put on her eyes was smudged on her cheeks. She wet and soaped the face cloth and scrubbed away, making her eyes sting and reddening her skin. Perhaps hot water would have been more efficacious.

In her cabin she stripped off her borrowed finery and put on her spare uniform, the one she kept for best. Nemle had given her the tunic and she loved its deep purple richness. Nemle had also embroidered over one shoulder in fabric and thread of almost the same colour but different texture so that she wore a subtle fall of leaves and flowers. The white shirt beneath the tunic had a fine purple thread patterning the stand up collar.

She pulled the pins from her hair and brushed it hard before confining it to its usual plait. It was a shame her boots were up at the house with her other clothes but her slippers were quite neat and serviceable. When she was dressed she folded Fali's clothes carefully and put them in her pack to take back to the house. If she needed them again she would also need Fali's help she thought. Then she went through to the saloon and Kel.

There were no questions during supper, but Marheh was very conscious of Greya's speculative gaze. She and Fali both admired her beautiful tunic and Greya returned her ordinary clothes washed and pressed. After supper though, as they sat around the table drinking sperit, answers and explanations were clearly expected.

Marheh tried to make a funny story out of her adventures and they laughed with her when she told of being ordered to flirt with the workman and stand in the corner, but she knew it was not enough. She had to share her thoughts and discoveries and listen to their suggestions too.

"I don't think Miss Dee can be very experienced," she said. "The control she tried to put in me was quite a simple one. She must have been pleased at being able to control me so easily."

"I wonder why she chose you rather than me," Kel commented.

Fali and Greya looked at each other and laughed. Kel and Tep looked puzzled but Sef nodded sagely. It was Fali who explained.

"You can't make Marheh look ordinary – she's beautiful, and she had you. That Miss Dee would have been envious of both. She would have wanted to make her look small. She would have thought a woman like the one Marheh was playing would be an easier target too."

"So that's what it was." Marheh spoke her thought aloud. "In the control," she explained when the others turned to her. "It was made with all sorts of bitter feelings," she continued, choosing her words carefully. "Once I would have said it was evil, and I suppose it was in a way because it used all the hatred, the desire for power she was feeling. I could recognise those and feel sad and ashamed because I've felt them too. It was the envy I couldn't grasp."

"Next minute you'll be feeling sorry for the woman," Tep said.

"Yes, in a way," Marheh said. "After all, she could have been Silberay, but she's gone too far down the other road now I think."

"And what is the other road?" Sef asked after a short silence.

"The desire for power," Marheh said. "Power to control other people. It's very seductive. You could tell Miss Dee was just loving what she thought she was doing to me."

Kel nodded. "A kind of malicious glee."

"The Silberay are right to be strict about it. It's too easy to slip without noticing. You go along unnoticed and you see things you know you could stop, just small things that are wrong. It's tempting to do it, just slide into a mind and interrupt the bad action, but it's too easy. Someone like Gul or Sybi would put themselves on the line if they tried to take action. We should too. Nemle always did. The first way might succeed at the time and make you feel good, but the second way has more chance of making real change and it doesn't inflate the ego."

"You sound as if you're speaking from experience," Sef said, smiling at her.

"Nemle did her best to drum it into me, even if I don't always live up to her teaching."

"Have you learnt any more about what's happening here? I don't suppose your Miss Dee is the only Yareblis about?" Tep asked.

"The more we uncover the more I think Lowcroft Heights is designed as a training ground. Create a place that will appeal to people whose values are lightly held or even similar to those of the Yareblis. Include Yareblis who need to hone their skills before being moved into a position of power in the world and let them wreak as much havoc as they like." She sighed a little. "They must have most of their resources invested in it, so they've a great deal at stake."

"So what next, do you think?" Sef asked.

"I think Mr and Mrs Mackenzie might have to revisit the estate agent and demonstrate their fitness for Lowcroft Heights and hope perhaps to be led to Miss Dee's superior. She must have one."

Two days later, resplendent in more borrowed plumage, they returned to Miss Dee.

The day in between had not been wasted. Marheh had gone to visit Gul and Sybi and keep them informed. They seemed to be in good heart and welcomed her warmly. She entertained them with the story of her vicissitudes under the supposed control of Miss Dee and shared her theories about Lowcroft Heights. They in turn told her how the attacks against them seemed to have waned since she and Kel had been singing with them, but that they were still conscious of the possibility of further trouble.

"I'm afraid the concentration is now on finding our supporters," Gul had said. "You've been very visible. You will be careful won't you?"

Marheh nodded, aware of the truth of his words. They would be looking for her, just as she was looking for them.

After she had sung with them she took the bus to Higham's Hill. Gul and Sybi had agreed with the possibility that Lowcroft Heights was being managed from there and she thought she would call on Blethan and see if she had any ideas.

Blethan gave her the same hospitable welcome she had done in the past, offered her lunch and laughed at the story of how she had visited the empty house three doors down. She did not have any real information for Marheh, but did not discount her theories and promised to keep a careful eye out.

"They would be people who keep to themselves," Marheh suggested. "Polite but distant and quite formal, even with each other, at least in public. Quite possibly they would have someone from the village visiting, someone who is fascinated by them and does not realise they are being used."

Blethan looked thoughtful at that, but she would not give Marheh a name when she asked.

"I don't really know," she said, shaking her head. "It's just that something rang a bell when you said that. I'll think about it."

Marheh had to be content with that. She thanked Blethan for her lunch and warned her to be careful before taking the bus for Deerford and the pottery.

Kel had spent the day with Sef. He knew he needed to have all the details of his story correct if they were to make a second visit to Miss Dee. Sef's experience and knowledge were at his disposal and together they invented a businessman who had made his money up north with a small printing works. At the urging of his wife he had put in a good manager and planned to move south. He was not perhaps wealthy, but up north he was thought of as a warm man. He owned the freehold of the printing works as well as a large house on spacious grounds, but his wife was delicate and found the northern climate trying. He would do anything to please her and keep her happy and healthy.

Sef explained some of the difficulties of small business, the extra skills that must be acquired, or employed, as well as some of the issues relating to property that Kel had no need of in his life as Silberay. Kel was grateful, not just for the information, but also for the opportunity to get to know Marheh's father.

Fali and Greya had spent the day shopping for clothes for Marheh. They had had Tep drive them to Bartelford, where there was a choice of shops. They had enjoyed themselves picking out a dress, another blouse, a pretty petticoat and even a pair of knickers with lace on. Then they found a pair of high heeled sandals, stockings and a suspender belt and laughed together at the thought of Marheh's face when she saw them. They had had lunch together in Bartelford and caught the bus home feeling very pleased with themselves.

In the morning, as they dressed her, Marheh had tried to be grateful, playing up to their teasing and letting them see the spoilt doll wife she was pretending to be. At least the playacting kept the fear at bay, and she was afraid. She had no doubt that Miss Dee would once more want to control her and she would have to perform again the delicate balancing act that would persuade Miss Dee that she had succeeded. Thank goodness Kel now knew what was going on and could prevent her from complying with the worst excesses. They had worked out a little signal too, so that she could reassure him that she was just pretending.

Although she kept them waiting Miss Dee was clearly glad to see them, or at least to see Kel. Marheh she ignored after one deliberate, coldly dispassionate inspection. Kel, carefully primed by Sef, had a multitude of questions about Lowcroft Heights. Miss Dee brought out a big roll of paper and spread it out on the desk. It was a simplified plan of the development showing the position of the houses and the community facilities, but it was not enough for the astute Mr Mackenzie. He wanted to know which house might be theirs if they did take up the offer and how long they might have to wait for it to be built. He had questions about landscaping and the siting of the community facilities as well as the on-going costs of maintaining these.

Marheh leaned against him and gazed at the plan.

"It seems like a lot of houses," she said. "Will we have to wait for them all to be finished?"

Miss Dee looked at her as if surprised that she had spoken.

"The first phase will be finished in six to eight weeks," she said to Kel. "That will be the five residences you saw when you visited."

Marheh took Kel's hand and looked up at him.

"But won't it be horribly noisy and dusty if we go there before it is all finished?"

Marheh felt Miss Dee try to enter her mind. Of course she would be expecting the control would be still in place. Would its absence make her suspicious, or would she attribute it to her own lack of skill? Kel squeezed her hand and looked at her fondly.

"We won't go anywhere unless you are perfectly happy darling."

Marheh simpered at him and allowed Miss Dee to place a new control.

"What assurance can you give us that the whole project won't just stop at the end of the first phase?" Kel asked. "Who is financing the development?"

"I'm not at liberty to say, but I can assure you that the finance is secure."

"That isn't good enough," said Kel. "Come along Kathleen, I think we can do better than this."

"But this is what I want," Marheh wailed at Miss Dee's prompting.

"Now don't fret sweetheart. We'll find just the thing, but you wouldn't like it if we lost money because it didn't get finished, now would you?"

"Don't be so mean! You said I could have what I want."

She made fists and began to batter his chest so that he had to catch her wrists and hold them.

Although Miss Dee had Marheh use all Kathleen's wiles Kel remained adamant. He could not possibly proceed further without more information about the financial backing of the project. Miss Dee excused herself to telephone and they heard her arranging an appointment for them.

Again they were to avail themselves of a pub lunch and then Miss Dee would drive them out to Lowcroft Heights where they would meet with a representative of the company that was managing the development, who, she was sure, would be able to answer Mr Mackenzie's questions and put his doubts to rest.

This individual turned out to be a man of about Kel's age, introduced as Mr Jay. He had white blond hair and sharp blue eyes and although not particularly tall, he took up more space than he seemed to need. He greeted them formally, but his glance at Marheh caused her a moment of fear. Miss Dee suggested that she take Marheh to look at progress in one of the houses and ordered Marheh to agree.

Kel did not intervene, so Marheh reluctantly left with Miss Dee. Once inside she made no attempt to show Marheh anything, although it was obvious that work was progressing rapidly. Instead she amused herself by practising her control over Marheh and having her humiliate herself in ways that seemed to afford her the same malicious glee as before. Marheh obediently followed her commands, controlling her longing to hit back by focusing on the reason for the masquerade. She even submitted meekly to being slapped though it cost her all her resolution not to retaliate.

When she was finally escorted back to Kel she was aware almost immediately that something had changed. Kel stood silently beside Mr Jay, not moving, but looking at her from trapped, angry eyes.

"This one put up quite a struggle," Mr Jay informed Miss Dee rather smugly. "He still resists everything I suggest. He'll be good practice for the more advanced."

Kel was being controlled. He could no longer prevent her from complying with anything she was told to do, and she could not free him, not now while she was containing the control placed in her. She dared not even reach her mind towards his for fear of discovery. Surely they must allow them to leave eventually though. She would just have to pretend for all she was worth.

"You've done well," Mr Jay was saying. "He'll sign up and pay up and they'll both be useful." He looked speculatively at Marheh. "Suppose you give me a little demonstration of what you can do with her."

Miss Dee giggled. It was an extraordinary sound coming from this very formal, rather severe exterior. Marheh suppressed a shiver. Resisting a little, she lifted her skirt to display the lace trimmed petticoat beneath. She saw Kel lurch forward then jerk back as Mr Jay applied his control. She wanted to reassure him. Whatever they made her do would only be superficial. All she could do was look. Then she was ordered to raise the petticoat to display the lace on her knickers.

She hoped it would not matter that tears ran down her cheeks as she slowly obeyed, helpless, angry tears that she passionately resented. She stood, skirt and petticoat lifted, while Mr Jay studied her then reached forward to hook his finger under the suspender nearest him. He pulled it towards him and let it twang back against her skin. She was allowed to lower her skirts then and left to stand while Mr Jay and Miss Dee talked about Lowcroft Heights.

At first they were only reiterating what she already knew and, desperately anxious for Kel, she allowed her attention to wander. Then they began talking about HQ and HH. They always used initials as shorthand. It seemed to be a way of reducing everything and everyone to some kind of formula, making them distant and de-personalising them. HQ was pretty easy though and HH too, given the vicinity of Higham's Hill.

It sounded as if Kel had been right to turn her attention in that direction. They seemed to be expecting the arrival of some nameless He. Marheh could see the capital letter as they spoke and she got the feeling that the two in front of her were expecting to be rewarded for their present activities by some kind of promotion up the hierarchy. Clearly too, neither of them resided at HQ which suggested there were others about as well.

The awaited He would be visiting Lowcroft Heights and would expect a gathering of prospective residents. These would come when ordered of course, but driving into Deerford, Mr Jay had seen a couple of boats moored. There were Sillies about and Miss Dee should be alert. Marheh knew they were aware of her presence, their various attacks had made that plain, but had hoped they would not have associated her with the pottery. Just as well she and Kel had been careful not to be seen coming from there.

A few more minutes of conversation and she and Kel were ordered back into Miss Dee's car for the ride to Deerford. Kel was very quiet, looking her with troubled eyes as she took his hand. She squeezed it gently and leaned against him. The control would be dormant now and Kel would have no memory of its operation. Surely she would be able to remove it though and he would be alright. She closed her eyes, then snapped them open again as Miss Dee ordered her upright and away from Kel. Thank goodness they were nearly at Deerford. She was so tired of pretending and of containing the control that nagged painfully at her.

It was probably only another hour before they were back at the mooring, but it seemed a long time to Marheh. She could hardly wait to put Miss Dee's control in the fire and be free of it so she could help Kel. She didn't stop to examine this new control but got rid of it as soon as she reached the saloon. Kel had followed her onto *Day Bringer* and she pushed him into the armchair and settled herself on the footstool in front of him.

"How much do you know?" she asked.

"What do you mean?"

She leaned forward against his knees.

"You have a control. That Mr Jay put it there. Can you identify it?"

If he knew, perhaps he could isolate it for himself. It would be better that way, if he could manage without her. She could see him turn inward and waited quietly. At last he shook his head.

"There is something, I can tell there is something, but I can't grasp it."

"Will you let me help you?" she asked.

"Who better?"

She gathered her focus and slipped into his mind.

The control was an obvious intruder, a sort of parasitic lump. It looked to be trying to strangle something within him. She wanted not just to remove it, but to show it to him, so that he could help her.

Silberay would fight, sometimes to the point of being broken, to prevent being controlled. Kel had not done that, probably because of their masquerade. She hoped he might be able to tell her about it once the control was gone. At least she was confident now that it would be gone, even if she had to do it all herself.

She reached towards it, wanting just to touch it, hoping that might show it to Kel. First she touched it, then began to pick a little at the edge of it, watching all the time for a reaction from Kel. For a few moments nothing, then suddenly there was a convulsive movement beneath the control.

"Yes!" She tried to encourage him and saw first the recognition and the pain, then the resolution as he tried to contain it the way she had been able to. She longed to help but held back for him, knowing that was the better way.

A few minutes of struggle then she could see it no longer. She waited for a moment or two to be quite sure then slipped out of his mind in time to move aside for him to reach the fire.

She could see the weariness in his face and knew that it was reflected in hers, but there was satisfaction too.

"Talk later," he said, leaning back and closing his eyes.

"Yes," Marheh said quietly, studying his sleeping face. Then she leaned against him and closed her own eyes.

She woke before him and got up quietly to put the kettle on for sperit. She prepared the mugs and regretted the lack of bread or biscuits. When she turned back to him, she found he was watching her.

"Alright?" she asked.

"Very much so, thank you, that was a costly gift."

She blushed and shook her head.

"You did it."

"But you showed me how."

She was glad of the kettle's urgent whistle so she could turn back to her sperit. She was suddenly aware that she was still wearing Mrs Mackenzie's clothes.

"I need to change," she said, thrusting a steaming mug at him and turning to go.

"Why?"

"I need to," she said again.

She wanted so much for him to hold her and kiss her and touch her. The wanting was like a pain and she had to be away from him to deal with it.

"It won't make any difference, you know."

He put his mug down on the floor beside the chair and held out his hand to her.

"I don't know what you mean."

"Yes you do. You want to run away from me and put on your Silberay armour, but it won't work. It's dangerous in more ways than one this masquerade."

"You feel it too then?"

"Of course I do."

He reached out, grabbed her wrist and pulled. She let herself tumble into his lap. When he had settled her comfortably he turned her face to him and kissed her lips, gently but thoroughly. She gave a little gasp when he released her but did not look away.

"You are very beautiful and desirable and I love you, but you have chosen the life of the Silberay and you still choose it. I do too."

"Oh Kel, not even once?"

"What do you think?"

"It didn't matter, doing without, until now."

"Speak the truth and shame the devil," he said, laughing at her just a little.

"I could make you," she said.

"Yes, you probably could, but you won't because you are Silberay and because you are Marheh, and have too much pride."

"No pride," she whispered, tears running down her cheeks.

He held her face in both hands and rubbed them away with his thumbs.

"Discipline, integrity, all those things you have struggled for."

She tried to shake her head but he wouldn't let her.

"We have been given to each other to be soul friends, not many have that.

We will belong to each other always. It is just Mrs Mackenzie making you want the other kind of loving."

She sighed and leaned her head on his shoulder.

"I expect you're right. Why do you have to be so sensible?"

"Because you are not."

She sat upright abruptly.

"It is one of your great gifts actually."

"How can being… not sensible… be a gift? Anyway, I am sensible."

He pulled her back against him.

"We'll sing, then we'll talk."

The singing was rich and joyous but brief, then they talked, sitting sensibly at the table opposite each other. Kel had no memory of what had happened while he was being actively controlled but he could tell Marheh how it had happened. He had recognised the incursion and begun to resist, as his Silberay training had taught him, then he had realised that this would reveal his identity, so he had allowed Mr Jay to place the control, not expecting to be able to deal with it as Marheh had done, but trusting that she would free him afterwards.

"What if I couldn't?" she said, rather overwhelmed by the extent of his trust.

"I knew you could."

Even with the control it had been possible to resist, he told her, possible but painful, increasingly painful as his resistance increased. He knew he had resisted, but not why or how.

If he didn't remember it was better he didn't know how she had been humiliated, but she could tell him what she had overheard.

Then of course there had to be a discussion. It might even have been an argument only Kel refused to get heated and just smiled and shook his head at Marheh's more outrageous suggestions. In the end they called a truce and went up to the house for supper and for Marheh to change back into the clothes she had left there.

Greya always insisted that meals should not be accompanied by discussions about strategy so for a time at least there was space to hear of the activities of the others and to enjoy the luxury of food she did not have to prepare, but Marheh could not forget that nothing was yet resolved. The Yareblis had to be stopped, they agreed on that, but could not even agree on what that meant. She wanted Lowcroft Heights to stop, the buildings to disappear and the lovely landscape she had rambled over as a child, to be restored. Of course that would not happen, could not, but Kel thought they were best to focus entirely on the Yareblis and forget Lowcroft Heights.

It was not until the dishes were done and the boys were in bed that Greya lifted her ban and Marheh was allowed to air what was uppermost in her mind, the fact that the boats had been spotted here, near the pottery. She was afraid for her family if they stayed, but they could not go. Sef and Greya, Tep and Fali listened to her fears. Sef was inclined to be sceptical about what they might do. After all he had never tried to hide his support of the Silberay and the pottery had never been threatened. Greya looked worried but said little. Tep and Fali were more concerned, not so much for themselves, as for their boys.

"I know you have to act against them," Fali said. "I expect nothing less of you, but what is it they might do? How might they threaten?"

"What they have done in the past," Marheh said carefully. "Is find someone vulnerable to control. It isn't necessarily a child but it could be. It might be best if you and Tep collected the boys from school and if they didn't visit with their friends until we know more."

"We can do that," Fali said. "Tith won't even notice, but Fen will, he likes to be independent."

"I know but…"

"But if we do everything we can to keep them safe that is one less thing you and Kel have to worry about," Sef said. "I'm sure Fen will understand. He's old enough for an explanation."

"I wonder if we could fool them into thinking we've left," Kel said. "Why don't we put the boats in the tunnel?"

"We could I suppose," Marheh said slowly, thinking about it. "But there's no towpath, we would have to swim to get off."

Kel shook his head.

"It's not wide enough to go breasted up, but if *Day Bringer* went in first, backwards, and *Storm Cloud* followed, we could tie the bows together so you could get across. Then we could have just enough of *Storm Cloud*'s stern sticking out so I could put out the gangplank. There's plenty of shrubbery around the mouth of the tunnel. Of course they would see it if they really looked, but a casual glances from the road is more likely and they'd never spot it."

Marheh grinned at him.

"And if they think we've gone, they're even less likely to associate us with Mr and Mrs Mackenzie."

"There is that too," Kel said gravely, teasing her.

"We should do it tonight then, don't you think?" She sounded as if the prospect of action pleased her. "But I still think you should all be careful even so."

. . . .

Mucking around in the dark was the sort of play challenge that felt like fun and adventure. Not that it was easy, but a ducking was likely to be the most serious consequence of a mistake and that was almost a joke compared with the fears of the last few days. When all was secured to their satisfaction they both tested the gangplank and examined their handiwork from the bank. They would know better how successful they had been in the morning, in daylight, but they went up to the house to report, feeling pleased with themselves.

When she finally scrambled back onto *Day Bringer* Marheh realised she would have to let the fire go out. The chimney was too close to the tunnel roof and the cabin was smoky. She opened a window to let the smoke away then closed it again as the cold damp air in the tunnel made her shiver. *Day Bringer* would be cold as well as dark, but if it fooled the Yareblis it would be worth it, and now the best thing for her to do was go to bed.

When she woke, late and a little disoriented because of the tunnel's dark, she knew she had to return to Higham's Hill. Blethen's hesitation coupled with Mr Jay's references to HH and Miss Dee's to HQ, suggested there was something to be found there. She dressed quickly, made her way through

Day Bringer and climbed across the bow to *Storm Cloud*. Kel was ready and waiting for her and she realised, with something like dismay, that *Day Bringer*'s position in the tunnel meant she could never go off on her own. Kel would always be able to keep an eye on her movements. If she really had to she could swim for it, she thought with a shiver, *Day Bringer*'s stern was not so very far from the other end of the tunnel.

She smiled a greeting and followed Kel through the dim saloon and out to *Storm Cloud*'s stern. Outside the tunnel was bright morning light and they both stood and blinked a little, letting their eyes adjust before tackling the gangplank. They made their way to the path and turned to look back. *Storm Cloud*'s dark painted hull was hardly visible in the dark arch of the tunnel mouth and the shrubbery disguised the gangplank well. As they continued up to the house Kel spoke.

"I won't question your comings and goings, I promise, though I hope you'll tell me what you're doing."

Marheh stopped and looked at him in surprise.

"How did you know what I was thinking? Am I so predictable?"

He laughed hearing the note of indignation.

"Only in your need for independence."

She made a face at him and darted away towards the house. He knew her too well. Swimming might still be an option.

At breakfast, having made known her intention to go to Higham's Hill, she was told firmly that she could not go in her uniform.

"You might as well bring the boats back to the mooring if that's what you plan," her father said. "I thought you wanted them to think you've gone."

She wondered whether she looked as trapped as she felt, but she knew it was sensible. She sighed and looked at Kel.

"You'd better come with me then. I don't think Kathleen would go alone."

Dangerous new shoes

Chapter Fourteen

An hour later they were sitting side by side on the bus. It was the driver she had helped, but he clearly did not recognise her. She clasped her gloved hands demurely over the little handbag that rested in her lap. How could she possibly achieve anything when she felt so imprisoned by the accoutrements of Kathleen? Kel bent his head towards her.

"Clothes do not make the woman," he whispered.

"It just feels like it," Marheh grunted.

Today the curious looks from the other passengers felt different. They were strangers so of course there would be looks, but no animosity now and even a few smiles, though she thought the smiles were mostly for Kel, seated protectively on the aisle. They could not talk about what was really on their minds, so they were mostly silent for the first part of the journey until Kel tried to start a conversation about their house hunting activities.

"Are you quite sure about Lowcroft Heights, Kathleen?" he asked. "I thought you wanted to live in Higham's Hill."

"I know that's what I said, but that was before I knew about Lowcroft

Heights."

They were both speaking a little louder than usual, but perhaps it was necessary in order to be heard over the engine of the bus.

"It means we would have to wait. Miss Dee said six to eight weeks, but I think that was a rather optimistic estimate."

"But we could stay in the district until then couldn't we? You know you promised to take a long holiday."

"Perhaps we could buy in Higham's Hill, the second house we saw would suit quite well, and wait to see how Lowcroft Heights develops. I don't like the idea of living on a building site."

Nobody seemed very interested in their conversation, although that did not mean that nobody was listening, so they continued to discuss the possibilities of the house in Higham's Hill as a temporary measure with Marheh becoming just a little bit shrill and Kel patiently firm.

At the edge of Higham's Hill the bus slowed and stopped for a couple to get off. Before it could set off again a small, dark blue car sped past.

"Oh look darling," said Kathleen. "Doesn't that look like Miss Dee's car? If she's in Higham's Hill maybe she could show us that house again."

"It certainly looks like her car," Ken said cautiously. "But there may be other cars like that."

Marheh and Kel just looked at each other, wondering.

When the bus reached the centre of the village they got off along with most of the other passengers. Arm in arm they strolled around the Green, decorous visitors admiring the local scene.

"It was her, wasn't it?" Marheh said. "I wonder if she stopped here. Perhaps we might find where she went."

"If it was her, if she stopped here, if the car is in the street," Kel teased her.

"Don't be such a spoil sport."

"Why don't we go and sit on that bench and watch for a bit?"

"We could I suppose."

Marheh felt curiously reluctant to revisit the seat under the tree where she had been so threatened, but she let Kel lead her there and even managed to enjoy feeling his arm around her. There was no more need for words between them. They both set themselves to listening and watching.

Marheh knew she ought to hold out her candle flame just to test the landscape but the memory of the last time she had tried it restrained her. She sighed a little and cuddled up to Kel then drew herself upright. She would not let herself be diminished by fear. Carefully she let herself into that other dimension expecting her candle to be a tiny spark against the encroaching darkness. Kel heard her gasp and tightened the arm that held her, bringing her back to him.

"There is nothing, not even darkness," she said turning to him. "It was like a blank wall, impermeable, my flame was just reflected back at me."

Kel nodded.

"I didn't get anywhere at all — no light, no darkness, my portal led nowhere."

"It's like... like a kind of parallel to Lowcroft Heights, a wall to keep out... or keep in. I've never seen anything like it."

"They're keeping us out, but what are they keeping in?"

Marheh shook her head.

"That's what worries me. If I was to try and break in what would I be letting out? Perhaps it would be imprisoned minds, but perhaps it would be the poison that enslaves them."

"You couldn't break in with out drawing attention to yourself. I think it is too soon for that."

Marheh looked at him.

"I might have to try in the end."

"I know, but not yet, not until we've thought it through." He turned her towards him. "If it has to happen there must be ways you can be supported, helped."

"I wonder whether there is anything in the archives... whether anyone else has experienced anything similar."

"We can contact the Harbour when we get back to Deerford."

Kel stood up and offered her his hand.

"For now I think we should walk a little."

Marheh grinned and stood up.

"And look for the blue car that *might* belong to Miss Dee, and *might* have stopped here, and *might* be parked in the street."

Kel laughed.

"Oh well… there's a chance."

They strolled on, arm in arm, across the Green to stand outside the shop and study the community notices placed in the window.

> *Gardener available, cheap rates, hard working,*

read one.

> *Accommodation vacant, long or short term, meals provided,*
> *apply at Westerway in Cowslip Lane,*

read another.

"Perhaps Kathleen and Ken would be interested in that," Marheh said, pointing it out.

"And perhaps not," Kel said. "Come on, let's walk."

But Marheh lingered to read that a litter of five cross breed puppies were freely available to a good home and the Old Rectory was in search of a live-in housemaid.

"It would be nice to have a puppy," she said, a little wistfully as she let Kel lead her away.

It wasn't forbidden, but not encouraged either.

After circling the Green once more they chose a narrow lane that ran beside the church and made their way along towards another intersecting road. They stopped occasionally to look at the church and the grave stones that surrounded it and to wonder about the glimpse of roof they could see behind the high wall that edged the opposite side of the lane. There were trees too and a vine that was beginning to appear above the wall. A little further along a narrow gate appeared and opposite it the lynch gate to the church yard.

"Perhaps it's the old rectory," Marheh said. "It looks like the sort of place that might want a house maid."

"Were you thinking of applying?" Kel teased.

Marheh gave him a little push and, forgetting Kathleen, began to run from him. The unaccustomed shoes caught in a rut, her ankle turned and she fell heavily.

Kel was beside her in an instant. She pushed herself to a sitting position and held on to him. For a moment she thought she might be sick.

"Are you alright?"

"I will be in a minute."

Her ankle throbbed as she tried to move it. She buried her face against Kel's supporting arm then took a deep breath.

"I seem to have done something to my ankle. You might have to help me up."

"Are you sure you're alright? You've gone very pale."

"My own silly fault," she said lightly. "I should have behaved sensibly... but of course I'm not sensible."

Her skirt was dirty, her stockings were torn and her ankle was already swelling up. Kel put his arms around her and helped her to stand, balancing rather unsteadily on one foot. She clutched him and winced as she tried to put weight on the other foot.

"Swear if you want to," Kel said.

She laughed a little at that.

"It's such a stupid thing to have done."

She tried again to take a step, leaning heavily on his arm.

"You can't keep on like that! Hold on!"

He lifted her in his arms, grunting a little with the effort. Marheh laughed a little at the sound.

"You're not supposed to let me know that I'm heavy."

"Mind your manners or I'll drop you."

"Now what?" she asked as he hesitated.

"We've got to get you home somehow and maybe to a doctor."

"No doctor," she said firmly. "But maybe one of these houses will have a telephone they would let us use."

Kel set off down the lane. The house behind the wall looked grand enough to have a telephone if he could find the entrance.

"This takes me back," he said, once he had got into his stride. "I seem to remember carrying you like this before we were even introduced."

"I expect I was lighter then."

"Not as bossy either."

"I've learned to be assertive," Marheh said with dignity.

Kel stopped walking so he could laugh without dropping her.

As soon as he turned the corner into the road they saw the entrance to the house, wrought iron gates open to a gravelled driveway and, parked close to the house, a small, dark blue car. Kel stopped again.

"What do you think?"

"It's the perfect opportunity to find out," Marheh said. "My ankle is swelling nicely. Anyone can see I'm not pretending. It will almost be worth it if we find out more."

"She could be here on business?"

"Even that will tell us something."

Kel started off down the drive. Marheh was silent, letting the pain in her ankle assert itself and show on her face, re-establishing Kathleen.

The doorbell was answered by a grave, rather colourless man of about Kel's age. His face registered no emotion at the sight of them, despite the unusual nature of their arrival. He did not speak.

"My wife fell and hurt herself. She can't walk. I was hoping you might have a telephone I could use."

There were spaces between each of Kel's short, clipped sentences but no suggestion of response from the man.

"Wait," he said at last, when Kel had run out of words.

He turned and went back into the house, but did not shut the door. Kel saw that Marheh's eyes were closed and knew she was listening, probing a little with her mind. He shifted her weight and allowed the strain and anxiety to show on Ken's face.

"Please come in."

It was a different man this time. Of average height and build, he nevertheless gave an impression of confident, easy power. He was conservatively, but expensively dressed, immaculately groomed and his voice, superficially courteous, held an underlying note of condescension. Clearly this was their host.

Kel allowed himself to stumble a little as he stepped inside. Marheh whimpered and clutched. The man led them into a spacious sitting room on the right of the wide entrance hall.

"If you put your wife down on this sofa she can rest while you telephone."

Kel put Marheh down carefully and stood to survey the room.

"Why, it's Miss Dee," he said. "And Mr Jay." He turned to his host. "Perhaps you are thinking of Lowcroft Heights too?"

"Mr Mackenzie," Miss Dee said graciously. "You are in some kind of trouble?"

"My Kathleen, she tripped and fell. Her ankle is already swelling up."

"Miss Dee," murmured Marheh. "How nice. Miss Dee has been so helpful," she informed the room in general. "She took us to Lowcroft Heights to see the work."

She looked wanly at their host and held out a limp hand.

"Kathleen Mackenzie. It is so kind of you to take us in like this."

"The name is Casey," said their host, just touching her hand.

"Mr Casey, so kind," Marheh said again, allowing her hand to fall to her lap and closing her eyes for a moment.

"Just be quiet and rest Kathleen," Kel said, thinking Marheh was in danger of overplaying her part. "If I could just telephone for a car to take us back to our lodgings we won't impose on you any further."

"Of course," Mr Casey said. "But the car will take a little time. You must come back and tell us your impressions of Lowcroft Heights."

"I think it is going to be lovely," Marheh said. "Kenneth promised me we can live there."

As she spoke the man who had opened the door to them reappeared.

"Show Mr Mackenzie the telephone," Mr Casey said.

The man inclined his head, waited a moment for Kel to join him, then walked out of the room.

The telephone was located in a small alcove further along the entrance hall. Kel was aware of the need for caution. Everything he said was likely to be overheard. He picked up the receiver and spoke quietly to the exchange "Deerford 572 please."

Marheh, left alone with the three who she knew to be Yareblis, continued with Kathleen's babble.

"I must look a sight, dirty and torn stockings. It was so unexpected to find someone we know here, and so pleasant."

She wondered whether Miss Dee would again attempt to control her, or perhaps one of the others. She knew she had to be prepared for that. Miss Dee might start being suspicious of her if she had to keep replacing the control she thought she had already established.

"Are you thinking of buying at Lowcroft Heights?" She repeated Kel's question. "Only surely you wouldn't want to leave this lovely home."

This must be the head quarters she had overheard them speaking of and possibly, even probably Mr Casey was the He they had been expecting. She looked at him, awaiting his answer, but he ignored her and walked across the room to confer with the other two. Not the He then, Marheh thought, but quite high up. Obviously he lived here. She gave a little Kathleen sigh and fell silent.

She could see the other three standing by the window and she thought they were speaking about her. She could feel their attention and see their glances. It was difficult not to feel anxious and she hoped Kel would be back soon.

Now that they had established where HQ was and discovered another of their enemies she wanted to be back in her own person again and not confined by Kathleen. Yareblis' power could be challenged and she and Nemle had discovered that their ability to control other minds could be excised, leaving them unable to see the water road, but it was a difficult and exhausting process and not feasible now while she was so outnumbered.

Then she felt Miss Dee attempting to activate her control. She was so confident of success that she had left her own mind completely undefended. For a moment Marheh was tempted to act against her. She could be in and out and none the wiser. Miss Dee would never know what she had had, only an inkling that something was missing. But the other two would know, and know where the attack originated. For now it would be better to accept the new control. She raised her right hand when prompted then let it fall in her lap. Miss Dee nodded as if satisfied and all three came towards her.

She was suddenly afraid. They stood around the sofa looking at her. Had she given herself away? She kept her face blank though her heart seemed to be beating so loudly she thought they must hear it.

"Controlling her might be quite entertaining," Mr Casey said. "Once we're established at Lowcroft Heights you must let me have her."

Miss Dee inclined her head. "I should like to see how you manage her."

"A pity ... but best to wait. It will be a pleasure in store."

The effort to keep still and unresponsive took all Marheh's self-discipline. Anger and lashing out were not ultimately effective, but she hated to feel herself still and frightened, like a rabbit in a spotlight. Then there were footsteps. They moved back from her as Kel entered the room.

"Thank you, thank you," he said, coming towards her. "Our landlord has kindly agreed to come for us, so you won't have to put up with us for much longer."

He perched on the edge of the sofa and took Marheh's hand.

"You'll be glad to get home Kathleen."

"I'm sorry to be such a trouble," she said leaning her head against his arm, needing to hide her face for a few moments. Please let them just get out of here before she lost control completely and started hitting out.

"No trouble Mrs Mackenzie." Mr Casey gave a stiff little bow. "We'll let you rest while we talk with your husband and look forward to meeting again at Lowcroft Heights."

She couldn't relax, not yet, in case they decided to test the control Mr Jay expected to find in Kel, but for the moment focus was off her and Kel was earnestly questioning Mr Casey about his thoughts on Lowcroft Heights. Kel had endowed Ken with a good head for business but also an eagerness for knowledge that gave him a kind of youthfulness. Marheh found herself distracted by the masquerade and Kel's ability to dissemble. It was just as well his character did most of the talking. She doubted she could do as well. She opened her eyes. There was a question she could ask though. She tugged at Kel's hand to make him look at her then turned to Miss Dee.

"Have you found lots of nice neighbours for us?" she asked. "People who want to live in the other houses?"

"Probably that isn't something Miss Dee can tell you Kathleen," Kel said.

"Not names of course, but just if there are any. After all neighbours are so important, aren't they?"

She nodded to Mr Casey.

"Maybe we have already met one nice neighbour," she said archly.

"I don't think that is any of our business Kathleen," Kel said.

Marheh pouted.

"I was just asking."

"I haven't decided yet, Mrs Mackenzie," Mr Casey said smoothly. "But if you are to be a neighbour that will certainly influence my decision."

"I think you will find your neighbours compatible, Mrs Mackenzie," Mr Jay said. "I don't think I would be breaking a confidence if I told you that the other houses in the first stage have been offered to couples like yourselves."

"With children? Not too many children I hope." She looked with large eyes at Kel. "It has always been a great sadness that Mr Mackenzie and I have no children and I find it difficult to watch others more fortunate."

"There will be children of course, but I don't think you will find them too intrusive."

She sighed.

"No? Perhaps not."

She let her eyes close and leaned back against Kel's arm.

It was probably no more than twenty minutes before a ring at the door heralded the arrival of their landlord in a car. It seemed a lot longer. Kel offered to wait in the street but Mr Casey would not hear of it and insisted on remaining with them making awkward small talk about the amenities to be expected at Lowcroft Heights, the joys and disappointments of parenting and the advantages and disadvantages of living in Higham's Hill. Marheh was aware that she still contained Miss Dee's control. Its nagging pain added to the pain of her ankle kept her quiet and still. She did not know whether she looked pale, but she certainly felt pale and a little sick.

She heard the footsteps passing in the hall and the sound of the door opening then Sef's voice inquiring for Mr and Mrs Mackenzie. Kel heard it too and stood up.

"That will be our landlord," he said. "Thank you so much for your kindness."

"Yes, thank you," Marheh echoed. "I'm so looking forward to Lowcroft Heights."

She put her arms up to Kel and he lifted her and went towards the door. The three Yareblis stood and watched in silence as they left.

When she saw Sef waiting in the doorway Marheh felt a rush of relief.

"I'm sorry to hear of your accident Mrs Mackenzie," he said gravely. "It won't take long to get you home where you can rest."

"Ken has looked after me beautifully," she cooed. "He's so strong."

They were almost out the door by this time and the expression on Kel's face was enjoyed only by Sef. He opened the car door for Kel to slide Marheh onto the seat and hid a smile as he heard Kel's low whisper. "Any more and I'll wallop you when we get home."

Marheh gave him her most enchanting Kathleen smile and closed her eyes. The two men exchanged looks and got into the front of the car. Sef put it in gear and they drove off.

They were silent until they were away from Higham's Hill and heading into open country.

"So," said Sef then, settling back in his seat and relaxing a little now the need for gear changing was past for a while. "What have you been up to daughter?"

"I haven't been up to anything," Marheh protested. "It's these stupid shoes. I forgot about being careful and turned my ankle. It hurts," she finished, not really expecting sympathy.

"How bad is it? Do you need a doctor?"

She shook her head. "It's just a sprain. Comfrey ointment and an elastic bandage should take care of it."

"You were very circumspect on the telephone," he said to Kel.

"We seem to have found the Headquarters. I had to speak as if anything I said would be passed on."

"Well, so not altogether an unlucky accident."

A short silence followed while he negotiated a slow-moving farm cart then he said "And what are the implications of that discovery?"

"It's something we'll need to think about," Kel answered. "It's all a bit unexpected really."

"We've got some new knowledge," Marheh added. "But we haven't had time to think what to do with it." She leaned forward. "At least we have a bit better idea of what we're facing."

"What I'm not clear about is your ultimate goal."

"Neither are we," Kel said.

Marheh wanted to disagree with him but when she opened her mouth she found she didn't know what to say. What was their ultimate goal? To get rid of Lowcroft Heights, to disable the Yareblis, to help the villages, to restore the Yareblis' victims, all that was part of it. She closed her mouth again and her eyes. Her ankle was throbbing gently so she didn't need to worry that she would fall asleep and she needed to think.

The journey home was short and her thought had not managed to break out of its circle of inadequacy and indecision before she was obliged to respond to exclamations of concern, offers of assistance and requests for elucidation. She found her temper disintegrating by the minute and clamped her mouth firmly shut, knowing she might easily say something she would regret later.

Greya stripped off the torn stockings, bathed the grazed knees and bandaged the swollen ankle and Marheh tried to be grateful when all she wanted was to be alone to manage in her own way.

It was Sef who rescued her, putting Greya gently aside and calling Kel to help him.

"A bit of solitary confinement I think before she spontaneously combusts," he said.

The two men carried her between them up the stairs to the spare bedroom and put her gently on the bed. She just managed to wait until the door had closed behind them before giving in to tears that came in such a passionate storm she almost frightened herself.

It was not until the storm had subsided that she remembered that she still held Miss Dee's new control. There was no fire here to destroy it but she shut it in the drawer of the bedside table, felt the release of tension that gave and a moment later was asleep.

In the kitchen, over a late lunch, Kel tried to explain what had happened and what they had discovered.

"We are learning more but we still don't really know where to direct our efforts to be most effective. Marheh is spreading herself too thinly as a result," he finished.

"She's never been very good at asking for help either," Sef said. "So I'm glad the Silberay sent you to support her."

"And I bet she's giving you a hard time because of it," Tep added.

Kel laughed. "My shoulders are broad."

Fali got up, went to one of the drawers in the bench and came back with a pencil and a notepad.

"Would it help if we tried to make a list of the things which are worrying for us, for people in the villages?"

"It might," Kel said cautiously. "What sort of things do you mean?"

Fali thought for a moment.

"I suppose I'm thinking of things that might be the result of Yareblis action – but of course they might not be as well – they might just be ordinary disagreements and … misdemeanours – only if there are more than usual…"

"Do you mean things like vandalism and graffiti in the village?" Tep asked, trying to help her out.

"I suppose so." She frowned. "I thought I knew what I meant but it's hard to put into words. I suppose it is things like money has become more important than it ought to be and neighbourliness less important. People don't smile in the street. People are afraid to let their children walk in the fields and woods. Sometimes I'm asked about Marheh and when I try to explain I say that Silberay nurture an environment where good things can grow, but at the moment good things aren't flourishing."

It was a long speech for Fali who was usually more of a listener than a talker. There was a brief silence before Kel thanked her gravely.

"Silberay nurture an environment where good things can grow," he repeated. "I think Marheh would like that. Will you tell her?"

Fali blushed and nodded. "If you think it's helpful."

Halfway through the afternoon Greya went up to check on Marheh. She was still sleeping. The marks of tears streaked the Kathleen make-up and her hair was tumbled around her. Greya put a light blanket over her but she did not stir. She crept away, troubled, carried in memory back to the impulsive, passionate, independent, difficult teenager Marheh had been. The passion and independence had not changed, only been directed during the years of her apprenticeship. She had learned to think first on the whole but she still took things hard and felt more about aspects of life that others took for granted. Sef could wake her for supper when he came in. He had always understood her best. She might talk to him.

She was just stirring when he went in. She looked at him, sleepy and a bit puzzled. He saw the moment when she came awake to memory.

"Are you ready for some supper?"

She blinked, rubbed her eyes and pushed aside the blanket.

"I'm starving," she said, after a moment of thought.

"You've had nothing since breakfast," he reminded her.

She sat up, swinging her legs off the bed and wincing as the movement stirred pain in her ankle.

"Damn," she said, trying to stand. "How could I have been so stupid?"

"Accidents happen."

He helped her up and supported her as she balanced on one foot.

"I like your Kel, he seems steady and sensible."

"Everything I'm not," she offered.

Sef turned her to him, holding her arms.

"What's the matter daughter? You feeling sorry for yourself?"

She tried to answer him but tears came again. His arms went around her. For a few moments she let herself be held then pushed him away.

"I feel like a failure," she said, sniffing and rubbing at her face. "I can't do what they expect me to. I'm in a fog and I can't see the way out…and …and I just HATE Kathleen."

The last words burst out of her and she almost wept again.

Sef passed her his clean, folded handkerchief and she blew her nose hard.

"I suppose," she said when she was calmer. "I suppose it's good for me. I've usually been able to do what I set out to do. Maybe I've been too confident. I know people think I'm arrogant. I just feel… I feel … lost."

"Perhaps you're expecting too much of yourself," Sef said when he was sure she had finished. "Think about what you've actually achieved, let yourself rest for a bit, you'll see the way, the fog will clear."

She sighed.

"I don't know, maybe it won't, but I have to go on anyway really don't I?"

Sef gave her a little squeeze.

"Come and eat, you'll feel better with something inside you. Can you hop to the bathroom? You might need to wash your face first."

With his help she hopped across the corridor to the bathroom and washed her face, making liberal use of hot water and soap before finishing with a cold splash. She combed her hair and confined it in its usual plait then studied her face in the glass. They would see she'd been crying, she thought, and no doubt they would be very tactful which would be difficult to bear, but bear it she would. She squared her shoulders, tested her weight on her injured ankle and hobbled to the top of the stairs.

Sef was waiting there to help her down to the kitchen. It was warm and bright and smelled of good food. Tep was dishing up and Kel passing the plates. Greya and Fali were already sitting at the table. Fali looked up and smiled.

"Come and sit next to me. The boys are already in bed so we can have a grown-up meal tonight."

Marheh couldn't find words but she managed a smile as Sef helped her across to the table.

"Don't be too nice to her Fali," Sef said. "Or she'll think you're being tactful and she'll bite."

"Father!" Marheh sounded outraged, but Fali was laughing and she had to laugh too.

"I'm afraid I've ruined your stockings. I'm sorry."

Suddenly it was easy to talk and when Kel slid a plate with roast beef and all the trimmings in front of her she found it was all she could do to wait until everyone was seated and served.

Sef had been right of course, she felt a lot better for the good meal, and she could see that the others were not being tactful, just kind because they cared for her. Tep, indeed, was quite rude in the tradition of younger brothers, and that was kindness too.

Nevertheless there was still the moment when she had to address the Yareblis question again. She understood they would wait for her to raise the subject but if she didn't she would have failed in courage and let them down. It was Fali's description of her work that helped her to begin. Nurturing the environment was mostly done by singing and lately she had been using the singing only for her own sustenance. She tried to explain to them.

"I think perhaps I've been on the wrong track," she acknowledged. "Because my mind has been threatened I've been trying to use my mind to fight back, but then I'm being just like them."

Kel shook his head.

Marheh's look silenced him.

"I need to be using my skills of the mind for healing, not fighting. I'll never be able to use my mind like the Yareblis without becoming Yareblis. What we have and they don't is the singing."

Kel nodded thoughtfully. The others looked at her with varying degrees of puzzlement.

"It's what Fali said," she tried to explain. "It's the singing that nurtures the environment and that's not really the mind, it's the soul."

"I don't entirely understand," Sef said. "But it sounds as if you know what you're talking about."

"And since you probably don't need two functioning ankles for singing," Tep said. "Now is a good time to test the theory."

Marheh laughed.

"Watch yourself, little brother!"

"That sounds more like the Marheh we know and love," said Sef. He looked at her affectionately across the table. "Can we help?"

She smiled back at him.

"Loving is what helps."

Greya offered her a bed in the house, but she wanted to go back to *Day Bringer*. Fali helped her to change back into her uniform and Tep and Kel assisted her down the path to the water road. She thought she could hobble up the gang plank, but while Tep was arguing with her about it Kel bent down and slung her over his shoulder.

"If you struggle you'll have us both in," he said, setting off.

"That's the way to deal with her," Tep said laughing. "Good night big sister!"

At the top of the gang plank Kel set her carefully down.

"Alright?"

"Just like a sack of potatoes, or a bag of coal." She spluttered with laughter.

"Two bags of coal, at least."

He went first into the back cabin and lifted her down.

"I can manage," she said, still laughing.

"You'll probably have to, getting through to the saloon – it's a bit of a tight fit – then you can sit down while I get to grips with this idea of yours."

He followed her as she made her slow way through the engine room, past the bathroom, into the galley and then the saloon. Kel lit their way from behind, holding his lamp high, but the darkness in the tunnel was deeper than the darkness of an ordinary mooring and odd shadows lurked. Kel had had to let his fire out too and *Storm Cloud* was chilly as well as dark.

"It's a bit Spartan, isn't it?"

Marheh shivered a little.

"*Day Bringer* is just as bad. Maybe we should just go to bed and talk in the morning."

Kel was busy lighting the big saloon lamp.

"I'll get you a blanket in a minute. You take the armchair and put your foot up."

A warm, bright glow filled the saloon.

"That's better. I'll help you across to *Day Bringer* now if you want, but it isn't going to be any warmer till we're out of here."

She was still standing, leaning against the small table that was fixed under one of the windows.

"Where are you going to sit if I have the armchair and the footstool?"

"At the table… would you rather sit there too?"

She hesitated. She wanted to be close to him but she didn't know how to say so.

"Stay there a minute," he said, making a final adjustment to the big lamp and picking up the small one again.

She watched the light fade as he moved back to his cabin then he was with her again, a bright checked blanked over his arm. He wrapped it around her, helped her across to the armchair, sat down and guided her onto his lap.

"We'll keep each other warm," he said gently.

She was silent for a long time, silent, not sleeping, and he waited patiently. She was conscious of every point where their bodies met, his right arm around her back, his thighs supporting hers, her left side against his torso, her head resting on his shoulder.

"If I were a boat," she said at last, lifting her head to look at him. "If I were a boat you would be my anchor."

She felt his arm tighten, saw his eyes warm, but he didn't speak.

"I need an anchor."

He smiled then. "I'll try to hold you safely."

Another long and comfortable silence followed before she spoke again, settling herself upright and turning to face him.

"I think we could talk about singing now."

She began to explain, sometimes haltingly, feeling her way to meaning, sometimes with confidence, sure of where her thoughts were taking her.

"It's what we do Kel, you know that, in every new place, at every mooring we sing and there's light, and darkness moves back a little, but singing with Gul and Sybi was different and I feel ashamed now that I had never thought to listen for other songs. And now I think I've got a bit complacent about singing. Singing this morning at Higham's Hill was a shock. I haven't cared enough if the Yareblis have been able to make a wall against my song. I know I've a talent for using my mind and I've been encouraged to use it and develop it, but Gul and Sybi showed me that the soul can learn and grow too. I think it's only the soul, the strength of the soul song, which can really… not exactly defeat, more negate, wash out, the influence of the Yareblis. The clever tricks I've been trying to do with my mind – well that's all they are, clever tricks."

"You're too hard on yourself. How many Yareblis controls have you removed and destroyed? That's not just a clever trick."

"No I suppose not, but that's using my mind for healing and I wouldn't be surprised if that helps the soul grow too."

"Do you want to sing now?"

She nodded.

"Both of us to sing together, one to keep steady and strong and one to spin the gold out further. Maybe I'm all wrong, but it can't hurt to try."

He held her a little tighter.

"I know you want to be out there adventuring and you've already told me I'm an anchor – but you will be careful, won't you?"

Lock near Deerford

Chapter Fifteen

The entry to the song came easily and they spent a few moments enjoying the harmony they made. Together they made a space of light, together they danced at the edges of the dark and knew that it shrank for them. Then, when they seemed to have reached the limit of their influence, one song changed key. There was a new dissonance that urged movement forward. For a moment or two a place in the light became a point of brightness that drilled into the darkness, trailing a glowing wake. Then it faltered, and fell back.

The song continued a little longer then gently faded.

Kel was not surprised when he woke to find Marheh still in his arms. Nor was he surprised that she still slept. Singing always drained energy and he couldn't imagine the effort Marheh had made. He wondered whether she would be able to explain it, and whether, if she did, he would be able to make a similar effort.

The darkness in the tunnel made it difficult to judge the time of day, but the lamp still burned softly. He thought about the singing and waited for

Marheh to wake. He was hungry and expected she would be too. Was hiding in the tunnel a necessary precaution? Would they be better off to move, moor closer to Higham's Hill or Willow Rise and practise this new approach? Would physical proximity to the centre of the surrounding darkness be an advantage?

Of course it would, he answered himself, it always is. That's why we keep moving.

He drowsed again, not wanting to disturb Marheh by getting up. He wished he knew the time. It might still be the middle of the night but, on the other hand, maybe breakfast was already finished up at the house.

Eventually Marheh opened her eyes.

"What do you think?" she asked. "It seemed to me that there was just a little … dint in the darkness."

Kel laughed.

"What, no 'good morning Kel, did you sleep well?'"

"Is it morning?"

"I've no idea."

"I'm hungry."

"So am I."

"What do you think?"

"Yes, there was a dint."

She grinned and tried to get up, found herself entangled in the blanket he had wrapped around her and fell back against him laughing.

"Let's try again."

"Not without something to eat first," Kel said firmly.

She shook her head and made a face at him then began to untangle herself.

"How's the ankle?" he said, reminding her as she was about to stand up.

She wriggled it experimentally.

"Not great, but I'll live. I'm going to have to use your loo though. It's too far to *Day Bringer's*."

She hobbled away as he stood up, smiling a little. Given the disposal problems, sharing a boater's toilet was a real test of friendship. He turned up the lamp and shook out the blanket.

"Kel, have you got a candle? It's pitch dark in here."

"Coming," he called.

When she came back he saw she had taken time to tidy her hair and straighten her uniform.

"I used your comb too," she said. "Almost like being married really isn't it?"

"If we were married I'd probably have to beat you because I'm hungry and there's no breakfast."

"I thought there was a catch somewhere. We might as well go up to the house then. Mother won't mind. Is it breakfast time?"

"I've no idea. I couldn't get to my watch to wind it last night and now it's stopped."

"Oh! Oh well, never mind. Come on then."

It was just beginning to be day, they discovered, when they emerged from *Storm Cloud's* back cabin.

"I don't think I can bear that tunnel too much longer," Marheh said.

She was leaning on the railing that surrounded *Storm Cloud's* back deck and gazing at the sky.

"It is a bit depressing isn't it?"

"We might go back to the mooring near Willow Rise, do you think?"

"I was wondering about that, but let's not make any decisions till we've eaten and talked."

"And maybe even sung again."

She limped down the gang plank and waited at the bottom for Kel.

"I wonder how the singing affects them," she said as they went slowly up the path to the house. "Do you think they make the dark on purpose, like we make light, or is the darkness a sort of side effect of their thoughts and actions?"

"If we knew that it would be clearer how we should act."

Marheh stopped to ease her ankle which was telling her to slow down.

"I think it is just a side effect. I don't think they would even believe in it. Nemle said they don't believe in the soul."

She started off again, leaning a little more heavily on Kel's supporting arm.

"But if it's just a side effect, then how can our singing make a difference to what they do?"

They had reached the courtyard made by the two wings of the house and the pottery itself. There was a wooden bench against one wall of the house and Marheh lowered herself onto it.

"Let's not go in for a bit." She gazed at the pale sky and the field opposite. "It's nice here."

Kel sat down beside her, thinking mostly of breakfast. Marheh yawned and stretched and settled herself again.

"I don't know, but it does. Perhaps it makes them feel uncomfortable, very uncomfortable when they do something that adds to the darkness."

"You mean we are their conscience?"

Marheh shook her head.

"I don't know what I mean," she said, frustrated.

"Why don't we have something to eat? Then we can sing again and see if things become clearer."

"Yes," she said, giving him a look that reminded him of his earlier words. "That's the sensible thing."

Greya appeared before they had managed to make too much mess in her kitchen.

"Sef will be down in a minute. You could set the table if you want to help."

"I'll do it," Kel offered. "Let Marheh rest her ankle."

Greya smiled at him and opened the cutlery drawer. Marheh thought she looked weary.

"I'm sorry Mother. You must be getting tired of having to look after me, or humour me, or all the other things you do."

"It's been a worrying time for us all and you do what you have to."

She turned back to her porridge pot. The kitchen was silent. Marheh saw each of them as separate. She saw each outline, sharp and clear, and she saw the space between them. It seemed almost tangible, keeping them apart.

"What's wrong Mother?" she asked, when the silence had gone on too long.

"There's nothing wrong," Greya said.

"Oh yes there is." Sef had come into the kitchen in time to hear the last comment. "You went into the spare room to see if it needed tidying and came out a different person."

"Don't be silly," Greya said sharply. "There's nothing wrong."

"I think I know what it is," Marheh said, remembering the control she had left in the drawer.

"There's nothing wrong," Greya said again.

"Did you open the drawer?"

"There was nothing in it."

"You wouldn't have been able to see it."

"I don't know what you're talking about."

Marheh limped across to Greya and put her arms around her.

"I'm really sorry Mother. I put a Yareblis control in the drawer yesterday because it was too hard to come back to the fire. I need to find it because I think it is influencing you."

"Controlling me?"

"No, I don't think it could, but it's poisonous." She turned to Sef. "I need to go up and look in the drawer, that's the place to start. I don't see how it could actually move itself."

"Why don't I bring the bedside table down here?" Sef said. "Then you won't have to manage the stairs and you'll be near the fire to destroy it."

Marheh shook her head.

"I don't know what it can do, on its own like that. I need to contain it."

She refused their offers of help on the stairs and limped slowly upwards trying to prepare her mind to refocus. How could she have forgotten something so poisonous? She sat on the bed, gathering herself, then when she felt ready she opened the drawer just a crack. The thing had changed. Instead of the neat, contained, box-like object she had removed from her mind there was something more like a loose grainy sponge, black and greenish grey. A scarcely visible, greenish vapour seeped from it. She shut the drawer again to give herself time to consider how to transfer what she saw into her own mind and contain it. Perhaps this was the time to make an illusion. Not a brazier, she didn't think she was skilled enough to destroy it with an illusion, but she could build something to contain it so it could be safely removed.

It was more difficult than she expected and required all her concentration, but in the end she managed to enclose it, building it into a wooden box that would burn with it.

Carefully, painfully she made her way back to the kitchen and disposed of it.

"That should be better," she said, staggering a little as she turned to the others who were watching anxiously.

Sef helped her to the table. Someone embellished her porridge with cream and honey and slid the bowl in front of her, all she had to do was pick up the spoon. The others left her in peace, busy with their own food, while she made the effort to re-orient herself and eat.

It was what she needed and by the time the bowl was empty she was able to join the conversation as well as start on a piece of toast.

Nothing important was discussed over breakfast, but Greya's dark mood lifted slowly and Marheh felt she had succeeded in destroying the control. She wanted to think about what it had become too. Would it change like that in someone's mind, leaking its slow poison? The ones she had removed from people in the past had been more contained, so perhaps not, but perhaps there were others left to fester in the landscape. The singing would act against those wouldn't it? She gave a little sigh of frustration. She wasn't an apprentice any longer. Why was there still so much she didn't know?

She and Kel didn't linger once breakfast was over but promised to return at lunchtime and explain their plans once another working session had helped clarify their thinking. Marheh had the feeling Greya wanted to doctor her knees again and re-bandage her ankle but she gave her no opportunity to say so. A hug and a thank you for the breakfast and she was away, limping down the path while Kel was still apologising for her.

"I think I can climb over onto *Day Bringer* now," she said when he caught up with her. "I need to be there to sing again."

He could see she was determined so he didn't attempt to argue, just lent her his arm for the last steep section of path.

Getting across from bow to bow was awkward in the dim light, and painful too, but *Day Bringer* was more than just home, *Day Bringer* was her refuge, her shell and even the cold and the damp atmosphere in the tunnel did not stop the lift of spirits she felt.

They had agreed to spend half an hour getting themselves and their boats sorted. After that they would sing. Marheh was looking forward to it, eager to try again to pierce the darkness. It was a new challenge. She lit her lamp and turned it low. With no dishes and no fire to attend to all she had to do was wash her face and clean her teeth. Half an hour was more time than she needed. She didn't even have a bed to make. She settled herself in the armchair with her cloak around her and picked up her journal, but she couldn't concentrate to write. Her mind was too preoccupied with thoughts of the singing.

She put her feet up and closed her eyes. It wouldn't matter if she began as long as she waited for Kel to join her before going adventuring. Perhaps Nemle's song would be there this time too.

She had to work quite hard to get past her portal and at first she seemed to be singing alone. There was a hint of melancholy in the melody she made, but gentle melancholy, silver weaving instead of gold. She allowed the thread of melody to dance where it would and found that there were other, distant songs making their own melodies from afar. There was no song to harmonise with hers, not at first, and darkness pressed from most directions. Then a new song entered, two new songs that seemed to belong together, and the mood changed, her silver reflected their ochres and umbers and seemed to brighten. Finally there was a third song that belonged with hers, complementing it in a way she recognised.

For a little time she acknowledged them all, weaving her melody through and around, then she knew it was time to challenge the dark. As she changed key she felt the other songs modulate beneath her, making a pad of harmony that supported her. It was light she was singing now, brighter and brighter, clear and sharp. Then she was cutting with it, the thick darkness falling away on either side. There was a place she must reach, a place that contained the source of the darkness, but the harmonies beneath her were fading now and she faltered and fell back. The light faded and the gentle melancholy melody she began with returned to ease her back to herself.

She slept then as she usually did, but not for long. When Kel climbed across to *Day Bringer* and called her name she was already stirring and eager to discuss what they had experienced.

"It was Gul and Sybi wasn't it... the other two?" she said. "It's only afterwards that you can name the singers, but I recognised the song."

Kel nodded. "They helped you too, didn't they? You seemed to go so far I thought for a moment you were lost."

"There was a place in the centre, I could tell there was something, somewhere that I needed to take the light, but I wasn't brave enough this time."

"What do you want to do?" Kel asked, willing to defer to her in this.

"I want us to take the boats and move up and down this section, a different mooring each day, and sing in every place... and I want to let Gul and Sybi know how they are helping and what we are trying to do."

"What about your family?"

"They'll probably be safer if we are not here. If we begin to make a difference then it's likely the Yareblis will look for us."

"You've already made a difference in the darkness we experienced today, but can you keep doing it?"

"I have to try."

Once their decision was made, it was time to go up to the house to let them know what they planned. Greya was concerned that they would be vulnerable if they left the pottery and more vulnerable if they needed to leave their boats for any reason, like purchasing supplies. She insisted on loading them with food from her pantry as well as feeding them lunch.

They would need to bring the boats back to the mooring before setting off so Marheh promised she would come and say goodbye. Kel would need to go through the tunnel and turn around at the next turning place, so he would be a good hour behind her anyway.

A little bit of juggling was needed before the boats were out of the tunnel and this time *Day Bringer* slid in beside the mooring with *Storm Cloud* on the outside. Marheh's ankle was protesting at all this activity so she was not sorry when Kel offered to walk up to the house to say his goodbyes and suggest the family came to her. He had suggested, too, that she wait for him at the top of the locks so he could work her through, and although she was reluctant to accept, she knew it would be sensible. Their aim was to moor for the night below the locks and they were already well into the afternoon.

The whole family trooped down to see them off. Fali had just arrived home having collected the two boys from school. There were hugs all round and Kel set off through the tunnel. Marheh lingered a little, taking the boys onto *Day Bringer* for a quick look and spending a few minutes reassuring Greya, before she too was away.

At *Day Bringer*'s tiller she felt whole again. She perched on the rail that went around the back deck and let herself expand into her proper shape. Past mistakes and future problems could be put aside for a time. Before long she found she was singing under her breath then, as there was no one to hear her, she let the song emerge full voice.

She didn't hurry, knowing she would have to wait at the locks for Kel, so it was more than two hours before she arrived. There were perhaps another couple of hours of daylight, which should be enough to see them down, if Kel wasn't too long. She nudged *Day Bringer* up against the bank and wondered about mooring but there was no wind and she was going to leave the engine running. She would go down and attend to her fire while she waited, and then she'd see. If Kel still hadn't arrived and her ankle felt reasonable, she might just start down herself.

It was good to spend time over the fire, cleaning out the cold ash, putting in a mixture of sticks and coal and lingering to watch as it caught and began to spread warmth into the saloon.

When the fire was going well she filled the kettle and put it on the edge of the stove. Then she went out to the well deck to see if Kel was in sight. Looking out over the wide landscape she felt a little shiver of apprehension remembering how she had been attacked as she came up the flight. The actions she and Kel were planning would probably draw them to her again, perhaps in greater numbers than before, but perhaps not. The singing might not diminish the Yareblis, but surely it would free the followers.

There was still no sign of Kel so she thought she might as well prepare the lock at least. She went back through the boat to grab her windlass from the engine room then out to the back deck. The thought that she might be afraid to step off was enough to make her pick up the centre line. *Day Bringer* had scarcely moved and she had no difficulty in reaching the bank even though she was favouring her injured ankle.

She carried the line with her as she went to open the paddles though she knew *Day Bringer* would do no more than move forward into the lock mouth as the water began to fill the lock.

Where was Kel? Surely he had had time to reach her by now. What if they'd targeted him already and he hadn't been able to defend himself?

She took a deep breath knowing her worries were foolish. Kel was on *Storm Cloud*. He was boating. This was when he was least vulnerable.

The lock filled. She saw that the water had equalised and leaned on the lock beam to open the gate. Pulling *Day Bringer* into the lock put significant strain on her ankle and she realised it would be a mistake to continue. As she was dropping the paddles she looked up and saw *Storm Cloud* in the distance. She had not realised how tense she had been until she felt the relief wash over her. She closed the lock gate behind *Day Bringer* and stepped on board. Kel would do the rest.

It was another ten minutes before he reached her and the lock had lost several inches through the leaky bottom gate. She looked up at him.

"No trouble?"

"No trouble."

He opened the paddles on the bottom gate and waved his windlass at her before disappearing in the direction of the next lock. She knew he would be running down to open the paddles before coming back to release her from the lock.

With Kel working the locks the whole operation went very efficiently and *Day Bringer* was tied up below the bottom lock after only about fifteen minutes. Marheh watched him start back up the hill to bring *Storm Cloud* down. She couldn't help him, not really. Even if he had let her steer *Storm Cloud* she would still have to climb the hill and he would be half way down by the time she reached him. Preparing the bottom lock wasn't beyond her though. She picked up her windlass and pushed it into her belt. She would go now and watch for him. Walking on the flat was not too bad, but the short, steep hill up to the lock had to be taken slowly and carefully.

She reached it at last and perched herself on the lock beam, glad to be able to ease her ankle. At least she had been able to get her boot on over Greya's strapping and that gave her reasonable support. She still felt a nagging sense of worry and was holding herself focused with Kel at the forefront of her mind.

Storm Cloud had just appeared, poised in the lock above, when she felt it. Kel was battling with something. His mind was struggling to defend itself against incursion. He was fighting with strength and skill, but he had been taken by surprise and had more than one mind trying to break him.

She flung her mind into the melee, felt Kel's pain, felt them turn on her. She knew she screamed, a fierce, wild cry of rage, anguish and determination. Kel was hers, they would not have him. She bared her teeth and snarled, a lioness, all gleaming gold, claws and teeth and supple strength. The attackers fled and she pounced, gripping the last, gripping and shaking, gripping and biting. Then Kel was beside her, calling her back to herself, his mind bruised and battered but not broken.

Her mind held something the lioness had taken. She offered it to Kel to destroy. That other mind would never know that it had once been Yareblis.

Dazed and a little frightened of what she had found in herself, she realised she was still sitting on the lock beam. Above her Kel had raised the paddles to release the water. She could see it gushing from the lock mouth. Unsteadily she clasped her windlass, fitted it to the mechanism and wound the paddles beside her, glad the task was so familiar.

A limping and exhausted progress brought *Storm Cloud* down to tie up at last just ahead of *Day Bringer*. There were no words exchanged yet, though Marheh knew there would have to be. She was so tired she could barely hold herself upright and she thought Kel felt the same. They would be safe on the boats though and she could sleep if Kel would stop looking so oddly at her.

She waited until he had finished tending to his boat then went to stand beside him. He swung around and seized her upper arms. If he had not been so tired she thought he might have shaken her.

"What on earth?"

The words were ground out.

"I don't know Kel. I think it might have been an illusion. Please Kel… I don't know."

She held herself together, just, because she was not going to cry, or fall over or do anything that might be construed as feminine wiles, anything that Kathleen might do.

He continued to hold her, looking down at her upturned face. He was grey with fatigue, and she thought she was probably the same. At last he drew her into a fierce hug for a few moments then thrust her away from him.

"Go and get some sleep. We'll talk later."

It was nearly midnight by the time they had slept, eaten and cleaned up. They had not spoken much. The silence was not uncomfortable, but Marheh was very conscious that Kel wanted an accounting. *Day Bringer* was very peaceful in the quiet evening. The curtains were drawn in the saloon and the lamp glowed softly. The fire was low. Marheh touched Kel's hand.

"If you sit in the armchair I'll take the footstool and try to explain."

He invited her onto his lap but she shook her head. She wanted to be there so much it was like a pain, but she needed to be disciplined. She could still hear herself snarling "he's mine" and was ashamed of that assumption of possession.

She settled herself on the footstool and leaned back against the chair. It was easier not to look at him while she told him of the eagle and the fire, of how she had tried to make an illusion of warmth and of how this new illusion had come without her conscious calling.

Only when she had finished her telling did she twist around to look at him.

"I'm glad to have told you. I couldn't talk about it to anyone else. I wish I know... I wish I knew how it happens. It makes me afraid because it comes without my calling it."

He reached down to touch her.

"It made me afraid too, at first, but you can't deny it was useful."

She gave a little grimace.

"And I think we've established that we are disturbing them with our singing," he added.

Her face brightened and she nodded.

"And we can sing again in the morning."

They couldn't hurry, not if they were to exhaust themselves singing with this new purpose each time they moored. It was the regular, steady pattern of Silberay life, a couple of hours of boating, time for work and time for the disciplines. Marheh could feel herself growing stronger and calmer and was grateful.

They had not been attacked again, but they both felt that another attack would come, because their singing was penetrating the darkness further and further now. Marheh continued to wonder just how they were affecting the Yareblis, but she was confident they were. Sometimes she thought she recognised Gul and Sybi's songs beneath hers and Kel's and on these occasions the brightness she carried seemed to penetrate further, but she had not yet reached the centre, the source of the darkness, although sometimes it seemed very close. Of course if the Yareblis were continuing their work then the dark would be renewed, just as they were renewing the light.

Although she had taken only two days to travel between Willow Rise and Deerford, this journey was slower, and it was not until the evening of their sixth day of boating that they reached the mooring for Willow Rise. Gul and Sybi's songs were very strong that evening and there was a new joyfulness that lit Marheh and intensified the brightness she carried.

Next morning over breakfast she suggested to Kel that she walk up to the village to visit them.

"I want to tell them what we are trying and thank them for their song," she said.

"I wish you had thought to go yesterday, before we sang. The song would have shown them where we are."

They were eating on *Storm Cloud* this morning and Kel got up to cut another slice from one of the loaves Greya had given them. It was rather stale now, but fine for toast.

"Do you think so?" Marheh gazed out the window beside her and chewed her own toast reflectively. "I mean, yes I suppose so, but do you think it matters? Surely it will be our minds that are at risk and that could happen wherever we are if we leave the boats."

"They might try and separate us from the boats."

Marheh nodded. "Yes. I don't think we should both go."

"Then I will," Kel said.

Marheh picked up her mug and took a sip.

"I knew you'd say that," she said. "But I think I should be the one to go. You're physically stronger than I am, you can look after the boats better and still have their protection. I can manage better than you if they try mind stuff."

"No Marheh…" he began, but she stopped him.

"You know it's true Kel."

"I suppose so," he said reluctantly. "But I'll worry about you all the time you're away."

"I'll be careful, I promise."

She was a bit surprised he had agreed so readily, but it did make sense and he was sensible – unlike her! She smiled a little, remembering how he had told her that that was a strength.

It was a nice morning for a walk and now her ankle scarcely bothered her at all. She had considered taking her pack and going to the shop as well as visiting Gul and Sybi, but in the end agreed with Kel that shopping would draw attention to them. She walked briskly, conscious that she was vulnerable out in the open, but the village was quite close and she had no real expectation of trouble.

It didn't take her long to reach the road and turn towards the village. She had only travelled a hundred yards or so when a car passed her. It was not going fast and she thought nothing of it. Even when it stopped a little distance ahead of her she was unconcerned and kept walking steadily on.

She had come within ten yards of the car when the doors opened and three men got out. One of them she recognised. It was Mr Jay. Well, J really, since he was Yareblis. They stood by the car, not attempting to enter her mind, just watching her. She stopped walking and stood poised. A noise behind her made her glance over her shoulder to find that a second car had drawn up behind her. D got out and then Owen Mitchell, Inmi's husband. Still no one had attempted to enter her mind and she wondered whether they might even be a little afraid. Then a third person emerged from Owen's car. It was Mr KC and pulled after him was Rebah.

At that moment everything changed.

There was a long silence. Marheh was determined not to speak first but she knew her danger. With Rebah as hostage they had the upper hand. They knew she would not save herself at Rebah's expense.

"Get in the car," KC said at last.

Marheh looked at the expressionless faces around her. As she hesitated Rebah gave a little wail, held out her arms to her then fell silent. Marheh knew she was being controlled and knew too that the child would be damaged if she did not comply with his request. She looked for a long moment at the quiet countryside around her then walked towards the car.

No one spoke during the drive to Lowcroft Heights. Marheh's mind was racing. She did not expect to emerge from this as herself, if she managed to emerge at all, but she would do her best to save Rebah. Even D did not seem to have recognised her as Kathleen Mackenzie and that gave her hope that Kel might not be targeted.

The thought of how she had managed the controls D had placed in

Kathleen gave her an idea for a bargaining chip, though she could hardly bear to contemplate what it might do to her. She tried to use the silence to sing and build courage, but she had time to do no more than rest in her portal for a moment or two before the two cars drew up at the gates to Lowcroft Heights.

Rebah had spent the journey in the front seat, squeezed between her father and D. Occasionally she whimpered a little and each time KC looked at Marheh as if to remind her where the power lay. Marheh wondered how Owen could allow his daughter to be used like this but knew he too was being controlled.

KC's servant from the house at Higham's Hill emerged to open the gates and the two cars drove slowly round to the edge of the space enclosed by the five houses already under construction. They drew up beside a big bulldozer. The houses had changed and grown since she was last here and seemed a formidable barrier around the unfinished courtyard.

The others got out of the car and KC came around to open the door for her with mock courtesy. She got out quietly, trying to show nothing of the turmoil within. Why had they brought her here? What did he want with her?

As she moved ahead of him into the space she saw that there were more figures sitting blank and still on the steps of the houses. Imni was there and with a little shock she recognised Nella and Wilda. Not Mek though, where was Mek? Each house had one or two people staring inwards and, as she watched, KC's satellites spread out to stand one at each place. D left Rebah in the centre of the courtyard and returned to KC's side.

Marheh remained still and silent. Whatever they had brought her here for it would not be good, but she would not give them the satisfaction of seeing she was afraid. Rebah turned in a circle, stiff and jerky like a little doll and stopped facing Marheh, her face blank and unrecognising. Then Marheh saw her face twist and grimace and she cried out. Imni jerked forward and slumped back. Marheh held herself tightly so she could speak calmly and deliberately and turned to KC.

"What do you want of me?"

It was the first time she had spoken and she understood he had been waiting for that.

"I want recompense for the trouble you have caused me," he said. "I will show the Silberay we are not to be trifled with."

Marheh smiled gently. "Is that how you think of yourselves, as trifles?"

Rebah screamed and she wished she had held her tongue but it pushed her to a decision.

"You don't need a hostage for that," she said and stopped, looking for courage. "If you will release the child and her mother I shan't defend myself against a control."

She saw him take in her words, saw a flicker of excitement in his eyes, saw his mouth open and his tongue pass once over his lower lip. She had no idea whether she could contain a control of his as she had done D's. Either way it would cost her dearly.

"Just the child," he said.

"The child and her mother."

"What makes you think you can bargain with me?"

"It is the only way your hostage will be any use to you. If she is not released to grow up her own way I will fly the eagle and run the lioness come what may, because her life will be no good to her if she is not free."

She had no idea whether she could do either of these things at will, and she wondered where the words had come from, but she saw they meant something to him.

"And if they are released you will accept a control."

"That is what I said."

"And once they are gone, will you remember what you said?"

"You have my word."

He studied her for a few moments and she looked back at him, her gaze calm and level.

He gestured to D and she brought Rebah and Imni to them. They stood passive and empty at first but then she saw their faces change. Imni reached for Rebah who cuddled in to her then turned her head to greet Marheh. She went to them, took a hand in each of hers and smiled. Quickly she checked to be sure they were really free of any control.

"Why don't you take Rebah to visit Nother Granny," she said, then turned to Rebah. "You'd like that wouldn't you?"

"You come too," Rebah said.

"When I can, not now." She turned to KC. "Have him take them to Lowcroft." She gestured to Owen. "When he reports back … then I will keep my word."

She believed that even under control Owen could not be forced to hurt his wife and child and this plan was all she could think of to get them far enough away. That it gave her more time was only an advantage if she could keep herself from thinking of what was to come.

She could see that KC and D were excited by the idea of controlling her and she knew the kind of humiliations D had enjoyed inflicting on Kathleen. She looked around the courtyard at the impassive on-lookers. If she managed to contain the control but convince them she was controlled could she perhaps help these others? Nella and Wilda didn't deserve this and Mek loved them. Probably the rest weren't bad people either and, bad or good, she was Silberay and they were her charge. She heard the sound of the car returning and flinched inwardly. Who did she think she was fooling? She doubted she could save herself. How could she help anyone else?

The car pulled up sharply. Owen got out, slammed the door and marched up with his report. He went to sit on the step where Imni had been and KC turned to Marheh.

"Now," he said.

She inclined her head and waited.

Bulldozer

Chapter Sixteen

Kel didn't know whether he was angry or worried. Where was Marheh? It wouldn't have taken her more than half an hour to get to Gul and Sybi. She had said she would sing with them. He had sung, but there had been no questing light though he thought he had detected Gul and Sybi's songs. Now she had been gone for close to two hours. She asked for trouble sometimes, went looking for it even, but surely she would have stuck to the plan they had made if she could. Unless she had deliberately misled him and gone off on some ploy of her own.

He would have to go looking for her he decided, even though she had not called him. At least he could see if she had visited Gul and Sybi.

He locked the boats and made his way up the hill to Willow Rise. The bus passed him just before he reached the church and he wondered suddenly whether Marheh had decided to go to Higham's Hill or Lowcroft because of something she had seen. It would be just like her.

A child and her mother got off the bus and were walking in his direction. The woman looked tired and worried. He was about to step off the path to let them past when he heard the child say "I wish Marheh would have come with us, don't you Mummy?"

He stepped in front of them so abruptly that the woman shrank back from him, but the little girl smiled and looked him up and down.

"Marheh has clothes like yours."

He crouched down, careful not to frighten her.

"I'm looking for Marheh," he said. "She's my friend."

"She's my friend too," Rebah said. "She gave me a present."

Kel looked up to Imni.

"I'm worried about her. Have you seen her?"

Imni nodded and seemed to be trying to say something. Kel noticed again how anxious she looked and how exhausted.

"I'm sorry," he said, trying to contain his own anxiety. "You look tired. Are you in trouble?"

"I don't know what to do," Imni said. "Something is wrong with my husband. Then I was at that place where he wants us to live. Marheh was there."

She rubbed her hand over her face.

"Rebah was hurting and I couldn't go to her no matter how hard I tried. Then Owen took us to Lowcroft and we got on the bus because Marheh said we'd be safe with Nother Granny, but then I remembered she has gone to stay with her sister and… and I can't seem to think straight. But Marheh was staying there."

"Will you let me take you to my friends?" Kel said.

How had Marheh got to Lowcroft Heights? What was happening there?

"They'll look after you and help me to find Marheh too."

He offered her his arm and, after a moment of hesitation, she took it. He wanted to break into a run but tempered his pace to hers. She must have been fighting the control all the time they had her child because he could see she was ready to drop. He was now so anxious for Marheh that it was difficult to think of anything else. Why hadn't she called him? What was she doing at Lowcroft Heights? Was she in trouble? Why hadn't she called him? The questions went round and round in his head as he walked but the answers wouldn't come.

Gul and Sybi welcomed Imni and Rebah in their usual hospitable way and Sybi led them away to the kitchen to be fed. Gul however stopped Kel from following.

"Marheh?" he asked.

"She was supposed to come here. She wanted to see you, to thank you for your support and to sing with you. From what the child said I think she's at Lowcroft Heights and…" He stopped, covered his face with his hands then looked at Gul. "I'm afraid for her but I can't see how to help her."

....

KC's initial approach to Marheh's mind was tentative, as if he was half expecting the eagle or the lioness, but when she remained acquiescent he pushed in his control with malicious pleasure. It was much more powerful than D's and Marheh struggled to contain it. The first shock of pain was almost more than she could bear, but she taught herself to endure and held herself ready to obey him.

It would be hard she knew, perhaps hard enough to break her, but he would only turn his attention away from her if he believed she was controlled.

Falling to her knees she crawled towards him as he backed into the centre of the courtyard. She stopped in front of him, her forehead on the ground then began to lick his boots. A tiny part of her wondered whether this was the extent of his imagination. Then she heard D giggle and was afraid all over again.

There was a moment when she heard KC consulting with D and another moment when the thought of Wilda strengthened her resolve then she stood up and began to take of her clothes.

What did it matter really? Clothes were only about the outside. Her boots, her trousers, her tunic, nothing mattered except containing the control, enduring that pain so it wouldn't overwhelm her. She removed the last of her garments and stood naked before them. Tears ran down her cheeks. It would not hurt so much if she stopped containing the control. Why was she bothering? What was the difference? There was a difference, there had to be. She kicked at her uniform, spat on it, trod it into the dust. Maybe it was easier because so much of her was occupied with the pain.

She found her belt and gave it to D. She dropped to her knees and began to crawl, D driving her with the belt. Crawl faster, crawl faster, crawl faster around and around the courtyard, past the silent onlookers, past Nella and Wilda with their blank eyes, crawl faster. And then she couldn't crawl, not faster, not at all. She sprawled in the dust, her breath coming in great panting sobs, her hands and knees bruised and bloody.

D struck her a few more times then KC came to where she lay and poked at her with his foot.

"More?" asked D.

"We might take a break for lunch."

KC's foot jabbed into her hip and encouraged her to roll onto her back. She had never felt so vulnerable.

"That will give you time to think up some more entertainment for our guest. Then when we're done with her we'll have Owen drive her to their headquarters. That will show them what we think of their star performer."

D sniggered and stepped over Marheh to take KC's proffered arm.

"Soft the lot of them," she said.

Marheh did not dare to turn her head but she heard their footsteps moving away, then more footsteps and the sound of car doors. Then an engine started up, grew louder for a moment, then faded into the distance. This would be her only chance if she could take it. He had left his control active. He expected her to be unable to move, but had he left anyone to guard her? If she got rid of his control she could probably deal with that.

She didn't know how she would destroy it but she removed the control and put it down outside herself, hoping it would not do too much damage before it could be dealt with. That pain gone, she was more aware of the pain of her body, but it was not more than she could bear, not debilitating, not really, she told herself.

Trying hard for focus, wanting to be prepared for the possibility of attack, she cautiously eased herself onto her side. When that did not provoke a response she struggled unsteadily to her feet.

The half dozen onlookers still stared blankly. She knew she had no strength yet to release them. Her clothes still lay crumpled and dirty where she had left them. She would feel more like herself if she were dressed. Then she would find a place to hide. Then she would sing. Kel would be so worried about her now.

.....

Gul looked anxiously at Kel.

"Does she ... communicate ... with you?"

"She can do, but only if her mind is free to focus. I need to talk to the woman. How did she get to Lowcroft Heights? What's happening there?"

Gul hurried along the corridor to the kitchen, Kel crowding behind him.

Imni's memory of the last six hours or so was confused, muddled by the Yareblis control. She remembered her husband getting her and Rebah up early to go for a drive. She had not really wanted to but he was insistent and he had been so strange lately that she thought it best to acquiesce. Rebah had been excited. She was having an adventure. But all that happened was that he drove to Lowcroft Heights. Other people had come there too and they had begun to look at the houses, but then things became confused. She knew Rebah had been taken from her and somehow she had been stopped from going to her. There had been struggle and pain when she tried.

Finally she had found herself with Rebah as if a nightmare had ended. Marheh had been there and a man and woman and Marheh had arranged for Owen to drive them to the bus stop at Lowcroft. Marheh had stayed behind. Imni raised worried eyes to Kel.

"She said we would be safe with Nother Granny, but why would she think we needed to be safe?"

"I think she would have known that you were being controlled by our enemies," Kel said. "She would have wanted to help you. She told me about meeting you and Rebah."

"But why would she stay?"

"I don't know, but I'm afraid I can guess."

He turned to Gul.

"You think so too, don't you?"

"It would be like what I know of her."

"What will be the quickest way to get there?"

"One or two of my parishioners have cars. I'll see what I can arrange but it might take a little time."

Kel groaned and put his head in his hands.

"They could have destroyed her already."

"Perhaps if you and Sybi sing while I'm finding someone to take us there. That might be her most immediate aid."

. . . .

Just walking about was hard, but at least her feet didn't hurt. Marheh was trying to be positive as she gathered her scattered clothes and put them on. She didn't know how long she would have before the Yareblis returned and the temptation was to hurry, but she made herself be deliberate and methodical and think. Where should she hide? How much would the silent watchers be able to tell if they were interrogated? If they thought she was nearby, would they use another hostage to force her to emerge? If she sent her mind to Kel, would he be able to help her or would they destroy him too?

Carefully she made her way across the courtyard towards the house opposite the bulldozer and Owen's car. There was enough space between each house for her to walk out of the courtyard to where she would not be seen by the watchers. She was struggling to think clearly and find any kind of focus, but she tried to send a picture of where she was to Kel. She knew he would be alert for her. From where she was she could see the gate. It was closed but not locked, she discovered, walking across to check. She opened it a little and looked up at the slope of trees above the road. Could she perhaps hide up there? Anyway she would leave the gate open so they might think she had gone that way. But if she left, there were still Nella and Wilda as well as Owen Mitchell and the other three she did not know. Left here, they would remain tools of the Yareblis.

She made her way around the houses looking for a place to hide. Out of the past she heard Nemle say "Your best defence is the discipline of the soul", but not if they could see her to act on her physical self.

The bulldozer and Owen's car still stood in the space, completing the circle around the courtyard. It was a shame she couldn't drive a car. That would get her far enough away. Owen could though. Perhaps it would be possible for her to control him and have him drive her to Willow Rise, to Kel and Gul and Sybi. She would be safe there. But the others wouldn't be. Hide first, then think, she told herself, anxious at the time she was wasting.

She looked at the bulldozer. Perhaps she could wriggle underneath it, between the caterpillar treads. It would be a better hiding place than inside one of the houses. It was dark and enclosed, unless someone started it up. Decide, do something. Her mind seemed to her to be slipping out of her control. Do something. She moved quickly behind the machine and crouched down, crawled on her stomach until she had tucked herself in behind the big scoop.

She found that with a little adjustment she could peer out through the crack between the treads and the scoop and see all six of the Yareblis dupes. They needed to be released but she doubted her ability to hold any more controls, her mind was still so scarred from containing KC's. Perhaps she could get them away though. If she controlled Owen could she have him put them in the car and drive away? It was worth a try, and then she would sing.

She could see Owen, in profile, unmoving, sitting on the middle step of the three that rose to the porch of the house behind him. His house, she supposed. Summoning all her concentration she made herself focus. She felt as if she was wrenching her poor, abused mind to attention. Holding it to her will was a huge effort.

As she entered Owen's mind she realised that she would have to remove the Yareblis control if she was to place one of her own, or he could be torn apart by the conflicting demands. Her own mind was nearly at the end of its strength and removing and replacing the control cost almost everything she had left, but she saw him get up and go up to Wilda and Nella. He seized an arm of each and marched them towards her hiding place. She heard the car doors open and close and saw him go back for two of the others. There was no finesse. Rough and ready was all she could manage.

Back he went for the last one. The car doors slammed shut and she heard the engine start. She managed to listen until the sound of the car had dwindled into nothing then she almost fell through her portal and into the soul song.

It was dark where she entered and, if she had thought at all, she might have expected her song to falter as her strength had, but instead it was strong, soaring and luminous, so that she burst through darkness to the other side where she found herself singing with other souls whose song danced with hers.

She was deep in the soul song when the Yareblis returned so she did not know of their anger at finding her gone with all their hostages. She did not feel KC trying to activate his control of her and finding it where she had left it, and she did not see how uncomfortable all of them felt in this place, now filled with her soul song. D barely left the car. J could only manage a cursory glance around and even KC could not bring himself to make any real attempt to search for her.

They left quickly, angrily and had only just reached Lowcroft when a small, elderly Morris passed them and took the turn off for Lowcroft Heights.

Gul's parishioner, Ard, was earnest and kindly and very careful of his car, so that Kel, squashed into the back seat, could hardly keep himself from controlling the foot that managed the accelerator. Gul, in front beside the driver, sat quietly, his eyes closed. Kel thought he was practising his own version of the soul song. Perhaps he should be doing that too but his anxiety was too great. He had received a confused, faltering communication from her that had been so unlike Marheh's usual sending that he was filled with dread.

The gates stood open when they reached Lowcroft Heights and they drove in very slowly, Ard making anxious little clucking sounds as he negotiated the rough terrain. He pulled up beside the bulldozer and Kel sprang out. He dashed into the centre of the courtyard and stood staring around. Where was she? She must be here.

Gul came more slowly to stand beside him.

"She showed you she was here?"

Kel nodded.

"But her sending was confused. Not like her, not precise, but definitely here."

"Then perhaps we had better start looking."

He eyed the unfinished houses with interest.

"They do have delusions of grandeur, don't they? I can see why you were disturbed by the place, but it doesn't feel malevolent."

Kel's anxious scanning paused while he considered.

"It doesn't now," he said with some surprise. "I wonder what she did."

He tried to call her with both voice and mind but there was no response.

"Are you sure she's here?" Gul asked again.

"Yes, she's here. I know she's here. I don't understand why she doesn't respond."

"Would she hear you if she was singing?"

"She should do unless…"

"Unless?"

"Unless her mind is damaged."

He could hardly bring himself to contemplate the possibility. Gul touched his arm.

"Why don't you look for her body while I sing for her soul."

"Her body!" Kel turned on him.

"I don't mean she's dead," Gul said hastily. "Look for her physical self. You're better suited than I to scrambling about a building site."

Kel headed for the first of the houses while Gul went back to the car to explain to Ard and sit quietly with his song.

When Kel returned to the car nearly an hour later it seemed as if the two elderly gentlemen in the front seats were sleeping, but as he approached the open window beside Gul he realised that he had been singing.

"I can't find her."

"She is here. It was her song I joined I'm sure. There was so much light."

He did not sound at all troubled and Kel wanted to reach in and shake him.

"I can't find her. What if her mind is damaged?"

Gul smiled at him. "Her soul isn't."

"I can't find her," Kel said again, pushing at the little car so that it rocked and the other elderly gentleman stirred and muttered.

"I'm sorry Gul." He passed his hand over his face. "I can't think where to look next. I've hunted through all the houses. I've even been under the floor."

Gul took in his dirty face and the cobwebs in his hair.

"Can you think like her?" he asked sympathetically. "If she had to hide what sort of place would she look for?"

Kel turned to study the landscape around him. Not the houses, he'd looked thoroughly, but they were the obvious place. She wouldn't be obvious. He stepped back from Gul and found himself leaning against the bulldozer. The cabin, he wondered, pulling himself up onto the step to peer inside. Where then? He walked around it, crouched down to peer underneath. It was dark and at first the mound at the furthest end seemed just part of the dirt, but as his eyes adjusted Marheh's huddled form became clear.

He called her softly first, then sent his mind to her, but with no response. A great surge of grief washed over him. Frantically he flattened himself under the machine and crawled towards her. He could hardly bring himself to touch her so afraid was he of what he might find. She made no response when he took her wrist, but he could feel her resting pulse, steady and even and he let out the breath he did not realise he had been holding. What mattered now was to get her out of here.

There was no room to lift her and dragging her would hurt her. He tried once more to call her back from wherever she was, then called to Gul. He explained the difficulty then heard Gul's voice explaining to his friend. Doors opened and closed and a bulky shadow blocked the light.

"Would a tarpaulin help? Could you roll her onto that and pull her out?"

It was Ard offering the covering he put over his car. Kel wriggled back until he could grab it.

It was not easy in the confined space but eventually he managed, spreading the tarpaulin out beside her and rolling her carefully onto it. Then, wriggling backwards, he could pull her slowly out into the light. Only then did they see the stained and crumpled clothes, the raw and bleeding palms and the tears and dirt on her face.

Kel crouched over her, about to try and lift her, but Ard stopped him.

"Lift her on the tarpaulin," he said. "It will be safer. Gul and I will take this end."

Between them they got her onto the back seat. Kel slid in beneath her, lifting her head onto his lap. Then Gul and Ard took their places and they were away.

As they reached Lowcroft, Ard stopped and looked back to Kel.

"Where to" he asked. "Do we need a hospital?"

Kel shook his head slowly.

"I don't quite know what is wrong but it might be that she is lost in the soul song. I've heard that it can happen, but it needs more wisdom than I have. I'd really like to contact the Harbour. Perhaps I could telephone."

"Willow Rise then," Gul said. "You can telephone from the vicarage."

Outside the vicarage was the puzzle of a parked car filled with people passively sitting as if waiting for something, but Kel's thoughts were only for Marheh. Gul led him inside to the telephone and went to tell Sybi what was happening. She was supervising Rebah with a biscuit cutter, making duck and rabbit shaped biscuits, while Imni slept in the spare room. Kel was quick to join them.

"There was a message," he said. "Jik is already on his way with Nemle. We're to take her to *Day Bringer* and keep singing with her. They're coming by car and will be here in a couple of hours."

Gul smiled at him and Sybi came to give him a quick hug.

"That's good news. Off you go then. I'm guessing you won't want to wait for a cup of tea."

The car could not get very close to the mooring but Gul and Ard helped Kel to ease Marheh out and into his arms, then held her for him, when he realised that he was the only one who could open *Day Bringer*. He hoped very much that later he might be able to make her laugh at the picture of the two elderly gentlemen anxiously managing her inert form between them.

It did not take him long to open *Day Bringer*'s back doors and slide back the roof hatch. Gul and Ard came with him as he carried Marheh to the water's edge. Gul, it seemed, could catch a glimpse of the boats. Kel heard him explaining to Ard what would happen. Getting down the steps into the cabin was a bit of a struggle but he managed it safely and rolled Marheh carefully onto her bunk. Then he went back for a quick word of thanks to Gul and Ard and his promise to keep them informed.

Afternoon sunshine filled the back cabin. Once he had made sure Marheh was lying straight he settled himself on the floor beside her, leaning against her bunk, one arm resting alongside hers, touching her lightly. If she was lost perhaps his touch might help his song to find her.

He was tired and anxious and at first he struggled to enter the soul song but he managed in the end. There was light and melody. Songs echoed joyously as if they were newly liberated from struggle, but they were not familiar tunes, and though they seemed happy to welcome him he could not find his place amongst them. Then, from further off, he found a harmony he could join and support. He could be steady and strong, a foundation for other reaching notes. He gave himself to the work.

As the song progressed, he felt his harmony linked with two other songs in particular and knew that all three were seeking, calling for another song that would dance with them, completing the harmony that would be uniquely theirs. For a time it seemed they would fail, but at last, from far away, there came a thread of melody that fitted. So faint and distant was it that it seemed as if it would never reach them, but suddenly, in a burst of joyful light, it took its place. The song soared in celebration for a timeless moment before the singers eased back into themselves.

When Marheh opened her eyes it was to find herself home on *Day Bringer*, not only safe but also surrounded by the three who loved her most. Jik and Kel were beside her on the floor and someone had brought in the footstool for Nemle. She too was opening her eyes and a loving glance passed between them, but they did not speak, still held in the music of the song.

Then the two men began to stir and the quiet eased into words of greeting and gratitude. Marheh found the thought needed for speech was painful and she winced involuntarily when Jik took her hand. Her whole body ached, but these three friends had brought her such a sense of well being that she could put the pain and weakness aside for the moment. She was grateful though when Nemle, who had been watching her carefully, took charge of the assembled company.

"Jik," she said. "I believe there is work waiting for you in the village. Kel will explain where to go I'm sure."

Jik got up, groaning a little and making a mock of his stiffness.

"I must be getting old." He touched Marheh's cheek. "I'm off to clear up after you niece, but I'll be back to hear all about it."

He and Kel left together. Kel was only away for a couple of minutes but by the time he returned Nemle had moved to Marheh's side, looked into the pain in her eyes and was examining the palm of the hand closest to her.

"Will you get me some hot water Kel?" she asked. "I'll need a cloth and a towel too. Then perhaps you might start to think about food."

Being patched up was never pleasant, but there were compensations. Nemle's gentle care brought with it the knowledge of being loved that was in itself part of her healing. Kel too, coming in to help Nemle undress her, gave her tenderness and strength. She couldn't seem to get any bits of herself to work, but Nemle was reassuring.

"Sleep, time," she said, feeding her mouthfuls of warm vegetable soup. "Don't worry, that won't help. It will all come back."

The soup finished, Nemle helped her to turn onto her side, kissed her and tucked her in as if she was still her young apprentice.

"Mama Nemle," she mumbled, already drowning in sleep.

"I won't leave you," she heard Nemle respond as she let herself go.

. . . .

So it was not until the next morning that explanations were permitted.

Nemle had refused the offer of Kel's bunk saying that she didn't need much sleep and would be perfectly happy in the armchair. Neither of the men was of a size to make sleeping in an armchair comfortable. Jik had suggested they toss for the bunk, but Kel's notions of hospitality would not allow that. He spent a broken night, mostly in the armchair, but sometimes stretched out on *Storm Cloud*'s floor. However none of these inconveniences seemed to matter given the knowledge of Marheh's safety and the sense that somehow changes had occurred, positive changes, bringing new light.

Marheh's night of sleep had gone a long way towards healing her mind, which enabled her to cope with the aches and pains of her body. She woke feeling refreshed and wanting to hear about Nemle and Jik's opportune arrival, about Rebah and Imni, and whether Owen Mitchell had delivered all the hostages.

Nemle helped her to wash, treated her hands and knees and massaged comfrey ointment into the bruises emerging from D's treatment of her.

"My hands aren't really strong enough for this now," she said, panting a little. "Perhaps you might let Kel take over tomorrow. Jik will probably want to go back to the Harbour in a day or so anyway."

Marheh just grunted a response. She was not quite sure she wanted to go where Kel's touch on her skin might take her.

The morning was well on by the time Nemle had helped her to dress in a clean uniform. Kel and Jik had spent the time preparing a splendid breakfast and waited to eat it with them. Only when the food was gone, having been awarded the attention it deserved, were explanations given and stories told.

"I knew you were suffering and in danger," Nemle said, when Marheh had given them a brief outline of what she had done. "That's why I made Jik bring me."

"Such a trouble you are niece," Jik teased. "I've left my duties twice in as many months."

She turned her head to smile at him. She had refused to take the armchair, insisting that it was Nemle's seat, so they had given her an extra pillow on the footstool where she sat half-turned to Nemle.

"And then you had to go and sort out the car load of hostages. I wasn't thinking very clearly by then, so I'm amazed they reached Willow Rise."

"It was Rebah and Imni coming to Willow Rise that made me realise where you were," Kel said. "They were just getting off the bus when I was coming to look for you. I didn't know whether to be angry or worried."

"What I don't understand," Marheh said slowly. "Is why my song was so bright when I felt so bad, and what happened, why I couldn't get back?"

These were questions for Nemle. Kel and even Jik wanted answers too, though Jik thought he might come close to part of it.

"What was it like when you were singing?" Nemle asked.

"There were a few moments of darkness, then an explosion of light," Marheh said slowly, reaching for the words. "It was as if the barrier of darkness had shattered and disappeared. Then there were songs, more songs than I could distinguish. They were kind but they were complete without me so they... deferred to me, let me go on singing but didn't join me. It was as if they sang around my song, not with it, so I had to keep singing to find the song that needed mine."

"Were you frightened?" Kel asked curiously. "It sounds, I don't know, lonely perhaps."

"Not frightened, not even lonely, I don't think, just not in the right place."

She looked to Nemle again.

"Why? I don't understand."

Nemle's gaze at her was full of a bright warmth that made her blush without quite knowing why.

"The brightness was because of the sacrifice."

"What sacrifice?" She really wanted to know.

"Of yourself," Jik said, showing he understood. "Exchanging yourself for Rebah and her mother could have meant your mind or even your life. You knew that and yet you still did it."

Nemle nodded. "But normally, even though we aren't aware of it, our mind is... is waiting for our return, influencing how we sing."

Marheh thought suddenly of how she and Kel had planned their singing.

"And my mind was not at its best by then." She grimaced. "So where was

I?"

"Safe in the soul song," Nemle said firmly. "Where we will all find our end and our new beginning, but your ending is not yet."

Sybi's kitchen table

Chapter Seventeen

Nemle was very aware that Marheh's mind had taken even more of a battering than her body. She would have liked to remain with her, caring for her, loving and sheltering her, but she knew the time for that was past and made no protest when Jik arranged for their journey back to the Harbour after only one more day. At least there was time to meet Gul and Sybi and experience their song. She sensed that Marheh was hesitant about entering and knew it was important for her healing, so she was grateful for the strong, grounded music they made as a foundation for the songs of the four Silberay.

She looked around the shabby, comfortable space that was the vicarage sitting room. Gul and Sybi had invited them all to stay and eat with them, but Sybi had refused her offer of help and Marheh's, and had gone to the kitchen with Kel as her assistant. Marheh and Jik were in earnest conversation with Gul, not excluding her, she didn't feel excluded, giving her time to savour the knowledge that she had been able to be of use to Marheh.

The work here was not finished, but it was not her work. The work here belonged to Marheh and Kel and she needed to remember that. Nevertheless, she was glad she had come and she knew Jik was too. Meeting Gul and Sybi was a pleasant change from the quiet life at the Harbour. Singing with them had given her new insight. It didn't matter how old you were when it came to new knowledge, something else to weave into the tapestry you were making of life's experiences. It was also good to know that Marheh had made friends. She was just at the beginning of what would be thirty years of solitary boating. It could be lonely, she knew from her own experience, and friends were important.

And Kel. She had been grateful for Kel in the past, for his supporting strength and his good sense, and now she was even more grateful. He and Marheh were bound together, soul friends, and he would anchor her beloved apprentice, her daughter, as she could no longer do.

Marheh looked across at her and smiled, stood up and walked, a little stiffly, to sit beside her.

"Tired Mama Nemle?" she asked.

She shook her head.

"Just thinking."

She reached out to touch Marheh. Her hands were twisted, misshapen with arthritis, but the fingers were gentle and loving. Marheh put her own strong hand over Nemle's and held it against her cheek for a moment.

"Thank you for coming."

"I feel very privileged to have been able to."

They remained together in silence for a while, resting in the closeness they had thought they may not have experienced again.

"Have you been making plans with Gul?" Nemle asked at last.

"Just exploring possibilities. Jik has been trying to impress on me that I still have some recovering to do, but we can't wait too long now that we have the initiative."

"I'm sure you'll be sensible," Nemle said firmly.

Marheh laughed.

"How much did it cost you to say that when you know I'm not always? Kel even said it was one of my strengths, not being sensible."

Nemle laughed too at that.

"You're a bad girl to be making fun of an old woman."

Kel appeared to call them all to the meal. Marheh helped Nemle out of her chair and, arm in arm, they led the way into the kitchen.

Like Greya, Sybi would not let them discuss Yareblis problems at the table and they were all able to appreciate the sense of her prohibition. The meal was not fancy but Nemle preferred simple and good tasting to fancy, and just having space to eat together in comfort was luxury.

She was about to say as much when Jik said it for her.

"I can remember a time when the four of us and Sul all squeezed onto *Storm Cloud* so we could eat together. This is such a privilege."

Sybi smiled at him.

"You've known each other for a long time then?"

Nemle nodded.

"Marheh was my apprentice. We were together for twenty years. She graduated and I retired only this year."

"Marheh is my niece," Jik added. "I first met her when she was two."

"Marheh is my friend." Kel smiled across at her. "We met twenty years ago."

Gul looked around at them all.

"So Marheh is the link."

"I'm the one that keeps getting into trouble," Marheh said. "I'm lucky to have such loving friends."

Stories of Marheh's past troubles entertained Gul and Sybi for the rest of the meal until Nemle realised that Marheh had been the centre of attention long enough and turned the conversation toward Gul and Sybi.

They had been fifteen years at Willow Rise. It would be Gul's last placement, a gentle one as befitted his age, or so they thought. Physically it was not demanding. The village was small and the number of parishioners not great, but there were always challenges. They had had time here to practise their song as they'd not been able to in their younger days in busier places. That had been rewarding and enriching and had helped to make them ready for the challenge of the last months.

It was both enlightening and humbling for the four Silberay to hear of what their music had been to them. Marheh looked from one to the other.

"I was a bit nervous about singing today," she confessed, getting a little nod of approval from Nemle. "And I was so grateful to find your song beneath me, holding me up."

"It has been a particular joy for us too," Gul said. "It seems there is no end to the possibilities or to the learning when we can sing together."

Sybi stood up then.

"Suppose we move back to the sitting room," she said. "I think Nemle might be glad of a more comfortable chair."

Jik and Kel insisted that they would do the dishes and Gul decided to remain in the kitchen with them to make sure things were put away in the right place.

"We shall withdraw like ladies," Nemle said, allowing Marheh to help her up.

When they were comfortably seated, close together, Nemle turned to Marheh.

"What is it you are not saying daughter? It will be better to speak of it. Sybi and I will listen."

There was twilight in the room now, and shadowy corners. Sybi had put a match to the fire too, but it had not yet had time to distribute its warmth and Marheh shivered a little.

"I can't keep from thinking," she said slowly, wondering whether she could bring herself to articulate what plagued her mind.

Perhaps if she had been younger Nemle might have insisted but Marheh knew she would not now. She looked from old friend to new friend and was aware of their loving attention. Nemle was right, it would be better to speak of it then perhaps the memory would not haunt her.

"I told you how I allowed him to place a control and how I contained it. Then I had to pretend to be controlled."

Nemle nodded.

"I told you how they ordered me to crawl around and around and how she hit me."

She broke off and covered her face with her hands then took them away again and looked at Nemle.

"I didn't want to tell you. He ordered me to take my clothes off first, to trample and spit on my uniform. I crawled around and around with nothing on until I couldn't crawl anymore. Then he made me roll onto my back."

She hugged herself and choked a little.

"I can't get rid of the way he looked at me."

She stared ahead of her, seeing only his gleeful satisfaction at her helplessness. When Nemle touched her she started then turned to bury her face in Nemle's lap, shaking with sobs.

Very gently Nemle rubbed her back, letting her feel her love. Having treated her grazes and bruises she had guessed something of what she had told them. She and Sybi exchanged looks but said nothing until Marheh sat up again and fumbled for her handkerchief.

"Sorry," she said when she could speak. "I didn't mean to do that. I was so terrified and ashamed and my mind hurt so much I hardly knew what I was doing, only that if I didn't do what he said he would have won."

"He didn't though, did he?" Nemle said quietly. "All the pain and humiliation that you accepted for Rebah and Wilda and the others became the brightness of love and sacrifice that was strong enough to banish the dark."

"I couldn't think what else to do."

Marheh sank back against the sofa where she sat with Nemle and closed her eyes. It had gone now, or almost, Nemle and Sybi had shared it and were helping her carry it.

The men came in soon after, ready to relax by the fire. There was no talk of work to be done, tomorrow would do for that. Instead there was easy discovery of each other. Ideas and experiences could be exchanged comfortably. Talk flowed as first one then another would highlight some event or issue that touched them all. Then, hearing that they were to leave in the morning, Sybi offered Jik and Nemle beds for the night. It made sense for them to accept, especially given the limited accommodation on the boats. So it was just Marheh and Kel who walked through the quiet evening down to *Day Bringer* and *Storm Cloud* waiting patiently at their moorings.

A warm hug and an offer of help gratefully declined and Marheh was alone on *Day Bringer*. There was enough moonlight so she had no need of her candle. She made her way slowly through to the saloon. The engine gleamed softly as she passed it and she reached out to run light fingers over its polished surface. She needed her friends and loved them and was grateful for their help, but *Day Bringer* was her home, her shell, and she could crawl into it for rest and solace.

Once in the saloon she lit the lamp and awakened the fire that had been carefully banked before they left for the vicarage. She was tired but a bit restless and not quite ready for sleep. Normally in this mood she would take up some clay, just to play with it and let it shape itself around her thoughts but her hands were not yet healed enough for that. What then? She didn't want food or sperit. Should she write in her journal? She settled herself in the armchair and picked it up but let it lie, unopened on her lap. Sing then, just to reclaim the joy of it, not for effort and pushing back darkness. She closed her eyes.

She was never really alone, she thought later as she made her way slowly to bed. Somewhere there was always someone singing, as well as those distant voices whose song was never-ending. Nemle would join them soon, she knew, and one day she would too, but tonight Nemle's had been the song that rejoiced with hers, rejoiced in the light that held them, rejoiced in the close and loving harmony. "My soul will sing with yours as long as I live," Nemle had written, and she had never failed to be there.

The morning came, clear and vibrant with new beginnings. The sun seemed almost impatient for her to wake. For a few moments she resisted, enjoying the snug warmth of her bunk, then for a few moments more, she lay watching the dancing light reflected on the ceiling, but there was work to do. She and Kel would go up to Willow Rise to say goodbye to Nemle and Jik and then they would tackle the cleaning up.

After breakfast, walking up the hill beside Kel, Marheh thought how good it was to be an equal partner, dressed in her uniform, contained and purposeful, instead of playing the doll-like Kathleen with her make-up, high heels and childish ways. She knew all marriages were not like the one she and Kel had pretended. There were plenty of good examples in her life, her parents, Tep and Fali, Gul and Sybi, but she thought of how Imni had felt constrained to obey her husband even when she thought he was wrong and then, on the other side, remembered Mek and Nella's attempts to have him deny the beliefs of his up bringing.

"It's good just to be ourselves, isn't it?" Kel commented, pausing a moment to look back over the valley they had just climbed out of.

"Just what I was thinking." Marheh smiled up at him. "A lovely morning and work we can do."

The walk was easing her stiffness and she stretched widely.

"We'd better go though, or we'll miss them."

They were in good time, however, and if Marheh's eyes were full of tears as she watched Nemle drive away with Jik there was no shame in that. She blew her nose and smiled when Sybi gave her the present Nemle had left her.

"Comfrey ointment, Nemle's panacea, but I think it's her healing hands that really make the difference."

Sybi nodded her agreement and invited them back inside for sperit and strategy.

"Because the darkness has broken up, we know that at the moment they are in disarray," Marheh said slowly when they were all comfortably seated around the kitchen table. "But that won't last unless we can intervene to reduce their ability to control. It has always been difficult to find a solution. Twenty years ago Nemle and I discovered a way to remove the water dimension from their minds and that seemed like an answer at first, but even without the water dimension they still have no values, or perhaps it would be more truthful to say they still have values we think are wrong."

Gul nodded.

"What you are saying is that if you and Kel remove the water dimension then it is up to the community to turn them into good citizens."

"Yes," Marheh said soberly. "Yes, that's really what I'm saying and that means you have the hardest job."

"Hard or not, it's our job," Sybi said. "And it wouldn't be possible without you doing your job."

"It may not be possible anyway," Marheh said. "But without the water dimension and the power to control, the damage they can do is… containable, and it gives them a chance of life at least."

….

Over a two week period Marheh and Kel scoured the villages, watching, listening with heart and mind and singing light. They found and removed Yareblis controls from several unsuspecting individuals and tracked down J to a cottage in Lowcroft. At the sight of their uniforms he tried to attack them, which made it easier to control him. Kel held his mind while Marheh removed the water dimension and when they released him it was as if he had never been Yareblis.

D they found on the outskirts of Higham's Hill, but when they reached the Old Rectory it was empty with a discreet sign offering it for sale.

It was always the way, Marheh thought rather wearily as she relaxed on *Day Bringer* that evening. The most powerful had the resources to begin again somewhere else. She had just about had enough of other minds and the dirt that she was addressing and the discomfort it caused. Without Kel's support she would have faltered, fallen even.

Well, they had done what they could and at least these villages would be safe for a while, especially with people like Gul and Sybi, Mrs Armstrong and Sandy, the bus driver and her own family too, acting like leaven, their efforts unhindered by controls they had few defences against.

Lowcroft Heights was another story. Work had stopped as far as they could tell and the place itself felt benign but the land still held the memory of pain. Probably the estate would continue in the end. Without the Yareblis influence it might have a chance to become a community but it would be months, if not years, before they would know.

She had her journal on her lap. She wanted to write something that would sum up the events of the last days and weeks but nothing she thought of seemed satisfactory. Tomorrow she and Kel would part to continue on their assigned routes. That thought brought sadness with it, more sadness than she had expected. He had cooked for her that evening and hugged her as they parted. She loved him and she would miss him. She could acknowledge that now. He complemented her and she knew he would always be there for her in a way she could not be for him. She didn't want another goodbye.

She scribbled something in her journal and stood up. In another hour the moon would be up. She would pull *Day Bringer* away around the corner to where the sound of the engine starting would not wake Kel. Carefully she made *Day Bringer* ready, checking the engine, attaching lines to hold the tiller steady, steering slightly away from the bank to counteract her tug towards it.

At the last moment she tore the page from her journal and went to tuck it under the neat, coiled end of *Storm Cloud*'s back mooring line. Kel would understand she thought.

She pulled up her mooring pins and tucked them away in their accustomed places then she took hold of the front line.

The first pull was hard and *Day Bringer* seemed reluctant, but then she began to follow Marheh like an obedient animal, slow and steady under the bright moonlight.

On she went, emptying herself into the night until she became part of its bright silence. When at last she drew *Day Bringer* into the bank she was almost reluctant to start the engine, but after the first burst of sound she could throttle back to almost nothing. On to the turning place she went then back to creep past *Storm Cloud* and away into the night.

. . . .

Next morning Kel was not really surprised to find her gone. He had a half remembered dream of a boat passing in the night and he had sensed her sadness in the hug she had given him when they parted.

He looked again at the paper she had left for him.

"On with the job," she had written. Then as he held it and thought of her he seemed to hear her add "No goodbyes."

ABOUT THE AUTHOR

Rosalind, like many Australians, loves to travel. She fell in love with the canals of England during her first visit there and this has remained a life-long passion. She spent nearly three years living and traveling aboard a 37ft narrowboat and this experience has informed her writing so that although the stories are fantasy the boating experience is authentic.

When not writing she enjoys walking her dog, practicing her violin, painting watercolours, choral singing, reading and of course traveling.

Marheh can be contacted at Marheh@gmail.com

www.ingramcontent.com/pod-product-compliance
Lightning Source LLC
Chambersburg PA
CBHW031303170626
46807CB00001B/287